NEXT
OF
KIN

The Janet Moodie series from L.F. Robertson and Titan Books

Two Lost Boys
Madman Walking
Next of Kin

NEXT OF KIN

L.F. ROBERTSON

TITAN BOOKS

NEXT OF KIN
Print edition ISBN: 9781785659126
E-book edition ISBN: 9781785659133

Published by Titan Books
A division of Titan Publishing Group Ltd
144 Southwark Street, London SE1 0UP

First edition: June 2019
1 2 3 4 5 6 7 8 9 10

A CIP catalogue record for this title is available from the British Library.

Printed and bound in Great Britain by CPI Group (UK) Ltd, Croydon, CR0 4YY

To Morgan

1

Harrison, California, isn't a place known for murders, the way, say, Stockton is, or Bakersfield. It's a typical Central Valley town, a generous sprawl of low buildings laid down over the last century and a half on the vast ancient seabed that forms the middle of the state. It has its old downtown, with fortress-like former banks now housing antique malls, boutiques in 1920s storefronts, and an old-fashioned movie theater, complete with a neon-lit tower, marquee and ticket booth, that now shows indie films. Off the beaten track these days, Old Town is a place where residents take visiting relatives to shop for California wine, olive oil, souvenirs, and Depression-era kitchen gadgets, and eat osso bucco and cannelloni at the old-school Italian restaurant or drink craft beer at the edgy new brewpub in a building that used to be a speakeasy. The neighborhoods around it are a mix of shabby apartment complexes and older run-down cottages, many of them rentals occupied by families who make their living as farmworkers or store clerks.

The present commercial center of town is Sequoia Avenue,

a wide boulevard edged with office buildings, real estate offices, law firms, and strip malls, flanked by subdivisions of placid suburban houses on generous, tree-shaded lots. Unlike some similar towns which have withered as railroad traffic diminished and highways bypassed them, Harrison got lucky: it's the county seat of Hartwell County, and a major highway runs along its edge.

Hartwell County came into existence in the great drought of the 1860s that broke up the vast Mexican land grants and opened the valley to Basque sheep herders and Swiss-Italian dairy farmers. During the Civil War the area held a pocket of Confederate sympathizers in a state that went with the Union; Harrison is named for a town in Arkansas. In the 1930s, in the middle of the Great Depression, Hartwell County attracted Dust Bowl migrants from Arkansas, Missouri, and Oklahoma, searching for any work they could get on the ranches, truck farms, and fruit orchards that support its prosperity. The Ku Klux Klan marched there as late as the 1980s, and the white people in Hartwell County (there are very few African-Americans) still retain something of the South in their speech, religion, and politics.

A few minutes outside town are the miles of well-kept orchards—peaches, walnuts, pistachios, pomegranates, oranges, lemons, grapes—set in a grid of numbered two-lane roads, and here and there a stretch of pasture behind an old wood and wire fence or a house and outbuildings down a long private drive. The rows of trees and tracts of open land along the roads are interrupted now and then by ragtag farm towns of small stucco houses with front yards of dirt and dry weeds, paint peeling from wood trim, air conditioners in their windows or old swamp coolers on their roofs, and pickup trucks parked in their driveways. The towns' main streets are a row of liquor stores, thrift shops, *bodegas*, churches, and shops that repair things: cars, farm equipment, wells and septic tanks, household appliances.

Sunny Ferrante grew up in one of those dusty little towns, a dot on the map twelve miles outside Harrison, called Sparksville. She may be the most famous of its alumnae; almost certainly, she's the only one to have landed on death row. A long time ago, she had been my client, and now she was again.

2

Carey Bergmann collared me during a continuing education seminar about criminal appeals, as I waited in line outside the restroom. "Janet!" she said, startling me from my reverie about the new changes in the felony murder rule.

I looked up. "Carey?" Not that I needed to ask; she hadn't changed much since I'd last seen her. I tried to remember how long it had been—seven years? Ten?

"I'd like to talk to you," she said. "When you have a moment."

I saw her a couple of minutes later, as I left the line of coffee urns with a fresh cup to get me, I hoped, through the rest of the morning. She was talking with Joe Hamilton, one of the day's speakers, but she excused herself and hurried over to meet me.

"I'm so glad to see you here today," she said, as we found our way to a couple of empty chairs. "I was going to call you." As we walked, I had a chance to look at her more closely. She really hadn't changed much—a little thinner, maybe, and more tanned in the face. She is taller than I am, perhaps five foot six, and she still moved with an athletic grace and physical confidence that has always eluded me.

"It's been a while," she said, when we'd both sat down. "I don't think I've seen you since Terry's memorial. That was really a shock. We all thought the world of him; he was an inspiration for me. How are you doing?"

"Not bad," I said, with a shrug. Terry, my husband, had committed suicide seven years ago. It wasn't something I generally cared to talk about. "I live a dull life."

"I hope not," she said. "Jim Christie says you're living way out in the woods in, like, Mendocino, and you and he have a habeas corpus case together."

"You know Jim?" The community of death penalty lawyers was really a small world, I thought.

"Yeah. I tried a case with him once, and we run into each other in court sometimes. Is he keeping you busy?"

"Not right now," I said, with what I hoped was a noncommittal shrug.

She gave a short laugh. "He's a regular Tom Sawyer. He has a gift for getting other people to do his work."

I nodded. "But we're almost finished. The petition in that case was filed—oh, God, two years ago—and we're waiting for the court to act. So I'm in a bit of a lull, I guess, doing appeals and not much else."

"Oh, good. You remember Sunny Ferrante?"

"Wow, Sunny. That was a long time ago."

"2002. She was sentenced in 2004."

"Right." It was a cold case—capital appeals move at

a glacial pace through the legal system—and a twisted, sordid one: on a spring day in 2002, Sunny's husband, Greg Ferrante, a local real-estate developer, had been found dead next to the swimming pool behind his house, a single bullet in the back of his head. Suspicion fell immediately on Sunny, especially since the local rumor mill had it that Greg had been about to leave her for a younger woman. But she had a solid alibi for the time of the crime. With no evidence and no other suspects, the case sat unsolved for several months, until a local petty malefactor in jail on a charge of his own told a guard that Sunny's daughter's boyfriend, a kid named Todd Betts, had confessed the murder to him, saying he'd been hired by Sunny to kill her husband. As bad luck would have it, Sunny had loaned Todd several thousand dollars to repair his truck, a month after the murder. And a month or so after that Todd had died of a drug overdose. The evidence against Sunny was thin, but enough to move an outraged jury to convict her of Greg's murder and give her the death penalty.

The state defender's office, where I was working, had taken her appeal, and it had been assigned to me. I'd been working on the opening brief when Terry killed himself. That had been just over seven years ago, now, in February. Somehow, I'd managed to finish writing the brief; in fact I'd thrown myself into it because absorbing myself in work seemed the only way I could temporarily push away the engulfing waves of shock, misery, and grief. But at the end of that year, I was too battered by hurt at Terry's inexplicable suicide and the fallout from it, particularly the murmured insinuations of blame from our colleagues in the criminal defense community, where Terry had been a respected trial lawyer. So I left the state defender, Sunny's case and all, and swore off death penalty work.

I'd retreated—there was no better word for it, except perhaps "fled"—to a little settlement called Corbin's Landing on the coast north of the mouth of the Russian River, where I bought a dilapidated vacation cabin on an acre of cleared land within earshot of the Pacific. I learned to graft fruit trees and build deer fences and started an orchard and a garden. I supported myself, a dog, and two cats by taking court-appointed criminal appeals, writing the briefs in a bedroom repurposed as my office. It wasn't a bad life, and over time it helped me recover some balance.

But death penalty defense, once undertaken, is something between a calling and an addiction. It gets a grip on your conscience that is hard, if not impossible, to disengage. So eventually it pulled me back, first to the case of a convicted serial killer, then to that of a man who'd been convicted of murder despite the fact that the real killer had confessed and exonerated him. And now, it seemed, to Sunny.

"Is Sunny okay?" I asked. "Has something happened?"

"She's fine, as far as I know. I've just been approved for appointment as counsel for her habeas corpus case," Carey said, "and the court has agreed to appoint you as co-counsel if Sunny will waive any conflict of interest from your having been her appeal lawyer."

"Wow, thanks. I feel honored. I like Sunny; I really was sorry to give up her appeal." I meant it, too, but even as the words emerged from my mouth, my rational mind told me I should know better than to get involved in another habeas corpus.

In California, every defendant sentenced to death gets counsel for their appeal and for a separate habeas corpus proceeding. The good news about habeas corpus is that, as the lawyer, you get to investigate the case all over again and present new evidence if you find it, something you can't do with the appeal. The bad news is that the courts don't generally give you enough money or time to do it all, to spend endless hours scouring courthouses, schools, hospitals, and social service agencies for records, traveling to a succession of dusty towns and state prisons, and talking to a lot of strangers, in the hope of finding something that might convince a court to give your client another trial. I'd been second chair on two habeas cases in the past couple of years, and I didn't have much appetite for jumping into another one. On the other hand, the client would be Sunny. I knew her and liked her, and I'd always had doubts about the case against her.

"Well, it makes sense," Carey went on. "You know Sunny and her case already. Plus I liked the work you did for Jesus Ortega; you were really helpful when I took the habeas. And Terry always said such glowing things about you."

"Really?" I said, and I felt a surprising small rush of tenderness. Terry's death had left me feeling not only broken, but angry and betrayed by his suicide and by the fact that he had never confided to me the pain that led him to it. Enough time had passed, it seemed, that I could feel touched by hearing how he had felt about me. That was progress, I guess.

The morning break was over, and Joe Hamilton was well into his lecture as we opened the door to the small auditorium. "I'll call you," Carey whispered, as we separated. We both stooped, instinctively, and I stifled a giggle as I thought of the picture we made, two middle-aged women, one tall and slender and the other short and, well, sturdy, creeping like guilty schoolkids to our seats.

I heard from Carey two weeks later. "It's all good," she said. "Sunny's appellate lawyer—you remember Toni Jackson?—visited her, and Sunny signed the conflict of interest waiver, so you can represent her. Evelyn Turner called; the court appointed us this morning. So the one-year clock is ticking as of now."

"How did you get Evelyn to give you Sunny's habeas appointment? Her appeal hasn't even been decided yet, and I thought Evelyn was trying to get lawyers for the oldest cases first."

Evelyn Turner was the state Supreme Court staff attorney in charge of assigning attorneys to capital appeals and habeas corpus cases. She was a tough negotiator, and once she had decided which defendants were getting lawyers that month from the roster of eligible attorneys, it was almost impossible to change her mind. It was also well known to everyone on the panel that there were a lot more defendants than there were qualified attorneys willing to take habeas corpus cases. Evelyn was working through a growing backlog of prisoners, some of whom had been waiting twenty years or more since their convictions for a habeas lawyer to be appointed for them. By my rough calculation, Sunny was still far from the head of that line.

"She's desperate," Carey said. "Almost no one is taking habeas cases anymore. The court doesn't pay enough, and you only have a year from appointment to file them. So she's a little more flexible. I read something about Sunny's case a while ago, and I told Evelyn I was interested in it, but she wasn't going to give it to me unless I took an old case at the same time."

"She's still tough."

"Yeah. But I was too busy then to take two more cases at once, and by the time things had freed up, this new law had passed, with the one-year filing deadline, and the pool of lawyers just dried up. Poor Evelyn hasn't got many cards to play. So she let me take Sunny's case if I promised to take another one after filing Sunny's petition."

I was impressed with Carey's powers of persuasion. "What made you want Sunny's case in particular?"

"Couple of things. First, looking at the appeal briefs, the case against her is shaky. Seems to me there's a real possibility she's telling the truth when she says she didn't do it. And there's this social prejudice against women killing their husbands—much more than when men kill their wives—and that may be part of why the system was so punitive with her. Since Betty Mateski, I kind of follow cases where women get convicted of killing their husbands or boyfriends."

Betty Mateski's case had been something of a *cause célèbre*. She had shot her husband as he slept, after some twenty years of unremitting abuse during which he had regularly beaten her and threatened to kill her if she left him. She had been charged with first-degree premeditated murder by lying in wait, essentially meaning that she had deliberately waited to kill him until she could catch him unawares. The prosecution sought a sentence of life in prison without possibility of parole. Carey, who was then a young public defender, had been assigned to represent her; and she had argued that Betty wasn't guilty of murder because she had killed her husband in self-defense.

At her trial, Betty testified about the years of abuse and terror Raymond Mateski had inflicted on her. His beatings had sent her to the hospital more than once; she had lied about how she had been injured, and the doctors and nurses treating her had largely taken her at her word. One or two surmised what had really happened and urged her to press charges, but she had shaken her head and gone back to Ray. She explained at her trial that she was so beaten down and afraid of him that in the years when her children had been living at home, she'd believed his threat that he would get custody of them if she left him.

All three of her children had testified to the violence Ray had done to Betty and to them, until one by one they had run away. After the children were gone, Betty finally tried to leave him. She left the house when he was at work and walked five miles to an old friend's house, but Ray tracked her down and showed up carrying a gun, threatening to kill Betty's friend and her husband. To spare them the horror of being menaced anymore by Ray, Betty had gone home.

On the night she killed him, he had gotten drunk on cheap whiskey and had accused her of infidelity with her friend's husband, and of plotting with her friend and her sister to leave him. He had refused to let her leave the house, punched her, pistol-whipped her, and repeatedly told her she would be dead before morning and that if she tried to escape he would hunt her down and kill her, her sister, and anyone who tried to help her. He had beaten her up and threatened her before, she admitted in her trial testimony. "But this time it felt different. There was something in his eyes and the way he was talking. I believed that this time he meant to do it. I thought I was going to die." Eventually, he fell into a drunken sleep, and she took a sawed-off shotgun he kept behind the door to their bedroom and emptied both barrels, one after the other, into his chest. When she felt sure he was dead she took his truck keys from his pants pocket and drove to her friend's house, where she called the police to turn herself in.

Carey had tried to present testimony from a psychologist who had studied victims of long-term abuse, explaining how a woman could be changed by constant terror and helplessness, could come to believe that her abuser was all-powerful against the efforts of anyone to help her, could become hypersensitive to her abuser's shifts of mood. The expert could explain that Betty's belief that Ray had crossed some line and was really about to kill her was honest and deeply held, as was her conviction that, once awake, he was unstoppable; so that her decision to kill him at the one point when he could not overpower her was motivated by a genuine, even reasonable belief that this was the only way she could save her own life.

Now, of course, the psychological effects of domestic violence on its victims are the stuff of talk shows and police dramas, but at the time of Betty Mateski's case, Carey's defense fell on unsympathetic ears. The prosecutor argued that the psychologist's evidence was incredible and, moreover, irrelevant, because Ray wasn't threatening to kill Betty at the moment when she killed him, and she could have escaped from the house while he slept. Ray's earlier threats didn't excuse her killing him when she did; the law was clear that a person could kill in self-defense only when she reasonably believed she was threatened with imminent death. The judge excluded the psychologist's testimony and refused to instruct the jury that they could consider whether Betty had killed Ray in self-defense.

The prosecutor argued to the jury that what motivated Betty to kill Ray wasn't terror but anger. The jury found Betty guilty of first-degree murder.

Betty's case got a lot of publicity and made Carey, indignant at the judge's rulings and the verdict, an activist for the rights of abused women. She left the public defender's office and started a public interest law firm that specialized in defending victims of domestic violence and advocating for changes in the law. Inevitably, some of those cases involved women charged with murdering their husbands, and eventually Carey also became involved in a couple of habeas corpus cases for women sentenced to death. She also got Betty Mateski a new trial and acquittal, after a law was passed allowing accused women to present evidence of domestic violence and its psychological effects in their trials.

Still I wondered why she had chosen Sunny's case. "But," I said, "there wasn't any evidence presented that Greg Ferrante was abusing Sunny."

"Yes, I know. This seems more like an innocent woman sentenced to death by male stereotyping—'hell hath no fury' and so on."

"Yeah," I agreed. "There wasn't really much evidence against Sunny except that 'woman scorned' motive and a story told by a snitch. The district attorney's theory was that she killed Greg for his money and life insurance—so she could inherit from him before he divorced her."

"Oh, right, the gold-digging wife," Carey said with a sigh. "I'd like you to come with me when I meet her. I think it'll be easier for her to have someone she knows there, too."

We raced through the arrangements. Pulled along by Carey's near-breathless enthusiasm, I had already offered to file a discovery motion. "We're on a tight timeline," I'd said. "I can finish one by next week."

"Great!"

We had hung up before I realised what had just happened. I'd started work on another death-penalty case, almost without thinking about it.

3

The Central California Women's Facility is farther north than Harrison, but still in the Central Valley. It's about a mile from the nearest town, in a landscape a lot like that around Harrison—a flat grid of country roads enmeshing orchards of peaches, pistachios, almonds, and lemons. CCWF contains the death row for women, the counterpart of the much more populous men's death row at San Quentin. But for the substantial sign in sober beige and brown identifying it at the head of the access road, it could almost be an office park, a campus of one-story stucco buildings and parking lots surrounded by lawns and landscape trees.

At a kiosk a little down the road into the complex, I showed my driver's license and bar card to a uniformed guard. When I told him I was coming for a legal visit, he pointed out the visitor center and the fork in the road that led to its parking lot.

The lot was huge and nearly full; I finally found a space fairly far from the building and, afraid I might be late, hurried across the blacktop and up the wide steps to the entrance. The air was bright and fresh, and the leaves on the trees were still a bright spring green. In the late morning sun, the buildings shone with the clear neutral light of a Diebenkorn landscape.

Inside, the visitor center was air-conditioned, and bright with light through windows that showed nothing more inspiring than the parking lot. Carey was inside, standing at the counter and talking to a uniformed woman.

"Oh, good," she said when she saw me, "you're here." She was wearing a gray pencil skirt and jacket, with a cream-colored silk shirt open at the collar. Her suit could have used a pressing, and her short dark hair was a little windblown. It was the look of a working lawyer; only on TV do we have perfect hair and designer clothes.

I walked over to the counter and took my driver's license and bar card out of my jacket pocket. Purses were not allowed inside, and I'd left mine in my car. "Good morning," I replied, with mock cheerfulness. "How was your drive?"

"Not bad—the usual collection of semis and a lot of maniacs in pickups. How about you?"

I made a grunt of sympathy. "The same," I said, and we turned to the business of getting cleared to go into the prison, signing the register and inventorying our possessions—pens, paper, money, jewelry—for the desk clerk. We took off our shoes for long enough to walk through a metal detector, and were handed plastic visitor ID cards to clip to our lapels. One of the guards, a round-faced fortyish man who had been chatting idly behind the counter, was drafted to escort us to the attorney visiting area.

We walked out a back door into the more familiar prison landscape invisible from the highway —a big cage surrounded by a tall metal mesh fence topped with coils of barbed wire.

"Where did you ladies come here from?" our escort asked, as we waited for the door behind us to close and the barred metal gate at the far end to open for us.

Carey gave him an appraising look out of the corner of her eye before answering, "Ventura."

"Corbin's Landing," I said.

"Where's that?"

"Up on the Sonoma Coast."

"Oh, nice."

His attention was diverted by the clank of the opening gate and a couple of prison staffers coming into the cage. "Have you had lunch yet?" one of them asked him. "We ordered pizza."

"Sounds good," he said. "Can you wait ten or fifteen minutes?"

"Sure," they said, and moved on.

Carey and I together, and the guard a little ahead, we walked out of the cage and down a concrete pathway across a lawn dotted with trees. The path was bordered with rose bushes blooming with red and pink flowers. Rose bushes are ubiquitous in prisons; San Quentin has them in rows along the approach to the gate and in beds outside the buildings, and so does Folsom. I'd tried growing them once, in a brief lapse into domesticity, when I lived in Berkeley, but I gave up after a year or two. They were too much work, between deadheading the old flowers, fertilizing, and pruning, and spraying for the myriad of pests that seem to live to eat or disfigure them. I suppose prisons have an ample supply of inmates happy to help maintain them, just to get outdoors and have something useful to do.

"Nice roses," I said.

"Oh, right." The guard sounded bemused, as if he'd forgotten they were there.

The light stucco building at the end of the path, with its roofed terrace and double door, was like something you might see on a state college campus. The guard selected a large key from a set at his waist, unlocked the door, and let us into a lobby with pale gray walls and a dark polished floor of some indestructible-looking aggregate. "Over here." He unlocked a second door and held it as we walked through.

The room beyond the door was auditorium-sized, with a high ceiling, an expanse of the same shiny floor, and metal tables, each with chairs around it, arranged in the space as if for a banquet. The tables were empty. At the opposite end of the room was a wall of windows with a view of a patio dotted with more tables. Inside the room, in front of the windows, stood a sort of dais with a counter, occupied by a female guard. Behind us was a row of interview rooms with glass-paned doors. Our steps echoed as we walked inside.

The guard who had escorted us crossed the room, spoke with the guard at the counter, and then returned. "She's on her way down," he said. "They'll be here in a few minutes.

When you leave, you need to get your paperwork from the sergeant over there." He gave a nod toward the counter. "I'm going back up front, if everything is okay."

We thanked him and reassured him that we were all right.

While we waited, Carey checked out a bank of vending machines. I could see through the window into one of the interview rooms. It was pretty standard-issue: an office-sized space painted an institutional off-white with brown trim, with a vinyl-topped wood table and wooden chairs in the middle and an empty bookshelf against the far wall.

A door past the attorney rooms opened, and Sunny Ferrante and a guard came into the echoing space of the visiting area. Sunny seemed heavier than when I'd last seen her, though it was hard to tell in her prison uniform of baggy blue pants and shirt. She spotted us in the gloom, and her face brightened. We walked over in their direction. The guard nodded toward one of the interview rooms. "I'll just put you all in here, if that's all right."

"We'd like to get some food and drinks," I said. Buying a meal or snack for your client on a legal visit is a sort of ritual. Not only does it give your client a taste of something different from prison food; it creates a relaxed environment, which encourages conversation and softens the tone of what can be a dry and even grim discussion of the law and your client's case. In the service of my chosen field I have eaten what seems like mountains of vendingmachine chips and cookies and drunk seas of terrible coffee.

"That's fine."

"Hi, Sunny," I said. "What can I get you?"

"Hi, girl," she answered brightly. "Long time no see. Some kind of salad and a diet Dr. Pepper would be great."

"You got it."

As the guard took Sunny into the interview room, Carey and I hurried to the vending machines and began easing dollar bills into their cash slots. After a few minutes, we returned, laden with trays of salads, drinks, chips, napkins, plastic forks, and a small bag of chocolate chip cookies I tossed onto the pile at the last minute. Sunny's escort, who had been waiting by the door, let us in and pointed out the button for the buzzer that would call the guard on duty when we wanted to leave, then went out, locking the door behind him.

Sunny was standing next to the table. She came over and hugged me and then backed up and gave me a smile. She had a great smile, lively and contagious. "You're looking really good," she said. I doubted that, but I thanked her anyway.

She turned to Carey and held out a hand, saying, "You must be Ms. Bergmann. It's really nice to meet you."

"Nice to meet you, too. Please, call me Carey."

When I'd last seen Sunny, seven or eight years ago, she'd been in her mid-forties, growing a little plump, but still lively and very attractive, with red-brown hair and the creamy complexion that so often goes with it. She moved a little more heavily now, and her hair was cut short and lightened by silvery strands. There were smile lines around her eyes and mouth, and she was still attractive, her face and eyes lit, as I remembered, by that dazzling smile. She was evolving, I thought, from a former beauty to a fairy godmother. What she didn't look like was someone who had hired her daughter's boyfriend to kill her husband.

She had one hand braced on the table as if to help hold her, and I saw a cane, which I hadn't noticed when she first came in, propped against a chair. She saw my glance toward it and explained, "Bad knee. I need a replacement and to lose about twenty pounds."

"Are you going to be able to get a knee replacement here?" Carey asked as we sat down.

"Eventually. They know it needs to be done."

"How are you doing otherwise?" I asked.

"Not bad. I'm kind of one of the old-timers here now. Though there are women who've been up here a lot longer. I don't know if you know, but I'm a grandmother, too. Brittany's married, and they have two little ones, a boy and a girl. She brings them to see me a couple times a year. Kyle is five and Brianna is three, and they're both cute as can be. Britt sends me pictures of the family. I've got a really cute one of the kids around the Christmas tree at home." She sighed. "I wish I'd remembered to bring them down."

Going to visit your grandmother in prison was hardly a typical family activity, I thought, though sadly all too common. We ate our salads, with more small talk about the food and prison life, and then turned to the business of our visit.

"So you're going to be my habeas corpus lawyers," Sunny

said. I'd emptied the little cookies onto a paper towel, so that we could share them, and she picked one up and contemplated it. "Just one," she said, and took a delicate bite, then turned to me. "Ms. Jackson came to see me and talked to me about the conflict of interest thing. I signed all the papers; I trust you."

"Thank you," I said. "I'll do my best to deserve it."

She smiled. "Some of the girls are really surprised I have a habeas lawyer already," she said. "One of them says she's been up here for twenty-two years with no habeas. Her appeal was denied, like, ten years ago, and mine isn't even over yet."

"I lobbied the court to get your case," Carey said.

"Really? Why?" Sunny took another small bite of the cookie.

"Well, I'd heard about it, and I feel strongly about women in the justice system."

"Hmm." She finished the cookie. "One of the other girls here, Maureen O'Donnell, told me you're her lawyer. She said good things about you."

Word gets around here, I thought, especially with so few women on the row. The last I'd heard, there were only about twenty. Carey, pleased by the endorsement, said, "I'm glad of that."

Sunny's smile dimmed to a look of concern. "You must be awfully busy."

"We should be fine," Carey answered. "We have a year to file a habeas petition, and I made sure my schedule was clear enough before taking the appointment."

"Oh, good." Sunny started to reach for the little stack of cookies, then shook her head. "No more," she said firmly. "I really do have to lose weight." She sat up straighter and gave a brisk nod, and glanced at Carey, then me. "So, where do we start?"

"With you. You and I talked a bit about your life years ago, but Ms. Bergmann—Carey—doesn't know much beyond what was presented at your trial. So," I said, "tell us everything."

"Hoo!" Sunny gave a little laugh. "I don't think my memory's that good. Not that there's much to tell. Born and raised in Sparksville. Not a lot happened before I met Greg."

"Your mother grew up there, too, right?"

"Yep. My grandparents came from Oklahoma with their parents when they were kids. My grandpa's people settled around Salinas. He met Nana while he was in the Navy in World War II, and they moved here near her family after he got out. Linda was born in 1947." I remembered that Sunny always called her mother by her given name.

"They were real Okies, Nana used to say," Sunny went on. "But not back then. When I was little, being an Okie was something people looked down on you for."

"Did you feel that growing up?"

"Not too much. I think Sparksville was kind of settled by Okies. Lot of the kids were, or Mexican. I heard about it more than I actually saw it. I think Grandpa and Nana felt the discrimination more. And Linda did, when she got pregnant."

"How was that?" I asked.

"Well, she had to get married right after high school, because she was pregnant with me. She said it was a shotgun wedding. She and my dad were going steady in high school, but he tried to break up with her when he found out she was expecting. She didn't want to marry him, either, after that, but their parents made them. Nana said his parents were pretty full of themselves—they had a big ranch outside of town. They called Linda white trash and as much as said they didn't think I was his baby."

"Wow," Carey said.

"Yeah. Linda said it was really hurtful. Grandpa and Nana never spoke to my father's parents after the wedding. Never forgave them for what they'd said about Linda."

"I don't blame them; I'd feel the same way," Carey said. "What about your parents? Did they stay married?"

"I don't think they ever even lived together. My father went and enlisted in the Marines. Kind of a stupid thing to do because it was the middle of the Vietnam War, but Linda said he did it to spite her and his parents. Anyhow, he was sent over to Vietnam and got killed there. The military gave Linda some kind of pension for her and me, so I guess some good came out of it."

"How did you get nicknamed Sunny?" Carey asked.

"I don't know—maybe my grandma and grandpa called me that first. I just know I've been Sunny as long as I can remember. No one I knew ever called me Cheryl—it's still true, even here."

"So did Linda raise you alone?"

"No—my grandparents brought me up. I guess someone told Linda she ought to think about being in movies—she was really beautiful, like a model or something; she'd been the prom queen at Sparksville High. So she left me with my grandma and grandpa and went to LA to try her luck. She was supposed to send for me when she got settled and was making money, but I guess that never worked out. But she stayed there, and she did get parts on TV shows and commercials; I remember seeing her in one or two. She came and saw us on holidays and stuff, and when I was old enough, I used to get to visit her in LA in the summer. I loved it." Sunny smiled at the memory. "She always seemed to live someplace with a swimming pool, and sometimes we'd go to the beach and have a picnic or walk around the pier, or even go to Disneyland and Knott's Berry Farm. I wanted to live in LA when I grew up."

"Did she move a lot, then?"

"I guess. She always seemed to be in living in a different place depending on who her boyfriend was at the time. I think she was married a couple of times, too. The last one took, and she settled down. Her husband's name is Pete Ottoboni, and they have a little house in Silver Lake."

"Did she have any more children?"

"No, I was it. She wasn't into motherhood, I guess."

"Did your grandparents have any other children?"

"Sort of. There was a baby born before Linda, but my grandmother had German measles when she was pregnant, and the baby was born with some kind of birth defect and only lived a few months. Her name was Mary Alice. We used to go now and then to visit her grave and put flowers on it."

"And what was your life like, growing up?"

"Ordinary, like I said. School, church, 4-H, sports, sometimes a concert. Hanging out with my friends. I had a good time in high school, got to be a cheerleader and prom queen, like Linda. She was proud of me, bought me a beautiful dress for the prom. Not that it was that big a deal." Sunny let out another little laugh. "Sparksville High was very small. There were only about fifty kids in my senior class."

"So you graduated?"

"Oh, yes. I wasn't a superstar, but I didn't get into cutting school or smoking weed like some of my friends, and my grades were okay."

Getting down to business, Carey asked her if she could remember the names of any of the kids in her class; after some thought, she listed a half-dozen. "I doubt that most of them are still around," she said. "Most kids leave Sparksville when they get a chance."

"What did you do after graduating?"

"Kept living with my grandparents. Went to work at an auto body shop in town. Ken, the owner, was a friend of Grandpa's."

"What did you do there?"

"I was the receptionist and answered the phones, and I helped with some of the billing and ordering. I was taking bookkeeping classes at the community college in Harrison in the evenings, so I could learn to do the books there. That's where I met Troy—Britt's father."

"At school?"

"No, sorry—he worked at the shop."

"What was he like?"

"Well, I fell in love with him. He was cute, kind of quiet and shy."

"How old was he?"

"A year older than I was, so I guess nineteen when we met."

"And you got married?"

"Yes. I'd been raised that that's what you did. I was kind of old-fashioned, I guess; I believed in saving yourself for marriage. We were engaged for about six months, and then we got married in my grandparents' church, at the end of our street, where I went all my life. We didn't have money for a fancy wedding and reception, but I had a white dress and my bridesmaids wore pale blue, and Linda had a friend who was a florist, so she drove up with a carload of flowers in coolers, and we decorated the church. It was just gorgeous— and such a beautiful day. And we even had a honeymoon, a week in Maui. Imagine!" She sighed. "I can't believe I was ever that girl."

"How long were you married?"

Sunny knitted her brows, thinking back. "A little over two years. We separated—let me think—in 1985, when I was pregnant with Brittany, but the divorce wasn't final until the end of 1986. Before Greg and I were married, anyway."

"Why did you break up?"

She shrugged. "We were really in love at first, but I don't think Troy was ready to be married. He kind of freaked out when I got pregnant with Brittany. Things got tense between us, and then I found out he was seeing another girl, someone he knew from high school in Harrison. We fought about it, and he moved out. It was awful because we were still working together. I needed the job, and no one else would hire me when I was pregnant, so I stayed until the baby was nearly due."

"What happened after that?"

"It was a really hard time. We were renting an apartment in Harrison so it would be easier for me to go to school. I had to give it up and move back in with Nana and Grandpa until Brittany was old enough that I could go looking for work. When I found a job in Harrison, Nana said she and Grandpa could take care of Brittany, but I didn't want to leave my baby like Linda left me. So I found another apartment and a babysitter for Brittany. It was tough. It was always like that old joke—'too much month at the end of the money.'"

"I haven't heard that one," Carey said, with a laugh.

Sunny laughed, too. "It described my life to a T."

"What kind of work were you doing?" Carey asked.

"Receptionist, a little bookkeeping—a lot like what I'd done at Ken's, but for a chiropractor, Dr. Ostrander. That's where I met Greg."

A guard knocked at the door. "Five minutes," he mouthed through the glass.

"They had to cut visiting short today," Sunny said. "Some kind of inspection or something."

Before the guard came back, we gave Sunny some records releases to sign, and I asked her for contact information for Brittany. "I'll call you," she said. "She lives someplace called Wofford Heights. She says it's east of Bakersfield. I never heard of it before she told me. Her married name is Ecker. Her husband is Rick, he's a firefighter with Cal Fire. She used to be an EMT, but she's taking time off while the kids are little. They're doing well."

"I'm glad things have worked out for her."

Sunny nodded. "Me too. All this has been awfully hard for her. But she turned out really well. I'm proud of her."

The guard returned, and I told Sunny we'd be back in a couple of weeks. "We still have a lot of questions."

"I'll be here." Sunny's smile broadened at the joke as she turned to go back to the cells.

4

Carey called me two days later, to say she'd made another appointment to see Sunny. "It'll be the day before the hearing on the discovery motion," she said, "so we can go from there to Harrison. I've arranged to see the trial exhibits afterward, and interview Craig Newhouse, Sunny's trial lawyer, that afternoon."

"Man, you're organized!"

"I can't help it; I'm constantly on edge about the timeline. Don't tell Sunny, but I'm starting to wonder if we did the right thing, taking a case with such a short deadline. But I have an investigator on board, Natasha Levin. She worked with me not long ago on a Russian gang case. She's an amazing young woman—fearless, and she speaks Russian. Not that we'll need it on this case."

No, I thought, *what we'll need is someone whom a woman in her fifties can relate to and confide in about the dynamics of a long marriage going bad.* I imagined Natasha as tall, classically good-looking, triumphant with youth—someone, in other words, whom I wouldn't trust to take seriously the confidences of a middle-aged woman. *Oh, come on, you haven't even met her,* I said to myself, and took a walk among my raised beds, with my dog Charlie in tow, to work off my attitude. There were lettuces growing up under row covers and sugarsnap peas climbing the cute purple trellis I'd bought from a garden supply catalog. Admiring them, I felt briefly like a modern pioneer woman, feeding my family of one from my garden—as long as I was willing to live only on greens.

I had a couple of weeks of my quiet, reclusive life, work on my other cases punctuated with one or two shopping trips into town with my friend and gardening mentor Harriet: to the supermarket for groceries and the hardware store for the wire Harriet's husband needed for the cage he was building to protect her blueberry bushes from voracious blue jays and raccoons. The urgency of the one-year deadline we were facing seemed to fade away; and it seemed too soon when I had to drop Charlie off with my neighbor Ed and pack to leave for the prison and Harrison.

The drive to anywhere from where I lived started with a perilous stretch of road along the cliffs above the Pacific. After that, the route to the Central Valley town where the prison was ran through hills and farmland followed by many miles of urban freeway skirting the cities of the Bay Area and crossing the valley beyond.

I started before daylight, because the urban stretch of my route was always a seemingly endless bumper-to-bumper crawl among other cars, menacing semis, and tanker trucks.

By the time I reached the prison, I was a toxic mix of road-weary and jittery from the sour coffee and packaged Mexican pastries I'd picked up during a pit stop at a gas station market.

The prison was the same, except that the bright day was warmer, though thankfully not yet the broiling summer of the valley. I arrived ahead of Carey, told the guards I was expecting my co-counsel, and settled down to read and yawn on one of the row of metal and plastic chairs in the waiting area. Natasha Levin was meeting us so that we could introduce her to Sunny. She arrived ten minutes after I did and caught my eye as I looked up to see who was coming through the door. "Are you Janet Moodie?" she asked.

I put my papers aside and stood up. "I sure am."

"I'm Natasha Levin."

As we shook hands, I sized her up. She was short—about my height, give or take an inch—and as cylindrical as a fireplug. Her face was a pale circle, slightly tanned, with a few barely visible freckles; her eyes were like bright black buttons over a snub nose and a firm mouth. Her hair, cut over her ears, was a shiny tangle of black curls, and she wore splashy earrings of silvery mesh that bounced and glinted when she moved her head. Her long black skirt and loose white shirt only somewhat obscured her stocky build and gave her the air of a gypsy dressed for a business meeting.

"Nice to meet you." I resorted to the cliché greeting of southern California. "How was your drive?"

"Not bad, for LA. Carey texted me she'll be a few minutes late; she got stuck in traffic behind an accident."

"Ugh. Sorry about that."

An awkward silence ensued. I tried to think of something to say, but all I wanted to do was close my eyes and rest for the interview with Sunny. "I'm sorry I'm not very social," I said. "I've been on the road since about five this morning."

"Where from?"

"Couple hours north of San Francisco."

"Jesus! That is a long way. I'll shut up and let you relax."

That made me feel guilty. "Is there anything I can tell you about Sunny's case?" I asked.

Natasha cocked her head and thought for a few seconds. "Not that I can think of. Carey gave me the appeal briefs and a flash drive full of other stuff to read. And she told me a little about what Sunny's like and what she told you last week about her early life—a pretty superficial interview, judging from her notes."

Was that supposed to be a dig? I resisted the urge to respond; there was no point in getting into dominance struggles with an investigator right now. The fact that she was probably right didn't make me feel any more congenial toward her. Fortunately, Carey walked through the door at that moment.

"Hi," she said. "Sorry I'm late. I see you've met."

"Yes." I gave a noncommittal half smile.

We walked to the counter together and went through the visiting protocol: the inventory of what we were taking in, the trip through the metal detector, sign-in, and issuing of visitor badges. The staffer assigned as our guide to the visiting room was not a uniformed guard this time, but a counselor. "Weather's starting to heat up," he said, as we walked in a cluster past the roses, whose warm scent rose to meet us, along with the smell of recently mowed lawn.

"Yeah," Carey said. "I don't feel ready for summer yet."

"I hear you," he answered. "It gets really hot here. I'm from Minnesota, and I've never gotten used to it."

He let us into the building with the visiting room; a guard inside escorted us into the big room, took our paperwork to the guard at the desk on the far side, and left.

Natasha surveyed the room. "I haven't been here before. It's actually nicer than I thought it would be. Looks better than my high school."

"It's probably a few decades newer," Carey said. "They're building more prisons than schools these days."

I headed to the vending machines, followed by Natasha, to survey the choices before Sunny arrived.

"Woah, Chinese chicken salad," Natasha exclaimed. "You don't see that in men's prisons. But they probably ought to rename it, don't you think?"

The possibility that Chinese chicken salad might be culturally insensitive had not occurred to me. As I began to ponder the differences between my age group and Natasha's, Carey answered, "No more than Russian dressing."

"You've got a point," Natasha said, and harmony between the generations was, I hoped, restored.

After Sunny met Natasha and was settled in an attorney visiting room with Carey, Natasha helped me get food and drinks from the machines and carry them back. As we moved cans, plastic-covered dishes, and flimsy white flatware from the trays we were carrying to the conference table, Natasha took the chair next to Sunny. *Nice move,* I thought; it was a more companionable arrangement than having Sunny face three interviewers across the table. Then we settled down to food and small talk.

"Where did you come here from?" Sunny asked Natasha.

"LA."

"What part?"

"I live in the Hollywood Hills. Near Griffith Park Boulevard; do you know LA?"

"Not really. My mother lives in Silver Lake. For a while when I was a kid I think she lived in Santa Monica, near the pier. We used to drive around to a lot of places when I visited her, but I couldn't tell you where most of them were."

"I like Silver Lake," Natasha said. "Cool place. Nice shops and restaurants."

"Is it still?" Sunny asked, a little wistfully. "It's been a long time since I've seen it." She became lost in thought for a moment, then asked, "You have to drive over the Grapevine to get here, don't you?"

"Yeah."

"Ugh," Sunny said, with a shake of her head. "I always hated the Grapevine. Greg used to say I was being stupid about it, there wasn't anything to be afraid of. But it made me nervous going over the mountains—all the curves in the road and cars driving way too fast—and the trucks! It still gives me the shivers just to think of it."

Natasha nodded in agreement. "It's not fun." She opened a plastic clamshell with a wedge of cheesecake in it. Sunny eyed it with interest. "Is that good?" she asked. "I've never tried it."

"Don't know yet," Natasha said. "Would you like some?"

"Just a bite. I really am trying to lose some weight, and the doctor says I'm pre-diabetic, so I should stay away from sweets." She turned to me. "I've lost two pounds since you were here last. Not a lot, but it's going in the right direction."

"Wish I could say the same," I said.

Natasha moved the clamshell across the table, and Sunny took a delicate forkful and chewed it slowly before swallowing. "Mmm," she said. "That's yummy."

"Would you like some more? I could split it with you."

Sunny smiled and shook her head. "Oh, no, that's fine."

"Anyone else?" Natasha asked. "Going, going, gone."

Carey shook her head, and I said, "I've eaten two *conchas* this morning; no more sweets for me for a while."

At some point, almost imperceptibly, we slipped into asking Sunny about her life with Greg.

"You and I have talked about your relationship with Greg before," I said, "but we'll need to go over it again, to fill everyone in."

"Let's start where we broke off last time," Carey suggested. "How did you meet Greg?"

"I was working at Dr. Ostrander's office, and Greg was a patient there. He'd done something to his back, and he was getting adjustments once a week. He'd stop at the front desk to make an appointment, and he'd say something nice—compliment my earrings or a top I was wearing, like that. He was flirting a little, the way men do; I didn't think it was anything more at the time. Then one time he asked me out to dinner. Later he told me he'd fallen in love with me at first sight." She rolled her eyes. "When you're young, you believe those things, I guess."

I think we all nodded.

"And you went to dinner with him?"

"I told him I didn't think I could because I couldn't afford a babysitter, and he said he'd pay for it. So after that I said yes."

"How did the dinner go?" Carey asked.

"It was *wonderful*," Sunny said, the "wonderful" becoming a sort of sigh. "He took me to this really fancy steakhouse downtown—Vincent's. White tablecloths, waiters, wine with dinner, amazing food. It was such an experience, especially then. All my money was going to rent and bills and the babysitter; just eating at McDonald's was a treat. I remember I was afraid to eat as much as I wanted to; I could have finished the steak and baked potato, but I didn't want him to think I was a pig." She laughed.

"How did he treat you? Did he want sex that night?"

"No, he was a perfect gentleman."

I saw Natasha blink; even to me, the phrase sounded old-fashioned, like something out of a movie from the 1950s.

"One of the girls at the office said he was a real ladykiller,"

Sunny went on, "so I was kind of prepared for him to try. But nothing happened. I don't think we kissed until the second or third time we went out. We didn't actually make love until the weekend he took me to his house on the coast. That's when I began to think he was serious about me."

"You didn't before?" Natasha asked.

"Not really. I couldn't figure out what he saw in me; he seemed so grown-up and worldly. I was dazzled, getting to go to nice places, being treated like a princess. He even took me clothes shopping."

"He was still married then, wasn't he?"

"Yeah." Her smile faded for a second.

"Did he tell you he was married?"

She shook her head. "Not at first. I must have asked him sometime because I remember him saying he was divorced. It took a little while for me to figure out that he wasn't as divorced as all that."

"Meaning?"

"Well, his wife—Pat—was in the process of divorcing him, but it wasn't final yet, so he was still married. Later I learned that she filed for divorce after she found out he was dating me."

"And at some point he proposed to you."

"Yes." Another downward glance.

"When was that?"

"Over the holidays—New Year 1987. He and Pat were separated at that point, but he spent Christmas with his kids. Then we drove to LA to spend New Year's with Linda and… I guess she was with Pete by then. I remember they were interested in buying the house in Silver Lake, but they were short money for the down payment. Greg offered to help them."

"He was in real estate," I explained to Natasha.

"Yes. Commercial real estate and developing properties. I never understood any of it," Sunny said.

"Was that the first time he met your mother?" Natasha asked.

"Yes. When he offered to help them get the house, they became fans of his for life."

"That's when he proposed to you?" I asked.

"Yeah. We drove up to the observatory in Griffith Park one day, just the two of us. I remember we took a picnic: sandwiches and drinks from a deli. He must have brought the ring with him, and I think he told Linda ahead of time what his plan was."

"Why?"

"She never could keep a secret, and she was walking around that whole time kind of smiling and looking at me. She even told me that if he proposed I should totally accept. So I figured at least that he'd been talking to her about it, probably getting her on board as his ally.

"When he asked me to marry him—he literally went down on one knee and offered me the ring—it was actually kind of funny." She shook her head and smiled. "But I said yes. I adored him at that point, and he seemed to really cherish me."

"And after that?"

"Let's see—a couple months later, the lease on my apartment was up, and the landlord wanted to raise the rent. I told Greg that I was going to have to find another place because I couldn't pay the new rent, and he said, 'Why not move in with me? We're engaged, after all.' So I did."

"When did you get married?"

"In the spring. May. We got married in Reno." She gave a small laugh. "I was kind of hoping for something a little more—so Grandpa and Nana and Linda could be there. But Greg didn't want to. I think his family didn't approve of what happened with him and Pat and me. But we went to Italy on our honeymoon—Venice, Florence, Rome. It was so romantic! Nana and Grandpa took care of Brittany while we were gone."

"Greg had you sign a prenup before the wedding, right?" I said.

Another eye-roll. "Oh, Lord, that! I couldn't believe they used that against me. I remember when his lawyer explained it to me I thought it was really fair. I never felt I had any *right* to Greg's money, anyway. He earned it, and in his eyes, what he made was his. But he was always generous to me and Brittany, with money anyway."

"Did you mind that?" Natasha asked.

"It didn't occur to me to mind. I was twenty-two and nobody; and he was giving me a life like I'd never had and taking care of Brittany and promising that I'd be provided for if we split up. I didn't think that would ever happen, but

I was grateful. It was his money; I didn't feel I had any claim to it.

"It's funny," she added, including Carey and me in her gaze, "but the idea that I would have killed Greg for his money still makes me angry. If they'd said I'd killed him out of jealousy or because I was tired of being played games with—I mean, I didn't kill him, but at least those are real reasons. But money—" she shrugged and made a "pfft" sound through pursed lips "—that was the last thing I cared about."

"You said you thought Greg's family didn't approve of his splitting up with Pat and marrying you," I asked. "Did you see much of them while you were married to Greg?"

"Oh yeah—all the time."

"How was that?"

"Well, they lived right in the area. The ranch was outside of Harrison. Papa and Mama Ferrante and Bob—Greg's older brother—and his wife Marlene all lived there; so did Greg's other brother Tony and his wife. His family were early settlers; they'd had the ranch since the 1870s. Robert—Greg's dad—was a good businessman, Greg used to say; he planted the land in wine grapes and olives. Anyhow, they had money, and they were pretty influential in local politics. Greg's brother Tony was on the county board of supervisors for years. They did things for charities and the community college, and they used to entertain a lot, dinners and barbecues on the ranch. The mayor of Harrison would come, and Alan Eldridge, the Congressman from the county, and a state assemblyman, too—I forget his name—and other bigwigs. Greg always wanted to be there, networking, he used to say."

"Did you get to know his family well?"

"Kind of, over the years. Not at first, I felt really shy. I mean, I knew they'd all known Pat for forever, and I didn't know how they'd feel about me. And Greg would tell me to be quiet and not talk unless he said so. I'd just kind of sit in a corner with Brittany and the kids and not know what to do." She hesitated, as if considering whether to say the next thing on her mind. Then, perhaps uncomfortable with silence, she spoke again.

"There were the clothes." She stopped again, then went on. "I was cute back then, and I had a good figure. Men hit on me. But I didn't much like it, that kind of attention, and I tried not to encourage it. I was careful what I wore and how I acted. When I was with Troy, I just wanted to be what I was, a married woman. But Greg wanted to show me off. I'd never heard the term 'trophy wife' when I met him, but I figured out eventually that that was really what I was to him. He wanted me to dress in a certain way, what he called classy but sexy. He'd pick things for me to wear different places. For barbecues in the summer, he wanted me to wear things like short shorts, and bikinis in the pool. And he'd call me over to sit next to him sometimes while he talked with his men friends, and pat me on the bottom, like 'see what I've got.' And what that meant was that all the time I was there, men would give me those looks, even the married ones. And the women mostly stayed away. I'd end up playing with the little kids, with Brittany, a lot of the time. That's how I finally began to make friends; women would come talk to me because their little ones were playing with me and Britt. That's how I met Carol—Carol Schiavone."

"Who was Carol?"

"My best friend. She was one of the first people who was nice to me after I married Greg. Her boy, Michael, was about Britt's age, and we kind of bonded over that and stayed friends afterward. She still visits me here."

"That's great," Natasha said. "Would she mind if we talked to her?"

"I'm sure she wouldn't. She lives in New Mexico now." She thought for a moment, then said, "I can't remember her whole address and phone number. I'll send them to you."

"How did the Ferrantes treat you?" Natasha asked.

"Okay, actually. Most of them tried to be welcoming, in their way. Papa was nice; Mama didn't approve of Greg remarrying. She was Catholic, and really religious. I always had the feeling she kind of tolerated me because she loved Greg, but that was about it. After I was arrested, she completely turned against me. Craig—my lawyer—said she pressured the district attorney to go for the death penalty."

"Really?" Natasha said. "I thought the Catholic Church was against the death penalty."

"I guess not. Or maybe she didn't care."

"What about the rest of the family? How did they treat you?"

"Like any other family, I guess. But to me it felt like everyone was older than me except the kids, who were all younger, so I didn't really fit in anywhere. But Aunt Cindy—Tony's wife—was always sweet, and so was Tony. And so were Bob and Marlene. They tried to make me feel like part of the family."

"Who were Bob and Marlene, again?" I asked.

"Oh, my," Sunny said with a laugh. "Bob was Robert Ferrante's—Papa's—son, Greg's brother. Rob was Bob's son. They were all named Robert, so the family gave them different nicknames, to help tell them apart."

"A big family tree," I observed.

Another light laugh. "Oh, yes. It took me years to get everybody sorted out."

Carey changed the subject. "You said something about jealousy being a motive for killing Greg?"

"If I had killed him. He was unfaithful, a lot. He hurt me, again and again. And in the end there was that girl Carlene who said he was going to leave me and marry her. But by then, I didn't really care."

"It sounds like you felt your marriage was just about over at the time he died," Carey said.

"Yeah, by then."

"But it wasn't like that at first."

"No, not at all. At first, it felt like a fairy tale. Greg didn't want me working after we were married, so I quit my job and was able to spend time with Brittany. He sold the house we were living in—he said he and Pat each got half as part of the divorce, and neither of them wanted to buy the other one out. We bought a new one—or rather, he bought it. We went together to look at places, but we ended up buying the house he liked. It was the same with the furniture and decorating it; he didn't like my ideas, he said they were too low-end. He ended up hiring a decorator. I think he was having an affair with her."

"Why did you think that?" Carey asked.

"Something in the way they interacted, the way he treated me. I wasn't sure then, I thought I was just being insecure. But when I got to know Greg better and see the patterns in how he behaved, I figured that's what was going on even back then."

"Did you confront him?"

Sunny shook her head. "Not then. I didn't say anything at the time. But I was a little scared—you know, he was married to Pat when we were seeing each other. Later, I got better at seeing the signs, and I started asking. He'd say there was nothing going on and get upset that I'd doubt him. And I'd keep doubting myself, thinking I had no proof, better to just let it go. But after a while there were too many late nights and weekends away, and once or twice he slipped up—I remember when some flowers he sent to one of his girlfriends got delivered to the house by mistake. When I brought it up, he'd get mad, say I was crazy and jealous. Later, when things cooled off between us, he didn't even bother to deny it; just said he was under a lot of pressure, and he worked his ass off to support me and my shiftless family. And we'd have an argument because I'd say it wasn't fair, Nana never asked him for any of the things he bought her, and Brittany was in junior high and what was he going to do, send her out to work? And he'd storm off into the night. After a while I just stopped saying anything."

She lowered her eyes, toward her hands clasped on the table in front of her. "I could smell it on him. He'd come home late and get into bed with that smell all over him. Or sometimes he'd have showered. They think they're being so smart, but why would a man shower somewhere away from his house in the middle of the night?"

"Did you still love him then?"

"For a long time, yes. But by the end I didn't feel much. I was just kind of floating along, not sure what was going to happen next. I had no idea what to do. He'd worn me down with criticizing me about so many things over the years; I had no confidence left. I think I was more afraid than anything."

"Afraid of him?"

She shook her head. "Not him… afraid of how I'd manage if he left me, how I'd be able to take care of Brittany. Not money so much; I knew we had the prenup. But I felt like I had no idea who I was anymore. I had no self-esteem by then; I didn't feel like I could make any decisions or do anything important on my own. He'd convinced me that I was too stupid. It's funny—" she looked up, around the room and through the window in the door "—I didn't really figure out how strong I was until I was here." She gave a small laugh and shook her head, baffled. "Prison—what a crazy place to find yourself."

"Was Greg abusive?"

"Physically, do you mean? No," Sunny said firmly. "Not that way."

"What do you mean?"

"He never hit me. He had his problems—the women, obviously, and he could be just so self-centered and mean. Not just to me and Brittany; he never got close to his own kids, either. But he wasn't a monster. He gave us plenty of money and a beautiful house. We traveled, had nice vacations. He was good to my family—he helped Nana after Grandpa died. He'd go himself and do repairs and stuff on her house. Put ceiling fans in the rooms, built her a deck, paid for a new roof and air conditioning. Nana thanked him, but she wouldn't use the air conditioning. Said it cost too much money, and she'd lived in Central Valley summers all her life. Linda and Pete mooched off him all the time, but he never cut them off. He really wanted to be liked."

"You said he wasn't physically abusive—was he in some other way?"

She nodded. "He was, but it took me years to finally realize that's what it was. I don't think I really figured it out until I was here. But all the time we were married, he made me feel like nothing. Anything I did was never quite up to his standards. If I cooked for him, he'd always find something wrong with what I'd made. If I put on an outfit to go out, half the time he'd make me change into something else. He'd criticize my hair; it needed cutting, I waited too long to cut it; it needed highlights; it was too straight or it was too frizzy. If we went out with his business friends, he'd tell me afterward that I'd laughed too loud or eaten too fast or said something I shouldn't have. He'd tell me I didn't discipline Brittany enough. So I was always doubting myself, wondering if I was good enough to be the wife he needed."

"That and his cheating—is that what did in your marriage?"

"That's about the size of it. We just drifted apart. He lost interest in me. He spent more and more time away from home, and I just stayed—went out with my friends, visited family, played tennis."

"What about Brittany?"

"She was okay until high school. Then she started acting out, cutting school, not coming home on time. She started seeing Todd Betts, hanging out with him and his friends. Sometimes she'd be gone all night. I didn't know what to do about it, and Greg took no interest at all."

"And at some point," I said, "you found out Greg was seeing Carlene Renner."

She nodded.

"When was that? Do you remember?"

She sighed. "Oh, Lord, I'm not sure now. Maybe just some time early in the year he was killed. He died in May of 2002, not long before our fifteenth anniversary."

"How did you learn about him and Carlene?"

"Well, Harrison isn't that big a town. My friends

sometimes knew when Greg was fooling around, but they didn't usually want to say anything, I'd just see it in the way they sometimes looked at me; you know, sometimes you can tell when people are talking about you behind your back. But one woman I knew, Mary Ellen, told me about Carlene because her hairdresser and Carlene's family were close. I remember she said Carlene was saying Greg was going to divorce me and marry her."

"How did you feel about that?"

"You know, I felt worse than I thought I would. I actually cried when I got home."

"Do you know why?"

"I guess, like I said, I was scared. It seems funny, because I wasn't happy where I was. Also, looking back, I'd always been afraid it would happen. Every time I knew Greg had another girlfriend, I'd wonder if this was it. And this time, I figured it was."

"Did you say anything to Greg?"

"No, I was afraid to bring it up. I thought if we got into a fight about it, he might really decide to leave me."

"And he didn't say anything to you."

"No. He was even more distant than usual, though, and of course that made me more worried."

"Did you talk to anyone else about it?"

"Carol. And I called Linda."

"What did they tell you?"

"Linda was saying, you need to fight for him; don't let her take him from you. But then she really liked Greg; he won her over early. He charmed her, gave her presents and money when she needed it, and she always took his side when I complained about him. She may have been almost as upset about losing him as I was. Carol said not to worry. She didn't think Greg really intended to leave. She said getting divorced would be expensive for him, even with the prenup, and she didn't think he'd really want to marry someone like Carlene. And even if it happened, there were plenty of people around, including her, who'd help me get a new start. That made me feel a little better."

"But then Brittany found out about it," I said.

Sunny stiffened a little, and she gave me a guarded look. "She heard about it from someone—I didn't tell her."

"How did she react?"

Sunny spoke a little more carefully than she had before. "I don't know how she felt when she learned about it. She told me what she'd heard, asked me if I knew and what I was going to do, and I said we'd figure it out." She paused for a second, as if considering whether to go on. "She was angry at Greg. She and Greg never got along. He was always critical of her, and she didn't like him."

Natasha asked the next question. "Do you think she had anything to do with Greg's murder?"

Sunny shook her head. "No," she said. "I can't imagine it. She was only sixteen. All the stuff between her and Greg—I know she said she hated him, but that was all teenage stuff. You get over it. I don't even know who killed him, really. I mean, everyone kept saying it was Todd, but they don't *know*." She faltered, a tiny fall of her voice, at the last few words, and shook her head again.

This was a subject I'd brought up before, when I was working on her appeal. She had jumped to Brittany's defense then, too, and pressing the point had only made her worried and defensive. I decided to change the subject for now, and asked a question of my own.

"What happened the day Greg was killed?"

This was old ground also, covered in Sunny's statements to the police and her trial testimony, but Sunny told the story again without complaint. "It was just a regular Saturday. Greg had a project going; he was planning to waterblast the deck out by the pool. He left in the morning for the hardware store. Brittany and I had plans to go visit Nana out in Sparksville, take her out for lunch and then to the mall."

"Did Brittany want to go with you?" Natasha asked.

"I said she should, and she didn't object. She loved Nana; even when I was having all the problems with her, she still went with me to see her once or twice a month. I went more often, a couple of times a week."

"So you left when?"

"About eleven. We picked Nana up and drove back to Harrison, to the mall. Ate lunch at a hamburger place there, then shopped for a while. When Nana started to get tired, we drove back to her place, after stopping for ice cream at Mitchell's—that was her favorite—and then at a supermarket to buy her some groceries."

"You didn't stop at your house that afternoon."

"No, no reason why we should. It was at the other end of town anyway."

"And after you dropped Nana off, what did you do?"

"We stayed at her house for a while and talked, and I put the groceries away. So we didn't leave right away."

"Did you go straight home from there?"

"Yes."

"And what happened when you got there?"

Sunny gave a small shiver. "Everything looked normal." She leaned an arm on the table and rested her forehead on her hand for a few seconds. In that interval I felt with her those last few minutes of ordinary life which you pass with no idea how precious they are or that everything is about to come crashing down, that somewhere miles away the car has veered off the road, the gun has fired, the airplane has struck the building. I remembered again the ringing of the phone. The receptionist's voice followed by Dave Rothstein's, telling me Terry had died. And how that fact tumbled me into a new reality where nothing would ever again be what it had been ten seconds before.

"I didn't see Greg or hear the water blaster; I assumed he'd gone out somewhere. Brittany went upstairs to her room; I figured she was calling Todd. I had a few things from the supermarket, so I took them to the kitchen and put them away, and then went upstairs. I'd bought a blouse and some sandals at the mall, and I wanted to take them to the bedroom.

"While I was upstairs I heard Brittany go back down. I

came down a minute or so later and went into the kitchen to start dinner. And I heard her scream, in the back yard. And then she ran in from the deck and said, 'Mama, Mama, Greg's out back. I think he's dead.'

"My first thought was that he'd had a heart attack. I went out with Britt, and she showed me where he was. He was lying on his back on the pool deck, and there was some blood under his head. I remember thinking, *Oh, God, he's cracked his skull.* I kneeled down beside him and checked for a pulse. There wasn't one, and his hand was cold. I felt his arm, and it was cool, too, and it felt stiff; and I knew then he was dead. His face, too—" She gave a small shake of her head and sighed. "His face was—it was kind of like a wax mask, like my grandpa's face in the hospital after he passed away. So I was almost sure. Britt was looking sick, and I said, 'Let's go inside and call 911,' and we did."

"You didn't see any sign he'd been shot."

"Except for the blood, no. I didn't know that until the police told me. Someone told me there was one bullet, and it hit his brain stem or something; anyway, they said he would have lost consciousness immediately and been dead in a few minutes. They said he didn't suffer; that made me feel a little better."

"The police suspected you straight away, right?"

"Yes. They took Brittany and me to the police station and separated us and asked us a lot of questions about where we'd been that day and what we'd been doing. One of them was really rude and kept acting like I was guilty. I was just in shock; he made me cry. After they took us home I called Carol and told her about it, and she said I needed to get a lawyer right away. She recommended Craig Newhouse. He was wonderful."

"You weren't arrested until—what, four months after Greg died?"

"Something like that."

"What was happening during that time?"

"I tried to go on living my life, but it got kind of crazy. Greg had life insurance, but the company didn't want to pay it to me because the police said I was suspected of killing him. Craig recommended a civil lawyer—he only did criminal then—and he straightened things out with the insurance."

"How much was the policy?"

"Two hundred thousand dollars."

"Not that much for someone with as much money as Greg had."

She shrugged. "It was enough for us. I thought it would last longer, but it turned out Greg had a lot of business debts and expenses that had to be paid. And Greg's family was contesting his will. We moved out of the house so the probate court could sell it, and rented a condo across town. Britt was kind of shaken up by Greg's death and having to move, and I guess I was, too. She asked me if I could loan Todd some money to buy a new truck. He was driving this horrible old pickup, with bad brakes and God knows what else wrong with it—just the thought of Brittany riding in it scared me to death. So I said, sure, and gave her a check made out to

Todd for five thousand dollars." She grimaced. "They said later that was a payment for killing Greg. And then Todd overdosed on heroin or something, and his mother kept the money, or what was left of it. I guess I was naive. I didn't even know Todd was doing drugs, or—I wouldn't have loaned him that kind of money. I felt sorry for him; he didn't seem like a bad kid, actually. He worked at the Ferrantes' ranch. He wasn't right for Brittany, but I felt if I didn't make an issue about him, she'd figure that out on her own eventually.

"After Todd died, Brittany was in terrible shape. She barely left the house, didn't want to see any of her friends. She kept saying she wanted to go away somewhere. We took a cruise up to Alaska together, and brought Nana along. I was hoping a change of scene would help her. Before we left I enrolled her in Sacred Heart, the girls' Catholic school in Harrison, because she didn't want to go back to Harrison High. After we got back, I signed her up for counseling."

"Sounds like you were doing a lot."

She shrugged. "I tried to; it helped keep the worry away. I looked for work, too, but wasn't having any luck; my skills were too rusty. I was thinking of applying for temp work, to get my foot back in the door, so to speak, when they arrested me."

Sunny's tone had been so matter-of-fact, we'd been lulled by her story. Even though we knew well enough it had happened, we all said, "Oh," almost involuntarily.

"Yeah," Sunny said. "It was kind of a shock. They didn't even tell Craig first, just came to the door around dinnertime, two detectives and a couple of women from Child Protective Services, who took Brittany. She ended up staying in a group home for almost a week, until the social workers allowed her to go live with Nana."

"Jesus," Natasha said.

"Yeah," Sunny said again. "It was as bad as it could be. God knows, Britt didn't need that on top of everything else."

The guard knocked on our door for the five-minute warning. Sunny seemed to shake herself back to the present. "I guess you know the rest."

"I'm going to be going out and interviewing people close to you and Brittany," Natasha said. "Can you give me some names of people you knew back then, and any friends of Brittany's you knew? Oh, and do you remember any of your teachers in school?"

Sunny thought for a moment and began slowly listing names and what she knew about where each of them might be now. Some I remembered as witnesses who had testified on her behalf at the penalty phase of her trial, but others, including the people she recalled as friends of Brittany's, were new. We took notes quickly. The guard came back.

"Thanks," Natasha said to Sunny. "If you remember any more, let us know."

We said our goodbyes and stood for a moment watching Sunny's retreating back before going to retrieve our forms from the desk.

"Glad you got those names," Carey said to Natasha. "Do you think you'll be able to locate any of those people in time to interview them while we're in Harrison?"

"Hopefully. I can do some locates online tonight."

I realized that after our exchange in the lobby I had been watching for Natasha to make a wrong step. But she hadn't; she had done well, I thought, at helping us touch all the needed bases in the interview. She might be a bit up herself, as they say in Australia, but she seemed to know what she was doing. So I decided it was best to counter the arrogance of the young toward the old with the tolerance of the old toward the young. "That went well," I said. "She seems comfortable with you."

"The way she talked about Todd Betts, I just don't believe she hired him to kill Greg," Natasha said.

"You're not the only one," I answered, "but the police, the prosecutor, and twelve good citizens of Harrison apparently did." And now, I thought, we had less than a year to convince a judge they were all wrong.

5

Harrison, where Greg Ferrante had been murdered and Sunny had been tried for it, is about a three-hour drive from the women's prison. Even fueled with more coffee, I was struggling against sleep before I reached the exit for our motel. As I got out of the car and walked to the building to check in, a cool breeze carried faint smells of dust, diesel fuel, and frying food. The sky over the flat plain of the valley was huge and clear, the afterglow from sunset silhouetting the distant hills on the horizon; and a planet or two shone like bright stars in an endless depth of deepening violet-blue.

Carey and Natasha arrived at the motel fifteen minutes or so after I did. Over dinner in a ranch-themed family restaurant nearby, with green and white gingham curtains on the windows and cowboy paintings on the walls, we discussed our plans for the next day—the discovery motion, the exhibits review. Natasha said she'd do some research at the library while we were in court. By the time we walked back, the sky was almost in full night, and many more stars had winked into view. A warm breeze came up, carrying other smells—orange blossoms, Chinese food, the tang of cow manure. In my neat, impersonal bedroom, I unpacked my suitcase, checked my email, watched a news program on the TV, and fell into a dreamless sleep until the alarm on my phone woke me.

We met in the motel's breakfast room. Carey, in her gray suit and cream silk blouse, a little rumpled from their time in her car, was the picture of a working lawyer. My navy blue skirt and jacket, from the small wardrobe of suits I'd been forced to buy for a hearing the previous year, were presentable enough for the discovery motion that Carey and I would be arguing that morning. Natasha had exchanged yesterday's flowing skirt and shirt for a neat gray-green dress and a short cardigan. Carey was bright and alert, Natasha and I both limp and largely silent.

We ate according to our fashion from the breakfast bar: steam table scrambled eggs and a waffle for Natasha, yogurt and a banana for Carey. I decided it would probably be a long, foodless morning, and fortified myself with the scrambled eggs, toast, canned peaches, and a couple of cups of bitter coffee with a lot of milk. I could feel the clouds clear from my brain as the caffeine worked its magic.

As we were gathering our paper plates and cups to toss them, Natasha said to Carey, "I had planned to go to the library this morning, but I think I'll stay here for a while and read through some more of Craig Newhouse's files on the thumb drive you sent me, and then join the two of you later to view the exhibits, if you don't mind. I don't know why you had to be the one to have them scanned. The state defender should have done it; it would have saved us a couple of weeks."

"Actually," Carey told her, "the state defender did have them scanned. I've just been too busy to find any flash drives with enough memory to hold them all. Why don't I call you when the hearing ends, and you can meet us in the exhibits room?"

We made the short drive to the courthouse in Carey's car. "What do you think of Natasha?" she asked.

I chose my words carefully. "Well, she's very sharp, and I liked the questions she asked Sunny yesterday."

"And yet—?"

"Oh, nothing much, just a generational thing. She seems like a bit of a know-it-all, a little too judgmental."

Carey nodded. "Yeah. Smart, but maybe lacking in life experience."

"What's her background in capital cases?" I asked.

"Well, she worked with Marianne Southern for a couple of years until she went out on her own."

"That would explain the attitude."

Carey nodded, with a laugh. "So you know Marianne."

"A little."

"I worked with her on a case, once. She's one of the best investigators out here, but—"

"Insufferable," I filled in.

Carey nodded in agreement. "Marianne's used to working for trial lawyers with a lot more money to spend than we have. Anyway, though, Natasha was taught well, and she did good work on my other case. I'm trying to tone her down a bit, acquaint her with the realities of work on a much smaller budget."

The County Government Center at Harrison, which held the county courtrooms, the clerk's office, the district attorney's offices, and the headquarters of several other functionaries, was a standard-issue government building: a light gray postwar block, durably built and minimally ornamented. It had three floors and a wide green lawn with shade trees. It occupied a street between the old town and the new that also held the public library and a parking garage.

Inside, past the squatters' village of metal detectors and uniformed guards at the entrance, the lobby, all wood-paneled walls and polished floors, announced itself as an institution of quiet dignity, an outpost of a large and prosperous state. High ceilings hushed the conversation of the small morning crowd of lawyers, litigants, jurors, and witnesses seeking out their courtrooms for that day's calendar. As many times as I had been in courthouses over the years, their psychological effect always impressed me: in the presence of whatever unmoving authority their architecture communicated, people grew quieter and better-behaved.

The courtroom itself, on the second floor, was windowless and even more hushed. The clerk and bailiff were working at their stations in monastic domesticity; and the elevated bench, with the judge's desk and the witness box beside and below it, resembled an altar of polished oak. The church-like tone of it struck me, and I remembered a hearing in a different courtroom, in another case, where my co-counsel, as the court adjourned on the final day of a long hearing, had been moved to say under his breath, "*Ite, missa est.*"

Two men in suits were standing at the prosecution side of the counsel table, talking quietly. They looked over at us as we set our briefcases on our side of the counsel table, and we traded introductions.

"Ken Cranston, Attorney General's office."

"Julian Maldonado, deputy district attorney."

Cranston was the older of the two, probably in his mid-forties, with a forgettable face and short, wavy brown hair starting to gray at the temples. Julian was surely hardly old enough to be out of law school. He gave his name its Spanish pronunciation, the "J" pronounced as an "H" and pronounced "deputy district attorney" with the consonants a little soft and slurred, the familiar accent of the Mexican-American children of immigrants.

"I saw your name in the case file," Ken said to me. "You were involved in this case in the past?"

"Back at the beginning of the appeal. I was Sunny's attorney for a while before I left the state defender's office."

"Ah. That was before I got the case. Dan Morgenthal had it then, right?"

It took me a second to remember the name. "That's right," I answered.

"I got the case from him a couple of years ago, when he retired. He's living on Bainbridge Island now, lucky guy."

"Lucky is right," I agreed, sincerely.

"Anyhow," Ken went on, "all the briefs in the appeal were filed when Dan had the case, and I thought I'd just be babysitting it until the court sets oral argument. I just started reading the file. You saw our response to the discovery motion, right? We're not going to contest anything but the two items I don't think the statute entitles you to."

Julian Maldonado, who had been listening, spoke up. "I'm new to the case, too," he said. "Sandy Michaud, the trial DA, is a judge now; she's in the juvenile court across town."

"Nice for her," Carey said.

"Yeah. I'm just here to hear the judge's rulings and supervise compliance with the orders. I'll be in charge of preparing DVDs of our files for you." He handed us each a business card. "Here's my contact information if you need to reach me."

The bailiff called for order, and we moved to our respective corners at the counsel table and stood as the judge came from the door behind the bench and took his seat. Even the judge was new; I remembered reading some years ago that the judge who had tried Sunny's case had been elevated to a seat on the Court of Appeal. The judge assigned to hear our motion was, as the bailiff intoned, the Honorable Armando Garcia. He was a small, middle-aged man who said almost nothing during our arguments on the motion but to extend a polite invitation to the other party to respond. His rulings, given from the bench in a quiet, level voice, were reasonable;

he gave us what we knew the law entitled us to, and one or two minor things besides. He asked Julian Maldonado how quickly he could provide the court-ordered discovery, "given the filing deadline under the new law," and when Julian said he thought he could finish in three weeks, gave a date three weeks away for compliance with the orders.

After adjourning the hearing, the two prosecutors left, and we met the judge in his chambers to discuss the request Carey had submitted for funding for the case. Our fees and expenses were paid by the state, but we had to get the judge's approval to spend money on investigators and experts. The discussion of money went as smoothly as the discovery hearing. Carey presented him with our claim for the work we had done so far, and a request that he authorize five thousand dollars more for future work for Natasha. "We're on a tight timeline," she explained, "and I think she'll be working almost full time on this case for a while."

Judge Garcia nodded. "You're probably right," he said. He read through the claim and request and then signed both. "Is that it?" he said, as he handed it back to Carey.

"Yes, Your Honor."

He stood, and we did, too, and we said our goodbyes.

The morning brought home to me how much time had passed since Sunny's trial, fourteen years ago. Between then and now, the entire cast of characters had moved on: transferred, promoted, or retired. The same would be true of witnesses; in a case this cold, too many would be dead or impossible to find or, when we found them, would remember all too few of the vital details we needed. And we had only months to try to talk to them all and put our case together. Carey was right to be anxious.

6

There must be a competition among courts to see how thoroughly they can hide their exhibits clerks. Some offices are in basements, others on the top floor, and they always seem to be at the end of a labyrinth of corridors. Hartwell County's was on the third floor of the courthouse, behind an unmarked door in a row of similar doors, at the far end of one wing. As we finally opened the right door, we were bewildered and surprised to have found the place at all. Our question whether this was the exhibit room was answered with a nod and a "Yep," by a round-faced young woman at a metal desk. She stood up, and it was clear from the bulge under the high waist of her short summer dress that she was pregnant.

"Oh, don't get up," Carey said quickly. "We're here to see Mary Jesperson and review the exhibits in *People v. Ferrante*. We're Mrs. Ferrante's lawyers, Carey Bergmann and Janet Moodie. Ms. Jesperson is expecting us."

"Oh, right!" The young woman sprang up again. Even heavily pregnant, her movements were almost effortless. *Ah, youth!* I thought. "I have those over here. Mary's at a meeting this morning. Just come in through that gate at the end of the counter. I'm Corliss, by the way—Corliss Howard."

"That's an unusual name," I said.

"It's a family name. I'm named for my great-grandmother."

"When are you due?" Carey asked.

"Two months. I can't wait." She smiled, looking down at her belly. "This gets really old after a while."

"Do you know if it's a boy or girl?"

"Boy. It's our second; our first baby was a girl. So we'll have one of each." Another smile.

The boxes, what there were of them, were on an otherwise unoccupied desk in a corner of the outer office. Natasha came in the door as I was plugging in my computer and attaching the cords to the scanner. "Sorry I'm late," she apologized. "I had a hard time finding this place."

"Oh, everyone does," Corliss answered. "We hear that all the time."

After more introductions, we began the work of looking at the exhibits, checking them off on our copy of the clerk's list from the trial, and photographing or scanning those that appeared to be worth preserving. The review was more for Carey's benefit; I'd seen them here once before, when I was Sunny's attorney in her appeal, and I didn't expect to get any new insights from viewing them again.

There wasn't much, for a capital trial: photos of the murder scene, of Greg's body lying on the concrete pool deck; autopsy photos showing the small bullet hole in the back of his head, the hair shaved to make the wound visible. The slug removed from his brain was in a small plastic bag inside a manila evidence envelope; it seemed a ridiculously small thing to have killed a man. There were also photos of Todd Betts's body slumped in an armchair, the tourniquet and syringe he had used on a table beside him. There were autopsy reports for both men, bank records and a copy of the check Sunny had written to Todd, and also some copies of criminal records of Steve Eason, the informant who had claimed Todd had told him he'd been hired by Sunny to do the murder.

Photocopies of the prosecutor's PowerPoint slides from her opening statements and closing arguments at the guilt and penalty trials had been made exhibits by the judge. More poignantly, there were photographs of Greg Ferrante, from childhood through middle age, that had gone with the testimony of his parents, to show the impact of his death on those close to him. I remembered there was also a video, made by the family, that had been shown at trial, with more photos and some home movie footage.

Sunny had also had her day, and the defense exhibits included school records, photos of her as a child; in junior high in her 4-H uniform, holding a brown and white rabbit and a red prize ribbon; as Homecoming Queen in the pink dress bought for her by Linda; as a new bride outside the Methodist church; more photos of her with Brittany, with Greg, with her mother and grandmother.

I was feeling the uncomfortable sleepiness of caffeine

deprivation as we closed up the last box and thanked Corliss for her help. Despite myself, I was a bit disappointed to find that there was nothing new to be discovered here—all was largely as I remembered, and nothing inspired me or suggested any new approach to the case. We would have to rely on Natasha's research and the long, uncertain process of interviewing witnesses, to perhaps throw up some new leads.

"Best wishes to you and the baby," Carey said, as we left. "Take good care of yourself."

"I will," Corliss said. "I have three months off, starting next month."

"That's good," Carey said. "Not a lot of time, is it, though?"

Corliss nodded. "Yeah, it's tough, having to go back to work so soon. But we need the money."

"You and that clerk really bonded over her baby," Natasha said to Carey as we walked down the hall.

I didn't see Carey react, but a beat passed before she answered. "My daughter's first baby was born this February."

After lunch at a sandwich shop near the courthouse, Natasha went her own way, to research high-school yearbooks and old city directories at the library, for names of neighbors in Harrison and Sparksville who might have known Sunny and her family, or Todd, or anyone else important to the case. She also had plans to interview a few people she had already found, including some of Sunny's and Brittany's teachers.

Carey and I had some time to kill after lunch before our

appointment with Craig Newhouse. We walked over to Old Town, which wasn't far from the courthouse, and spent a quiet half-hour strolling the old main street and window shopping. It was still spring; the leaves of the trees and shrubs that lined the street and shaded the sides and back yards of the old buildings were fresh and bright green, and the air under the shade trees was warm, but not yet hot.

"So you have a grandbaby," I said, regarding her with new eyes. Carey had seemed to me so professional and driven that I'd never seen her as particularly maternal, let alone grandmotherly.

Her eyes brightened. "Yes, indeed."

"Boy or girl?"

"Girl. They named her Rachel, after my mother."

"That's a nice gesture."

Getting back to business, Carey said, "I've got a few thoughts for questions for Craig Newhouse, but not many."

I agreed. "I've been going through his files again, and he did a decent job investigating the case and presenting mitigation. The woman he hired as his mitigation specialist knew what she was doing, too."

"Joan Simon. I know her—another one of Marianne Southern's alumnae. She is good."

"I could see that. She interviewed a lot of people—even got Sunny's father's family to talk to her—and compiled a history of Sunny's ancestors going back to the Civil War, with records and everything. It was impressive."

Carey nodded. "It sure was. But no smoking guns. It

must have been really hard for Craig. It's always a balancing act, trying to present background evidence that might make your client appear less blameworthy, when your whole case is that she didn't do the crime at all. And Sunny's past looks uneventful compared to most clients. She lost a father she never knew, and her mother skipped out on her, but her grandparents seem to have been good to her, and she seems very normal, as a kid and adult—no history of childhood abuse that we know of, no drinking, no drugs, no especially risky behavior, no signs of mental illness. Greg was a womanizer and emotionally abusive, but Sunny was no Betty Mateski."

"No."

"It's a tough case."

Craig Newhouse's office was near the courthouse complex, an easy walk back from Old Town, and we got there a few minutes early. He was a partner in a law firm that apparently occupied an entire building, with its own parking lot. The building, in Mission Revival style, was finished in cream-colored stucco with accents of oak and terrazzo tile. The sign above the massive oak double doors read "Eldridge, Saperstein, Newhouse, and Walti, Attorneys at Law."

The theme of the building's façade was continued inside it. The waiting area was decorated with polished terrazzo floors, blocky wood and leather chairs and magazine tables, and a wagon-wheel chandelier. Filtered light came in from a couple of tall windows framed in dark wood. An attractive young receptionist behind the counter took our names and said, "Mr. Newhouse is on the phone right now. I'll let him know you're here."

Carey and I sat in side-by-side blocky chairs and reflexively checked our phones for messages. I picked up a copy of a month-old *People* magazine from a side table and leafed through it, and Carey pulled a notepad from her briefcase and studied something written on it.

Lawyers and clients came and went through the lobby and into and out of the offices behind a doorway to the left of the receptionist's counter. After ten minutes or so, a man opened the door and walked a ways into the lobby, scanning it for someone. He was a little taller than average, and middle-aged, with salt-and-pepper hair cut short. He had probably been strikingly handsome when he was young; even now he was good-looking, with a suntanned face, a clean, square jaw, and the posture and easy movement of an older man who has kept in shape. Seeing us, he brightened. "Ms. Bergmann and Ms. Moodie," he said, striding toward us. "I'm Craig Newhouse. Sorry to keep you waiting; I had a phone call that took a while."

We stood and shook hands. "Which of you is Ms. Moodie?" he asked.

"Me," I said.

"Ah—we talked on the phone a few years ago. Nice to meet you in person."

"Nice to meet you, too," I said lamely.

"My office is back here." Craig gave a nod toward the door by the receptionist.

As he led us down a corridor lined with offices, he asked over his shoulder, "Does your being here for the habeas case mean Sunny's appeal is over?"

"No," I answered. "It's still pending. All the briefs have been filed, and they're waiting for it to be set for oral argument."

"That long," he said, bemused. "Here we are."

Craig's office was nice, but not luxurious: a large desk of polished dark wood at the left, a window at the right with a view onto leafy landscaping, a leather sofa under the window, dark wood bookshelves on the far and near walls. The furniture was plain and not brand-new, but good-quality and well-kept. It was a look that told clients the firm gave value for their fees.

A smartly dressed young woman stood up from the farthest of the chairs in front of the desk and reached out a hand. "Hi, I'm Alison," she said.

"Alison's our paralegal," Craig said. "She's working with me on Sunny's case." We exchanged more handshakes.

I doubted Craig needed a paralegal for whatever he was still doing on the case. My guess was that she had been asked to sit in as a witness when the conversation moved to Craig's representation of Sunny. However friendly we seemed, in any discussion between trial and postconviction defense attorneys, the possible claim of ineffective assistance of counsel was the elephant in the room.

"Can I get you something to drink?" Craig asked. "Coffee or tea? Water?"

Carey said water sounded good, and I opted for coffee.

"I'll get them," Alison said, smiling.

The surface of Craig's desk was uncluttered: a couple of photos, presumably of family members, an inbox with a few pieces of mail, a few manila files stacked to one side, a yellow pad in the center, a notebook computer on an L to Craig's left. Next to the computer stood a sleek metal water bottle. Above the credenza behind the desk, and below his framed college and law school diplomas and certificates of admission to the state bar, was a shelf of trophies and medals. "What are the trophies?" I asked, curious.

"Competitive swimming." He seemed both proud and a bit shy about it. "I just won best in my age class in two categories in the state competition."

Alison reappeared with a bottle of water, a mug, and a couple of small creamers and set them down in front of us. I carefully opened the creamers, trying not to spritz any drops from them onto Craig's shining desktop, and poured their contents into my coffee.

"Here, let me get those." Alison swept up the empty containers and dropped them in a wastebasket.

I took a sip of the coffee, which wasn't bad.

"So," Craig said. "Where would you like to start?"

"Well—" Carey inspected her notebook "—I can see you put a lot of work into Sunny's case."

Craig nodded. "We did our best. We were all shocked by the verdict; we were surprised enough when they found her guilty of murder, but none of us really believed the jury would find for death." He shook his head. "It should never have been a death case, but Mrs. Ferrante—Greg's mother— pushed really hard for it and got some victims' rights groups on board. She raised the profile of the case, made it hard for the DA politically."

"Had you done other capital cases?"

"Yes." He glanced at me; we'd gone over this ground before, years ago. "Before coming to Eldridge Saperstein I was a solo practitioner, working on criminal cases here in Harrison and in Tulare County. I did three capital trials there; none of them ended in a death verdict. Sunny's was the last case I thought we'd ever lose. I felt so bad that I pretty much gave up criminal practice after that. Now I do mostly personal injury and some criminal work now and then for clients of the firm—mostly DUIs and white-collar crimes, juvie cases when their kids get in trouble, things like that." He shrugged, and Carey and I nodded sympathetically.

"You were appointed by the court on Sunny's case," Carey said. "How did that happen?"

"Well I wasn't at first. She retained me, but then she ran out of money. Greg Ferrante didn't leave as much of an estate as everyone thought, and his relatives contested his will; and the life insurance company sued for return of the payout. So I ended up asking the court to appoint me. The judge wanted to appoint the public defender, but they declared a conflict; they'd represented Steve Eason, the informer, in an old misdemeanor.

"It was such a crazy case," he mused, with another shake of

his head. "There was almost no evidence connecting Sunny to the murder except that check to Todd Betts and Eason's testimony. Sandy—the DA—had this cockamamie theory about motive, like something out of a soap opera: greedy wife kills her rich husband because he's about to leave her for another woman. Hokey as hell, but it works on Hartwell County jurors. She knew her audience. The smartest thing Sandy did was to attack Sunny as a mother. She made a huge deal about how Sunny used her own daughter's boyfriend to do the killing. And she brought in the witnesses who testified about Todd Betts's admissions and what a good, hardworking kid he was and how he was wracked with guilt about it afterward. She ended up turning Todd and Brittany into victims along with Ferrante."

I nodded agreement. The strategy had been clever, and obviously successful. The prosecutor had called a couple of Todd's friends to testify that he had changed after the murder; he seemed shaken and frightened, and before his death he had started using a lot more drugs, "like he just wanted to stay high all the time." One said Todd, while high, had mumbled something about having done "something horrible." Brittany had been called to testify that she had seen the change in him. The district attorney told the jury, in her closing argument, that Sunny had used Todd and destroyed him, and that she was responsible for his overdose death, saying, "She may as well have put that needle in his arm herself."

"We tried to discredit the informant, Eason," Craig

went on, "the guy who told the police that Todd said Sunny had hired him. We investigated him and found he was pretty much a professional snitch. Harry Markman, my investigator, turned up several other cases in which Eason informed for money or leniency, including a couple where he claimed the defendant confessed to him. But the judge kept all that out. Said it wasn't relevant unless he'd lied in his other cases, and when we said we could show that he had been lying in some of them, he said he didn't want to hold a series of mini-trials about a bunch of unrelated crimes. But you know all that."

I remembered that exchange from the trial transcript. "Yeah. We argued that as a claim of error in Sunny's appeal," I said.

"Good," he said. "I felt strongly about that. The judge's ruling really hurt us; Eason's testimony was the strongest evidence the DA had. We could argue away the check Sunny wrote to Betts. You don't use a check if you're paying someone for a murder. But Betts's confession to Eason made everything fit. It pointed right to Sunny."

"How was that?" Carey asked.

"Well, if you assume Betts was the killer," Craig said, "the question became, who put him up to it? No one was going to believe Betts did it on his own; he didn't have any motive to kill Ferrante. And who would hire him for something like that? He was just a dumb kid, someone you'd have mow the weeds in your field or help pull a stump—not something like this. So if it wasn't Sunny who hired him, who did?"

"Maybe Brittany," I said. "The thought did occur to me back when I had Sunny's appeal."

"Right. I thought of that, too. But it would have been a hard sell—she was sixteen, and Todd was twenty. And Sunny wouldn't go there—what mother would?"

"Todd was working for Greg's father and brothers, wasn't he?" Carey asked.

"Yeah."

"What about them?"

"Again, what would be the motive?" Craig explained. "They're probably better off than Greg was. Ferrantes have been ranchers on that land since the 1800s, and Bob and his sons have turned it into a very profitable concern: wine grapes, olive oil, prime beef. Put it this way—even if they wanted to get rid of Greg for some reason, they wouldn't have to hire someone like Betts."

"Do you think Greg's family will be willing to talk to us?" Carey asked.

"It depends. Greg's mother decided Sunny was guilty and wouldn't have anything to do with us. Joan Simon interviewed his father and brothers, though. His father liked Sunny, as I recall. Greg's brothers weren't really close to Greg. I recall they thought he was a little shady. One of them told Joan in confidence that he had doubts about whether Sunny really did it. But none of them had much to say. Joan thought they were afraid of antagonizing Mrs. Ferrante. None of them testified at the trial, only Greg's parents and his kids."

"Huh," Carey said. "You'd think the DA would want them all as victim impact witnesses."

"Yeah. Joan said Sandy probably thought they wouldn't say they missed him that much."

"You said Greg was a bit shady. What did you know about him?"

Craig sat back in his chair and thought for a few seconds. "We got that impression, too, when we asked around. We got the feeling folks involved with him in business dealings didn't like him. I remember we found he had some trouble with the city over some rental properties, about upkeep and such. And he'd been sued a few times over real estate deals. He was leveraged when he died, lot of mortgages, a lot of debt; after all the business creditors were paid, there wasn't much left of the estate." Another pause, and then he went on. "And he wasn't a great human being on a personal level, either, is my guess. Sunny was reluctant to say anything bad about Greg, but you get hints, you know, from the way she talked about him."

"Was he physically abusive to her?"

"She said no. We asked, naturally. But she was firm, said he never hit her. There was something there, though. If you ask me, the abuse was more psychological. Brittany said he was 'mean' to both of them, and I recall Joan Simon interviewed some friends of Sunny's who said he bossed her around and was rude to her in public. We didn't pursue it that much; we had to be careful what we said about Greg at the trial. You don't want to trash the victim, usually, and talking about him treating her badly could backfire; it would just be more evidence that she had a motive to get out of the marriage and make him pay. Maybe that was a mistake; I don't know."

"Is there anyone in particular who it would be helpful for us to talk to?"

Craig thought for a minute. "I don't know, offhand," he answered, slowly. "Maybe Brittany, now. We didn't talk to her much back then. Joan said it was hard to get anything out of her. She was traumatized and depressed—not surprising when you consider what she'd been through. And Sunny asked us to leave her alone; she was afraid Brittany was going to harm herself." He paused again. "I have two daughters; I sympathized with her. Let's see, who else might there be? Bob Ferrante Senior died a few years ago. He was in his nineties. I believe his sons, Bob Junior and Tony, are both still alive; they run the business, live outside of town on the old ranch property. And they knew Greg and Sunny. Braden, Greg's son by his first marriage, was somehow in the picture when it happened. He was staying with the Ferrantes, and there was some scuttlebutt that he was doing drugs with Todd. And there were some young guys, friends of Todd's, down in Beanhollow. Joan will probably be able to help you; she knew the case inside and out. Harry Wardman, my other investigator, lives here in Harrison. He's retired now, but I run into him once in awhile. There were a lot of people we interviewed. I don't remember all their names, but they're probably in the files I gave you."

He stopped talking and reached for the bottle of water on his desk. He opened it, took a drink, closed it again, and brought his attention back to us.

"Look." His eyes met Carey's and then mine. "If you find there was anything I did wrong, or didn't do that I should have, let me know, and I'll sign a declaration for you. I want the best for Sunny out of this. I hope you can get her a new trial; she doesn't deserve to be where she is." He took a breath and moved to an easier subject. "How is she doing, by the way?"

"All right, all things considered," I said. "We've seen her a couple of times recently, and she seems to be getting along well. Getting older, like all of us, but doing okay."

"That's good to hear. She sends me a Christmas card every year, usually with a little note about something. I guess Brittany is married now and has a couple of kids."

"She told us," I said. "Brittany stays in touch, visits her mother once or twice a year."

He seemed pleased to hear that. We didn't know enough yet about the case to begin asking the tough questions, the ones about stones left unturned, what could have been done but wasn't. Those were never comfortable conversations to have, but they were still in the future—whatever future there was between now and when the petition had to be filed. For now, I was relieved at Craig's professionalism about the likelihood that we would at some point be making an argument that there were deficiencies in the way he had represented Sunny.

Craig shifted in his chair, and we all stood as if on cue, including Alison, who'd been quietly taking notes. He walked around from behind his desk and shook hands with Carey and then me; there was genuine warmth in his handshake. "I wish you good luck," he said. "If there's anything I can help you with, let me know." Carey and I thanked him.

Alison, to one side, said, "Nice to meet you," a little shyly, and turned to the door. "Here, I'll show you the way out." Carey and I followed her down the hallway, and I glanced through a couple of open doors: an outside office for another lawyer, smaller inside offices presumably for paralegals and secretaries. As she opened the door to the lobby, Alison said, "I really admire the work you do."

"We do what we can," Carey said; and with another round of handshakes and goodbyes, we stepped out into the large, quiet room and walked toward the massive doors. "Have a good afternoon," the receptionist said, and I nodded thanks to her over my shoulder.

"Man, times have changed," Carey said, outside. "Can you imagine anyone twenty years ago saying they admired what we did?"

"No way."

There had been a time when telling a stranger you defended people on death row usually got you an enthusiastically vituperative lecture on why certain people should be written out of society. I remembered seeing young men at law conferences wearing T-shirts that said, "Don't tell my mother I'm a public defender; she thinks I play piano in a whorehouse." I tried to find ways of avoiding telling strangers what I did for a living. Exonerations through DNA evidence began to change people's thinking; now, to at least some of the public, we had been elevated from shills of a system that elevated criminals over victims to noble defenders of the innocent. I reminded myself not to be cynical; most of the men I knew on the row weren't innocent, but they benefited from the new perception, too, as people on the outside learned about the flaws of the justice system. *Whatever works,* I thought.

As we reached the parking lot and Carey's car, I asked, "What now? Anything else we can do while we're here?"

"Natasha got an address for Harry Wardman, Craig's investigator," Carey answered. "I figured we might go see if he's around."

Harry's address was a small apartment building on a quiet street. The building wasn't new, but its tan stucco walls and dark green window trim were freshly painted, and the landscaping around it was simple but well tended, trimmed juniper bushes and creeping rosemary studded with blue flowers and buzzing with bees. Harry's name and apartment number were on a row of metal mailboxes next to a walkway leading to an outside staircase to the second floor. We walked up the stairs and rang the doorbell for his apartment. No one answered, and there were no sounds from inside.

As we turned to walk downstairs, we saw a middle-aged

man walking up them, carrying a pair of handle bags of groceries. "Are you looking for Harry?" he asked.

"Yes," we answered together.

"You probably just missed him. He works swing shift at the Vallarta Market downtown."

"Oh, okay," I said. "Guess we'll try back later."

Despite having been an investigator, Harry didn't appear to see any reason to be cagey about where he could be found.

7

That evening, we decided to try the brewpub in the Old Town. The pub was a typical example of its type: warm lighting, a lot of rough wood paneling and posters on the walls, industrial-looking tables and chairs, a blackboard with the food specials and the day's featured drafts, and a couple of big steel fermentation tanks behind a glass wall at one end of the room. It smelled invitingly of broiling meat and french fries and rang with the shouts of servers and the voices of the happy-hour crowd, mostly young, fit, and white.

A server, a slender young man in a white shirt, black jeans, and a black apron with the pub's logo on it in red, met us just inside the door, and when Carey asked if there was a table where we could talk, led us to one at the opposite end of the room from the tanks.

"How did your afternoon go?" Carey asked Natasha.

"Sucked," she said. "There's no one around anymore. I found one of Sunny's high-school teachers, but his memory's shot. He remembered Sunny's name, but he didn't recognize the photo I had. He said just about everyone he knew from that time has died or retired and moved away. The body shop is still there, but there's no one around who knew Sunny or Todd Betts. The guy who owns it now said he bought it ten years ago, and the man he bought it from told him he was planning to travel the country in an RV.

"I looked for her classmates, found one, but all she remembered was that Sunny was a sweet girl and was in 4-H for a while. She remembered the murder case in the papers, said she wondered how Sunny could have changed so much."

"We had a good meeting with Craig Newhouse," Carey said. "Do you have plans tomorrow morning?"

"Nothing that can't wait till later in the day; why?"

"Could you go to the courthouse and order the files on all the civil cases you find involving Greg Ferrante? Craig said he was always getting sued by someone or other."

"Sure."

Our drinks and food arrived, and the conversation stopped while we ate. By the time we'd finished, I was feeling a little sleepy from the stout I'd ordered. "I'm glad you're driving," I told Carey.

Natasha seemed more relaxed, with less of a chip on her shoulder. "Me, too," she said. "I should have paid attention to the alcohol percentage on that IPA."

"Not a bad day," I said, as we watched the server leave with Carey's credit card.

"I don't know." Natasha shrugged. "I hope I'll have better luck tomorrow."

"We've all had days like that," Carey told her. "I remember once driving the length and breadth of Illinois for three days before we finally found any of the people we were looking for." A thought struck her. "When we're both back in LA, why don't we arrange to see Linda? We know where she is, at least."

"Okay," Natasha said, brightening a bit.

Carey turned to me. "I can take care of talking with Joan Simon, too, when I'm back home. We're old friends, and her office is in downtown Los Angeles. When do you want to meet tomorrow to see Harry Wardman?"

"Nine, maybe? I don't know how early he'd get up, since I'd guess he works until eleven o'clock or midnight."

We agreed on eight thirty, to give us time for breakfast. The server returned, and Carey paid the bill, and we walked, a little unsteadily on my part, out to the car. When I got to my room, I decided I'd wait until morning to pack my things. Instead, I undressed, leaving my clothes in a heap on a chair, and collapsed onto the bed.

I woke up a little after five the next morning, with a guilty anxiety over everything I hadn't managed to do the night before. Showered, dressed, and fortified with coffee from the pot in the room, I fluttered around, clearing clothes, bottles and tubes from the room and bathroom and fitting them into my suitcase. I spent the time left before I was to meet Carey scrolling through the pages and pages of Craig

Newhouse's files on my laptop. Harry Wardman's files were in there somewhere—he had told me when I called nine or ten years ago that he had given everything he had to Craig after the trial—but I couldn't be sure which papers were his. There were multiple copies of nearly everything—discovery from the prosecution, notes of witness interviews, records obtained from schools, hospitals, and courts. I saw pleadings from some civil suits against Greg and realized, resignedly, that Natasha would probably spend part of the morning making copies of documents we already had.

When I brought my suitcase and backpack downstairs to the lobby, I found Carey at the desk checking out. After breakfast in the motel we walked together to our cars.

"We can take mine this morning," I offered.

"Sounds good."

We headed back to the tidy apartment building where Harry Wardman lived. The wide window next to his door was partly open, and I could hear a vacuum cleaner running and faint music from what sounded like a radio playing inside. When we rang the bell, the noise of the vacuum cleaner stopped, and a few seconds later the door was answered by a man who looked to be perhaps seventy, wearing belted jeans with a white T-shirt tucked into them over a small paunch. His hair was a mix of gray and black, thinning at the front, and his face was tanned. His eyes, behind horn-rimmed glasses, appraised us with a glance that was both friendly and watchful. I'd read somewhere that he had been a police officer before he was a PI.

"My neighbor said two nice young ladies were asking after me," he said cheerfully.

We both offered up a chuckle in recognition of his attempt at a compliment. "We are, if you're Harry Wardman," Carey said.

"That would be me," he said. "How can I help you?"

"We're the lawyers representing Sunny Ferrante," Carey said.

A hint of surprise crossed his face. "My! Now, that's a name from the past."

"I'm Carey Bergmann," Carey said.

"We talked on the phone once a long time ago," I added. "I'm Janet Moodie, used to be with the state defender."

As he shook my hand, Harry gave me a questioning stare, as though he ought to recognize me, even though we'd never met face to face. "Oh, right," he said, finally. "I remember. That *was* a long time ago."

"Nice to meet you at last," I said.

"Good to meet you, too. Please, come on inside."

His apartment had a bachelor's tidiness, with no clutter to speak of and everything in its place. A couple of library books in their plastic jackets were stacked neatly at one side of the coffee table. The patterned throw pillows on the brown sofa—probably a set that had come with it from the furniture store—were plumped and in their places. The wall-to-wall carpet was clean and freshly vacuumed. Behind a small island with two bar stools neatly set in front of it, the counters in the little kitchen area were bare except for the essentials: a coffee maker, a knife block, a dish drainer with a bowl and cup drying in it.

"Have a seat," Harry said. He walked over to a television stand, stooped, and turned off the radio on the shelf beneath the TV. "I can't offer you coffee or anything for a bit; hope you don't mind. I just finished mopping the kitchen floor, and it's not dry yet."

"No problem; we just had coffee with breakfast," I said.

Carey and I sat side by side on the sofa. Harry pulled an armchair up to the coffee table and sat on the edge of its seat, leaning a little toward us. "So what's up with Sunny?" he asked.

Carey explained. "We've been appointed on her habeas corpus case, and we're working on the investigation."

"Ah," he said. "How is she doing these days?"

"Pretty well, under the circumstances," Carey said. "We saw her just the other day."

"She was a sweetheart," Harry said. "Nice lady. Best client I ever had. What do you want to know?"

"Well," I said, hesitating. "To be honest, we're not that sure yet. We're just trying to get a clearer picture of her case and how she ended up on death row, what we can tell the court to convince them she should get a new trial."

Harry shrugged and shook his head. "She shouldn't be where she is, that's for sure."

"What do you think happened?"

He lowered his head in thought for a long moment before answering. "I think several things." Another, shorter pause. "It was—well, as things go around here—kind of a high-profile case. Family with money, developer with ties to city politicos, Hollywood-style plot. If the same thing had happened with a bunch of lowlifes over in Beanhollow, it would have been no big deal, just all in a day's work, if you know what I mean. But because it was who it was, the paper and the TV news got hold of it. In the courtroom at every hearing, with cameras. Once that happens, especially in a place like this, you can't really get a fair jury.

"That was one thing." He thought a little more. "Then there was Ferrante's family—actually, I guess, his mother. She was obsessed with getting 'justice' for her boy, and the police and DA convinced her that Sunny was guilty. She stirred things up, gave interviews on the TV news, leaned on the DA.

"And Joe Hansen, the detective on the case, decided early on Sunny was behind the killing. I don't think he really thought about whether the snitch—Eason, right?—might be lying, because what he said fit with what Hansen had already figured was the truth. I'll tell you, I was a detective for a long time, and that happens a lot—someone gets attached to a particular theory about how a crime went down, and then they only pay attention to what supports it and ignore all the loose ends.

"And then there was Sandy Michaud. She was probably the best lawyer in the DA's office—sharp, good in court. Ambitious. The office gave her her orders and she carried them out. Not to fault Craig. He did a good job, but she was just that much better. I guess all in all it was kind of a perfect storm. Everything just broke the wrong way for Sunny."

"It sure seems that way," Carey agreed.

"There was that juror," I said. "Do you remember him?"

"The evangelical preacher?"

"Yep."

One of the trial jurors had been the minister of a small church outside of town. After the trial, Harry had spoken with a half-dozen jurors who were willing to talk with the defense. In those interviews, it had emerged that during the penalty deliberations the minister had read passages of the Bible in the jury room. Not only that, he had told the jury that Sunny deserved the death penalty because in killing Greg she had not only flouted the commandment against killing, but worse, had committed an act of rebellion against the Bible's injunction that a wife must submit to her husband as to the Lord. Two jurors had signed declarations confirming this. Craig had made a motion for a new trial, arguing that a religious injunction was not a proper legal basis for sentencing a defendant to death and that the minister had committed misconduct by telling the jurors they should base their verdict on the Bible rather than the law. The judge had denied the motion on the ground that the jury had been properly instructed to follow only the law in the jury instructions given to them, and no evidence had been presented that they hadn't done what they were told.

"I remember those interviews," Harry said. "A couple of the jurors told me they actually believed the biblical injunctions Reverend—Jeffers, wasn't it?— had preached, but they wouldn't sign declarations. Most of them wouldn't talk to us, including the preacher. Craig said we couldn't have done anything with the information anyway, and I knew that from other cases. The law says the judge can't consider jurors' mental processes. That never made any sense to me."

"Not to me, either," I said. "But we're stuck with it."

"Maybe we can do something about it in the habeas petition," Carey said.

"I hope so," Harry said. "And I hope you can get the court to take another look at Steve Eason. I'm sure that guy was lying. I checked him out, and he was basically a snitch by trade. He had a history—get arrested, find or make up something on another guy he could trade for leniency. He got lucky this time because he was Todd Betts's uncle or something like that, so he could claim Todd confessed to him and be credible. Craig tried to get the guy's snitching history into evidence, but the judge excluded it."

"I remember," I said.

"I followed every lead I could find about Todd. People who knew him, his family—everyone who would talk to me—till I think everyone in Beanhollow knew me on sight. People said he was in bad shape before he OD'd, but he didn't talk about what was bothering him. He was getting high a lot, and his friends didn't see him with Brittany as much. There was a kid that Joe Hansen dug up, who said Todd told him when he was high that he'd done something he felt horrible about; and I found a couple of others who talked about him crying. His roommate said he was having nightmares. Some people said he suddenly seemed to have a lot of money and drugs around then and talked about buying a truck. My guess is that had to do with the loan from Sunny. But if he did kill Greg Ferrante, he didn't tell anyone I found. There was a theory floating around among them that Todd's overdose wasn't an accident, that he was killed to keep him from talking. But no one could point to anything beyond the timing. Those guys in Beanhollow are a bunch of stoners and tweakers, and it just seemed like the kind of conspiracy theory they'd concoct from any kind of coincidence."

"Kind of a dead end, then?" I asked.

"Yeah, unfortunately. Craig and I started thinking about following the money, asking who besides Sunny would benefit from Ferrante's death. Brittany, maybe, because her mother would get an inheritance instead of whatever she'd get in the prenup if Ferrante divorced her. And of course, Todd was her boyfriend. Then there were Greg Ferrante's other kids. But we understood that Ferrante's first wife had money of her own, and the kids were well off through her, so I couldn't see why they'd risk killing him." He stopped talking. A breath of morning air, with a hint of the day's coming warmth, floated in from the open window, bringing with it the faint, ordinary sounds from the streets—passing cars, the growl of a lawnmower.

I was impressed by his memory of the case, and I told him so.

"I have three kids of my own," he said. "I remember how it felt to be considering the possibility that one of Greg's own kids, or his teenage stepdaughter, would have killed him for his money. It wasn't something you like to think about."

We both made some sympathetic murmur.

"But it may not have been that far-fetched, after all," he added. "You may have already heard, but Ferrante's son is doing life in prison, for soliciting a murder."

That was news to me. "We didn't know that, " I said, surprised. "Do you know any of the details?"

"It's a while since I read about it, but it was in the Fresno paper that he tried to have his business partner murdered."

I think Carey and I both gulped. "Really! We'll have to follow up on that," Carey said.

"Hope it helps," Harry said.

It felt as though the interview was winding down. Carey asked Harry if there was anything else he could think of that might help us. He thought, brows knitted, for a few seconds before answering. "Nothing I can think of. But I'll let you know if I do. And feel free to come see me again if you have any more questions."

We all stood, and Harry walked ahead of us to open the door. "Give Sunny my best when you see her," he said, as we turned toward the stairs.

8

Carey said she'd stay and touch base with Natasha, so I could head for home. Feeling the first stirrings of optimism after the bombshell Harry had dropped about Braden Ferrante's attempted murder conviction, I decided, instead of heading directly home, to take a detour to Sparksville.

The town is twelve miles outside Harrison, down a two-lane highway through orchards and gently rolling rangeland. The business district was a reduced speed zone on the highway itself, a scatter of worn commercial buildings and small houses, with a few streets extending out on either side. I passed a lumber yard, construction and plumbing companies, a well-digger, the auto body shop where Sunny had worked after high school, an American Legion post, a small Mexican *supermercado*, a bar, a fire station, a motel, and at the end, in the middle of a parking lot of bare earth, a Kingdom Hall. Beyond that, before the highway went on through more farmland, I could see the playing fields and low buildings of what I guessed was the high school. The place was apparently too small for chain restaurants, but it had a taqueria and a diner with signs in its picture windows saying "Breakfast Served All Day," and "Two Eggs, Toast and Hash Browns, $3.95." The parking lot of the supermarket was about half full, and there were several cars parked on the street outside the coffee shop.

I turned down a side street, and then another. The streets ran about three or four blocks before ending at culverts or fences with orchards or pasture beyond. They had no curbs or sidewalks, just dirt shoulders with parked cars and pickup trucks, and beyond them well-trodden dirt walking paths bordered in rank weeds. They were lined with little houses of painted wood or stucco. Most of them were one story, though a two-story Victorian house towered over one corner lot.

Some blocks were better than others. On the worst of them, the paint on the houses was worn and the trim pitted with dry rot; the front yards were bare, compacted earth littered with faded plastic kids' toys or old furniture, and the sides of the houses piled with old junk: pallets, more furniture, bits of pipe and lumber. On the better streets, the houses were tidily kept, with small front lawns and wisteria or bougainvillea climbing beside their doors and in front of their windows.

The house where Sunny had grown up was on one of the nicer streets, dominated by a Methodist church at its far end, a plain building with an unassuming steeple, a blacktop parking lot on its right, and on its left a neat house that I guessed was the rectory. Sunny's grandparents' house, in the middle of the block, appeared fortuitously to be vacant and had a "For Sale" sign in front of it. I got out of the car and walked around it.

It was a bungalow, possibly a hundred years old, one that could have been built from a Sears kit, or at least modeled on one. The wooden building, painted white, sat on a raised foundation. A set of worn wooden steps led to a roofed front porch as wide as the front of the house. There was a door in the center and windows on either side. The windows were dark, but there were no blinds or curtains inside them.

I took a couple of photos with my phone, then walked down the little driveway to the left of the house, opened a gate in the low picket fence and followed a narrow concrete path to the front steps. The front yard had been covered in a cosmetic layer of dyed bark. Brick-edged flower beds, untended, bordered the fence, with red geraniums and honeysuckle spreading along the ground inside them. A flourishing pink jasmine vine climbed the post at the right corner of the porch.

I walked up the porch steps and crossed the porch to the windows, noting that the flooring had at some point been replaced with durable artificial wood. Inside, the rooms were bare of furniture. I pictured them as they might have been when occupied, in a sort of perpetual gloom from the shade of the porch. The room on the right would have been the living room; it had a fireplace on the right wall, with a small window high on the wall on either side of it. At the end of the room a wide opening led into the dining room.

Through it I could dimly see the built-in hutch that filled the far wall. The front room on the left would probably have been a bedroom.

I walked back down the path to the driveway and turned right toward the back of the house, passing the little detached garage. The back yard was bigger than I thought it would be, extending some distance behind the house. On the left, behind the garage, I saw the remains of a big brick barbecue. It didn't seem to have been used in a long time; a couple of loose bricks had tumbled from it, and it was half overgrown with vines. An orange tree was dropping the last of its winter fruit, split and dried out, onto the ground; and a dying peach tree had thrown out a leafy branch or two from its skeletal scaffold. At the back of the yard, there had clearly once been a garden, with neat raised rows, now growing weeds, and a small shed in the right corner.

Some owner had built a raised deck outside the back door of the house; a white plastic chair sat to one side, as if waiting for someone to come out and sit for a few minutes between chores. There were windows, unshaded, at each side of the door. I climbed onto the deck and peered through one into an enclosed sun porch, walled with shelves and with a hot water heater and hookups for a washer and dryer. Inside, another closed door probably led into the kitchen.

It was a house in which I could easily imagine Sunny growing up.

As I stood on the deck, a dog in the house next door gave a desultory bark and then stopped. No one came out to ask me what I was doing; the neighborhood seemed to nap under the warm sun of a spring day. I took a few more photos of the sides and back of the house, and left, and then walked up to the end of the street to photograph the Methodist church.

On impulse I decided to ring the doorbell of the house that appeared to be the rectory. After a moment, the door was opened by a gray-haired man in old khakis and a green short-sleeved sweatshirt.

"May I help you?" he asked. There was no challenge in the question, and his face and voice were mild. He was thin and a little round-shouldered, with the slightly underfed appearance of a man who has lived a long time on a small and carefully budgeted income.

"I'm not sure where to begin," I said, truthfully; I hadn't really thought this through. "I'm one of the lawyers for a woman in prison who grew up in that house over there, with her grandparents. I'm hoping to find some people who may have known them."

"Oh," he said. "Why don't you come in? I'm David Jessup—the minister of the church here."

"Janet Moodie."

He led me down a hall and into a room toward the back of the house, obviously his study, a room long lived-in, with stacks of papers, magazines, and books on the desk and shelves. A door in one wall led to the outside, in the direction of the church.

There were two armchairs in front of the desk. "Have a

seat," he said. "Can I get you something? Iced tea or water?"

"No, thank you," I said. "I'm fine." I sat in one of the chairs, and he took the other.

"Who were you looking for?" he asked.

"I don't really know. My client's grandparents lived on this street, but they've passed away. Their names were Al and Marie Sizemore."

"Marie Sizemore," Reverend Jessup said, thoughtfully, calling up her memory. "I remember Marie. She was a member of my congregation. Her husband passed before I came here, in 1998."

"Did you ever meet her granddaughter? Her name was Sunny."

He gazed past me, his brow slightly knitted. "I did, a couple of times, now that I think of it. She used to come visit Marie." He hesitated for a second, and then asked, "Was she the woman who went to prison for murdering her husband?"

I nodded. "She grew up here. She and her first husband were married in your church. Back around 1985," I added, so he wouldn't have to wonder if he had married them.

"Oh," he said, his expression a study in warring emotions. "Marie came and talked to me a few times about what had happened with her granddaughter, and I counseled her. It was very difficult for her. You know, for people in her generation, it brings real shame on them to have a family member convicted of a serious crime. She felt she couldn't hold her head up in the congregation. And she loved her granddaughter—if I remember correctly, Marie and her husband raised the child after her mother moved away. Marie wondered whether she was somehow to blame for what happened. Of course she wasn't. From what she told me they had brought the girl up with good principles and a lot of love."

"That's the impression I have," I said.

"And, you know," he went on, with a shake of his head, "she wasn't the only person in the congregation with a loved one in prison. These days, with all the drugs around, and, if you don't mind my saying so, the lack of solid morality to guide them, too many young people end up in trouble."

"Do you remember a teenaged girl who lived with Marie?"

He paused and thought for a few seconds, then nodded. "There was a girl," he said, "who lived there for a while. Her granddaughter's child, Marie said. About high-school age. She moved in with Marie and took care of her until Marie had a stroke and had to move to assisted living. Nice girl, quiet, a little sad, but no wonder. She used to come to church every Sunday with Marie. My wife has a Bible study group for young people, and she was in that, too. You could tell she loved her great-grandmother—unusual in a child her age. I don't know what happened to her after they moved. I heard Marie passed away."

I nodded. "Brittany's doing well," I said. "She's married now and has a couple of children of her own."

Reverend Jessup smiled. "That's always good to hear." He pondered for a few seconds, and then said, "I'm not sure there's anything more I can remember about the family. Is there anything I can do?"

"Not that I can think of, but thank you; you helped me understand some things." I rummaged in my purse, found a business card, and gave it to him, and we both stood.

"It was nice to meet you," Jessup said, shaking hands. "Please let me know if I can help in any way."

Before starting for home, I drove further down the highway, past the high school, and stopped to take a few pictures. It was small, but typical: a parking lot with shade awnings topped with solar panels; a single-story main building with a flat roof and a tan stucco façade; and two or three prefab buildings of the same tan color along one edge of the parking lot. Behind them I could glimpse the flat, fenced expanses of the baseball and football fields. Practice of some sort was happening on the track, and a faint shout or two reached me from a small group of kids in shorts and T-shirts clustered there.

Back in the business district, I stopped at the diner for a cup of coffee to go, with milk. The place had clearly been around for a long time, but it was clean and well kept. A radio played country oldies in the background. A couple of men in jeans and plaid shirts sat at the counter and chatted with the middle-aged waitress. About half the booths were occupied, the customers in them gray-haired—couples or groups of three or four. The server who brought me the cardboard cup of coffee handed it to me with a, "Here you go." In a glass case near the cash register I'd noticed a couple of trays of homemade cookies, cinnamon sugar and chocolate chip. I bought one of each.

Back in my car, I took a swig of the coffee and a bite of the cinnamon sugar cookie. It was a lot like the sugar cookies I'd baked with my son Gavin when he was small, and the taste opened up Proustian memories of rainy Saturdays in the big messy kitchen of our house in Berkeley. The coffee was about what I'd expected, and there wasn't as much milk in it as I'd have liked. But it would get me through the first leg of the trip home.

As I headed back down the straight highway toward the freeway, I mused a little about what it might be like growing up in someplace like Sparksville. I'd spent my childhood in the suburbs and a small city—the San Fernando Valley and then Anchorage—and my experiences didn't give me much of a handle on how it would feel to be a kid in someplace so small and isolated. In the end, I gave up trying and put it on a mental list of questions to ask Sunny when I saw her next.

9

I should have felt happier than I did to get home, a week's worth of groceries jostling with my suitcase in the back of my car, and a whole Sunday ahead of me to wind down from the trip. Instead, I felt exhausted, out of sorts, and old. It wasn't that long ago that I'd finished with an evidentiary hearing in another case in the Central Valley. The prospect of another year of long drives down the Interstate, gas station coffee, commercial country music, pickup trucks with right-wing slogans on their bumper stickers, and cookie-cutter motels made me weary just thinking about it. Less than a year to file Sunny's habeas petition, and these first few meetings had told us little we didn't already know.

As I lugged my bags and baggage from the car, almost tripping over the cats miaowing and weaving their way down the path in front of me, I could see lights through the woods from Ed's house. *Good,* I thought; *I can pick up Charlie.* In the house, I ignored the message light on my phone and called Ed.

"You're back," he said.

"Yep," I said. "Need to ransom a dog."

"He's here; come on over."

I picked up a flashlight, put a gallon of milk, a rack of lamb, a dozen eggs, a basket of strawberries, and a pound of coffee into a handle bag, and made my way down the path that wound through the tanoaks and redwoods between my house and his. Ed answered the door as soon as I knocked, and Charlie made a mad scramble from the kitchen and did his best, from corgi height, to knock me over. Pogo, Ed's big yellow dog, followed him and stopped, panting hopefully, a foot or two away.

"Down, ankle-biter!" Ed ordered Charlie, to little effect. He took the grocery bag from my hand, so I could stoop and scratch the two dogs' ears.

"You'd think you'd been away longer," Ed said. "He was starting to pine."

"I guess I've been deserting him a lot these last few months. First the Henley hearing in Wheaton, now this case in Harrison."

"Not much difference between them," Ed said. "Or is that just northern California prejudice?"

"One's an oil town, the other's big agriculture, is about it."

"Lucky you," Ed sympathized. "Would you like a beer? Got a growler of some new brown ale from Vlad's place down the road. Or we can try the cider we made, see how it's aging."

"Think I'll go for the ale tonight, have something made by professionals."

Ed chuckled, then disappeared into the kitchen and came back with two glasses.

"You're watching a show," I said, noticing the image on his TV, a small cadre of musicians frozen in mid-performance.

"Yeah, an Alison Krauss concert I recorded a while ago."

"I like her; want to turn it back on?"

"Sure." Ed picked up a remote from the table next to his favorite chair, and I sank into his sofa—to say it was sagging probably didn't do justice to its unique texture, a bit like an upholstered marshmallow with a few hidden steel springs. We listened to bluegrass and drank our beers in companionable silence, with the dogs asleep at our feet.

I finished my beer, and when the show paused for a break, pushed myself up from the sofa and took the glass into the kitchen. "I should let you get on with your evening," I said. "I'm in your debt again for taking care of Charlie."

"It's never a problem," Ed said. "You'll be okay walking back?"

"Sure—thanks. I have the Hound of the Baskervilles with me."

Ed glanced at Charlie and gave a short laugh. "Well, he is tough, I'll give him that. None of the dogs around here mess with him. You take care."

"You too."

The combination of beer, music, and undemanding friendship worked some magical transformation on my state of mind, and the night breeze, with its slap of chill fog, lifted some of the weight of exhaustion from my head and shoulders. Back home, I fed the cats, made myself a cup of instant cocoa, and settled comfortably into my own bed, the cats at my feet and Charlie on the rug beside me. Everything could be dealt with later. "Yep, Scarlett," I thought before I fell asleep, "tomorrow really is another day."

Sunday I started a pasta sauce and meatballs in my slow cooker with frozen tomatoes from last year's surplus, did laundry and overdue vacuuming and dusting around the house, and thought for the thousandth time about retiring and spending my days like an old cat, sleeping late and napping in the afternoons. Instead, I went outside to look at my garden and thin the fruit on my apple trees.

Something—birds or rabbits—had found a way under the row cover in my lettuce bed, and most of the greens I had been so proud of a few days ago were eaten down to green nubs. I'm not inclined to be philosophical, and I spent a few minutes swearing and lecturing Charlie on the need, from now on, to kill any wildlife he found in the yard. I pulled a few weeds from around the peas, which seemed to have escaped the raids, watered the tomato plants starting to sprawl in their pots in my popup greenhouse, turned the raised bed in which I'd decided to plant them, and moved on into the orchard.

My trees were still young, but several of them had clusters of nickel-sized green apples. Older hands with apple trees had told me that I needed to cull most of them so that the rest would grow to normal size. But I felt like apologizing to each one as I faced one branch after another, clippers in hand,

and decided, godlike in arbitrariness and finality, which fruit would live and which would end up in the compost.

After that, feeling a little bored with my own company, I drove down to the cliffs above the ocean to take a walk with Charlie and stop at Vlad's for a growler of the ale I'd had at Ed's. Tomorrow might be another day, but it was coming all the same, with more days like it; and it would be nice to have something in the fridge to take the edge off the evenings.

Warm smells of tomato sauce and beef greeted me as I returned home, reminding me I was getting hungry. After a break for lunch, I decided to follow up on Harry Wardman's remark about Braden Ferrante's arrest. Braden Ferrante was an unusual enough name that a simple search online immediately brought up links to newspaper articles about his case. He'd been charged in Fresno, his hometown, with soliciting the murder of his business partner. Braden and the intended victim had invested in a winery, but couldn't agree on how to run it. Unable to buy his partner out, Braden had tried to have him murdered. He had been caught by a sting, in that the man he'd tried to hire for the crime had been an undercover police officer. The similarity in *modus operandi* to Greg's murder, if you assume, as Craig said, that Todd Betts had probably done the killing for someone else, was just enough to make me wonder. Later articles said Braden pled guilty to some of the charges, and others were dropped, and that he had been sentenced to fifteen years to life in prison. Eventually we'd have to interview him; that much was clear. But at least he wasn't going anywhere.

For the hell of it, I decided to do another search, this one about the Reverend Robert E. Lee Jeffers, the Bible-thumping juror at Sunny's trial. It seemed that a few years after the trial he had found his moment of fame: several newspapers, including the *Los Angeles Times*, ran stories about threats from the Internal Revenue Service to revoke the nonprofit status of the little church he had founded, because he had spent the 2008 presidential election season sermonizing against the idea of women holding public office. An archive search found a video loop of Jeffers in full cry at the podium, his shirt limp with sweat and his white hair a short spiky halo around his head, fulminating about the evil of a world where women flout the Bible's command of subservience to their men. It was more or less his last hurrah, since he had died less than a year later. Given that and the timing of the IRS suit, I didn't think it would add much to the investigation, but I emailed the links to Carey and Natasha, along with those to the articles about Braden.

I spent Monday catching up on work: writing part of an opening brief in one case and a request for an extension of time to file the reply brief in another. In the middle of the day, after taking my outgoing mail to the private mail service at the real estate office on the highway, I spent an hour planting out the tomatoes from my little greenhouse, mostly because I knew that if I didn't, Harriet, who had given me the plants back in March after growing them from seeds, would ask if I had them in the ground yet. And if I didn't she'd be disappointed in me. Not that she'd say much—she never did; she'd just give me a "you really ought to get it together" look and say, "Okay." And I'd be crushed. For a lawyer, I thought, I crush pretty easily.

Some time after four o'clock, I tore myself away from the computer screen, changed into a T-shirt and yoga pants and dug through the clean laundry heaped on my bed for a newly washed sports bra. *Onward!* I thought, as I gave Charlie a pat on the head and marched out to my car.

Harriet, slim and strong at seventy-five, was waiting at her door when I pulled up. "So, did you plant the tomatoes?" she asked, and gave a nod when I said I had. "Good," she said. "What about fertilizer?"

Fertilizer. Of course. "Oh, shit," I said. "Sorry."

"Not a problem. Just give them some fish emulsion tomorrow to get them off to a good start, and then follow it next week with tomato fertilizer. I guess you've been busy," she said, a little tartly. "You haven't been around much lately. Are you still working on that case with the Aryan Brotherhood?"

"No, that's wound down; we're just waiting for the judge's findings. I have a new one, over in Harrison."

"That's a long way, too. Why can't you get a case someplace closer?"

I laughed. "I ask myself that at least once a week."

"Zoe asked after you at the exercise class."

"That's nice of her." I was surprised it mattered to the instructor that I wasn't there. But that was the kind of place Corbin's Landing was, sometimes. We lived scattered through the woods, but somehow we were in each other's business like a family.

"She's a sweet girl."

Molly Cordero met us at the bottom of the potholed private road that led to her house. I'd offered several times to pick her up at her front door, but she always said she didn't want people driving up there. "It's a mess," she'd apologized. "None of the neighbors will chip in to have it graded, and we can't afford to do it ourselves. Someday someone's gonna break an axle; maybe then they'll do something."

As we waited for Zoe to set up her CD player, the talk among the women and the couple of stray older men in the class was mostly about a sighting of a mountain lion up on the ridge the previous morning. "It walked across the ridge road right in front of some bicyclists," one of the women said. "My husband heard them talking about it at Vlad's."

"Better keep your cats inside at night."

"I do anyway; the coyotes will eat them otherwise."

"They don't eat chickens, do they?"

"Coyotes? Absolutely."

"No, I knew that. I meant mountain lions."

"Haven't heard of it happening. I don't think they like to come close to buildings."

It was what passed for news in our neck of the woods.

After an hour of stretching and sweating, Molly, Harriet, and I drove home in exhausted silence. "I can't believe I still have to cook dinner," Molly said.

"Doesn't Bob cook?" Harriet asked.

"Sometimes, but he was out in the field today and didn't think he'd be back before seven."

"I made a pan of cornbread and a salad before I left, and Bill is supposed to be heating up some chili, if he remembers," Harriet said.

"I'm not that much of a planner," Molly said, a little ruefully.

"I'm not, either, but it's easier now I'm retired."

Their small talk was comforting; and the thought made me aware of how often I felt alone, watching other people's lives from somewhere outside. After dropping them off, I'd drive back to my own little house and a dinner of leftovers, with a glass of Vlad's ale or red wine to put a little glow on the day's end. Then I'd get a fire going in my wood stove and finish my drink in the living room, cats on the sofa and Charlie at my feet, watching satellite television or reading a book. There was a time when that was just about all I wanted. But now it was feeling a little lonely being me. A thought rose in the back of my mind—and when it did I shook my head in disbelief—that a trip to Harrison or Sparksville now and then wasn't such a bad thing.

10

I am not careful enough what I wish for.

The next day—literally—Carey Bergmann called me.

"What's up?" I asked.

"Natasha's going to Harrison to try to talk to people who knew Todd Betts. I'm wondering if you could help, kind of divide the work, go with her as needed. Some of these folks live in sketchy places."

"Sure." I thought she was being a bit overprotective of Natasha, but I'd felt the same way sometimes when I'd worked with young investigators, an almost maternal need to see them warm and fed and safe.

"Thanks for the material about Braden, by the way. And old Reverend Robert E. Lee Jeffers was a stitch—or he would be if there weren't people out there who believe that stuff. I think we should include some of that in the petition, as evidence that the trial jurors were right about the things he was saying in the jury room."

As soon as Carey and I had said our goodbyes, I called Natasha.

She picked up on the third ring. "Hi, Janet, what's up?"

"Carey called. She wants us both to go to Harrison. She says you have some interviews planned there."

"Sure—okay." I could hear the question in her voice.

"She figures we can get more done in Harrison if we split up the work. And," I figured I might as well be honest, "I'm guessing that she's worried about some of the people we'll be seeing there and thought it would be good if there were two of us on some of the interviews."

Natasha laughed. "She's cute," she said. "Such a tough woman herself, but she acts like a mom."

"It's a good thing to take care of your team."

"Yeah," Natasha conceded.

"When are you free to go?" I asked. "I need to make some overdue visits to San Quentin, but other than that my schedule is clear."

We settled on a date to meet.

With an inward sigh, I sent an email to the clerk in charge of visiting at San Quentin, asking to see three inmates. Two were currently clients, and one had been years ago. They were each struggling with mental illness, which wasn't helped by the limbo of death row and ongoing appeals, and it wasn't easy to spend time with them, but I was in some ways their only hope of another chance. It often seemed a heavy burden.

I've never been someone who confides easily in other people. I don't tend to pick up the phone and call a friend when something is bothering me, and as a result I don't know anyone I can regularly unburden my troubles to. Feeling a little sorry for myself, I packed Charlie into the car and drove to the county park, where we took a walk along the bluffs above the ocean. A half-hour of hiking with the damp wind snapping at my face and hair didn't do my mood much good, but it made Charlie happy and made me appreciate the comforts of my home when I got back. That evening I picked enough peas from the garden for dinner for one, poured myself a glass of brown ale, and sat for a while shelling peas and listening to quiet jazz before moving on to the kitchen to make a lazy woman's dinner: the peas, an omelet, and a half-batch of baking powder biscuits. *Tomorrow*, I thought, *I'll make a loaf of bread and share it with Ed.*

After a drive that began at dawn and seemed to go on forever in a purgatory of stop-and-go freeway traffic, I finally made it down the potholed road to the San Quentin parking lot. I sat for a minute in my car, drinking the last of my coffee and staring out at the breakwater beyond the lot, the teal blue of the bay beyond that, and then the hills, half hidden by streaks of morning fog, and the sky the color of a bluebird's egg. Visits to San Quentin were indelibly linked in some corner of my memory to the aftertaste of tepid coffee and the sour buzz inside my head from sleep deprivation. But the sight of the bay, rippling with small whitecaps in the morning sunlight, revived me, and I gathered my files and plastic purse of cash, squared my shoulders, and marched bravely to the visiting office.

Generally, over the years, I've managed to remember all the arcane details about what I'm allowed to wear and carry into San Quentin on a legal visit, and my mishaps have been minor, such as accidentally having a five-dollar bill in my stack of singles (fixed by changing it for a fistful of quarters in the lobby change machine). But on the criminal defense attorney forums I read, I see occasional posts from people turned back because the color of their slacks was too much like the denim worn by the inmates or a jacket too close to the color of the guards' uniform. Once, at San Quentin, a woman guard at visiting decided that the outline of my brassiere could be seen through my shirt. I was saved from rejection by another guard who waved me through, as I wondered what disruption could possibly be caused to inmates' psyches by the hint of a utilitarian sports bra under the clothing of a woman manifestly on the far side of middle age. The upshot is that the visitor center at San Quentin always makes me a little apprehensive.

Everything went smoothly this time, and after recovering my papers, shoes, and jacket at the far side of the X-ray machine, I headed out the door and down the long path to the actual prison, feeling unburdened and even a bit lighthearted.

Passing through the pair of metal gates to the prison visiting area, I knew without looking that the wind from the bay had uncombed my hair into strange spikes and curls and reddened my nose. A trip to the restroom confirmed it;

I combed my hair with my fingers to push it into some kind of order, but the nose was, sadly, beyond hope.

The men I was seeing today were all, at this point in their lives, lonely. Arturo Villegas, once a gangbanger from Los Angeles, missed his family, who couldn't visit him because his parents were Mexican and undocumented and fearful of being arrested and deported. Walter Klum, a former client, had killed his wife, and the rest of his family wanted nothing to do with him. A motorcycle accident a few months before the murder had left him with permanent brain damage. I visited him from time to time—his current attorney had asked me to because Walt, in his isolation, tended to brood and become depressed and suicidal.

For the hour and a half allowed by the prison for visits, we made awkward conversation about whatever was on their minds. My first visit was to Arturo, whose case was still relatively early in its long progress through the system. He wanted to know how it was going—how long before the Attorney General would file their brief, how long before the case would come up for argument. He was also anxious for his parents, his sister in college, and his little brother, who he feared would turn to the gang life and end up dead or in prison like Arturo.

Walt, when I saw him this time, fell into reminiscing about his childhood on a farm in Minnesota, a hardscrabble life that he remembered as if it were some Eden from which he had been expelled into the harsh mundanity of adult life and work.

As we talked I felt in each of their voices their pleasure in getting a visit from outside, a continual, pleading undertone: *please don't let go, don't desert me, don't leave me here with no one.* I knew too well how little I could do to solve the great problem before them, that they had committed the worst of crimes, and society was collecting the rest of their lives as repayment. But I could, at least, do that one thing, and I promised to be there when needed, to send Walt some stamps, put a little money on Arturo's books and call his sister to find out how his family were doing.

It wasn't much, and I managed to get it done in the turnaround time before leaving home again and heading back down the road to Harrison.

11

"So you and Carey got to meet Linda," I said, as Natasha and I waited for our dinners at the diner by the motel in Harrison. "What was she like?"

Natasha tilted her head back to one side and made a *moue* with her lips as she considered where to begin.

"She was a trip."

"How?"

She rolled her eyes heavenward. "Oh, my God, she was so LA. She and Pete live in this tiny little cottage in Silver Lake. It's really sweet, with a little deck and back yard and a view, and full of, like, artifacts. Just this little hippie place, with lots of tchotchkes, plants in macrame hangers, bright colors everywhere. I have pictures on my phone. I guess she and Pete have lived there, like, forever."

"Sorry I missed it," I said. "What is Linda like?"

"Let's see—she's, what, about seventy now? But she looks amazing. I'll show you the pictures—here." She opened the camera app on her phone and handed it to me. "There are five or six, of her and her house. Pete was away playing a gig in San Diego so we didn't get to meet him."

I scrolled through the photos. From the outside, Linda's home was an unassuming cottage, pale green with white window frames, and a tiny front yard that seemed to be full of succulents. Inside, it fit Natasha's description, a prettily cluttered, comfortable space, with light-colored walls covered in paintings, framed photos, and woven art pieces and plants in pots and hangers near the windows. "She has a hummingbird feeder on her deck," Natasha said a little wistfully.

Natasha had also photographed Linda herself, alone and with Carey. Linda was slender, wearing a long skirt in a batik print and a white Mexican blouse with embroidery around the neckline. She had masses of dark red hair, like Sunny's had been, though it was all but certain that Linda's hair, upswept with attractive carelessness and held with some sort of clasp at the back of her head, was dyed. I couldn't help thinking that I had never been able to do anything like that with my hair before I gave up and cut it short.

"God, you're right," I said. "She does look amazing."

Natasha nodded. "She says she's never had any work done, just eats carefully and does a lot of yoga."

"That, lots of sunscreen, and good genes," I said. I couldn't resist adding, "And not worrying about pesky things like raising your children."

"Yeah," Natasha said. "She was so self-centered—it was all about herself, and sometimes Pete. She asked how Sunny was doing and said she's been to see her a couple of times because Pete said she really should, but she can't do it often because going to the prison is just too painful."

"Aargh."

"Yeah. She did say how grateful she was to her mom for taking such good care of Sunny. She said she tried her best, sent money and all when Sunny was a kid. Apparently she had a reasonably successful career in acting; at least she was able to make a living at it. And Pete was a soundman or something, though she says he's retired now and 'pursuing his passion'—her words. He plays guitar and mandolin in a group that does old time and some bluegrass. I guess they're pretty good; they play gigs around the LA area and go on tour up the west coast to Oregon and Washington a couple times a year. She told some funny stories about her career. She said when she first got to Hollywood she took acting classes, but had trouble finding work because she actually looked too much like Sharon Tate. Then Sharon Tate was killed by the Manson family, and after a while people kind of forgot about the resemblance. She had small parts in a couple of movies, but she did mostly television work and some commercials. She said she kind of specialized in being murdered."

I had to laugh. "Really?"

"Yep. She said cop shows liked to cast her as the cute girl at the beginning who has a fight over the phone with her boyfriend or leaves to go to her car after a party, and turns up dead the next morning. When she got too old for that, she sometimes played witnesses, grieving mothers, that sort of thing. She seemed very proud of one *Law and Order* episode where she was the villain, a nurse who was having an affair with a doctor and framed him for stealing drugs from the hospital where they worked, or something like that. Anyhow, she says she's mostly retired, but she still has an agent and gets a part now and then. Now she's into aromatherapy and sells oils and lotions at a couple of farmers' markets. Her house smells incredible, like roses and lavender and cocoa butter. It was kind of a high just being there."

"I'm sorry I missed it. Did she have anything to say about the case?"

"When we finally managed to talk about it with her, not too much. She talked about Sunny, said she was the sweetest little girl and she loved it when she visited, that she was never any trouble to anyone. She was delighted when Sunny married Greg, because he had money and she thought he was very in love with Sunny. Sunny never talked to her about any troubles with Greg. But then I'm not sure she would have. Linda seemed really smitten by him. Apparently he was always charming and funny around her and Pete, and he was generous with money, which Linda clearly liked. He negotiated a great deal for them on their house, found them a mortgage broker who got them a mortgage they could afford, and even loaned them money for work on the place, said they could pay it back whenever they could. She said they still owed some when he was killed. She didn't believe Sunny had anything to do with his murder. She didn't know of any problems with their marriage, and she didn't see Sunny as someone who would ever be capable of such a thing. That was about it."

"That's more or less what she said at Sunny's trial, too."

"That's what I remembered. Carey and I tried, but we didn't get more out of her than that."

Our food came, two giant bowls of salad that appeared to contain half the lettuce harvest of the Salinas Valley. We stopped talking while we tunneled through our respective mountains of greens, chicken, cheese, avocado, sliced supermarket cucumbers, and rubbery cherry tomatoes. "You know," Natasha said eventually, tilting her head again, "Greg was really manipulative—putting on a charm offensive with Sunny's family, to keep them on his side. So when he hurt her, she couldn't go to them because they'd be all, 'oh, but he's such a nice guy.'"

I was starting to like Natasha a lot. I could see why Carey thought she'd be good for Sunny's case.

"That makes sense. Sunny talked about all the things Greg did for Linda and Pete, and her grandparents. It could all have been a strategy."

As we sat convivially finishing our dinners, I wanted to ask Natasha something about her life outside this case, to get to know her better. Most people, I thought, would have known how to turn the conversation seamlessly into a casual chat about personal lives. But moving a relationship between levels, from business colleague to acquaintance, from acquaintance to friend, was a skill I'd never seemed able to develop; and fear—of taking a chance, smothering a possible friendship with the wrong question, or inviting assumptions of closeness I couldn't control—choked me up when I wanted to speak and move forward. So instead of inviting Natasha to say something about herself, I asked, "So how is the investigation business going?"

"Good. We're actually having to refer some things out. John—my business partner—is thinking about hiring another person, maybe someone good with cyber investigations. If you know anyone good who'd like to live in LA, let us know."

"Sure."

"What do you do up on the coast?" she asked. "You're like way out in the woods or something, aren't you?"

"Sort of; that's why I moved there."

"Where were you before?"

She's a lot better at this than I am, I thought. "We lived in Berkeley, but then my husband died, and I didn't want to be there anymore."

"Huh. I'm sorry." A man or woman my age would probably have asked more about my husband's death, but for someone as young as Natasha, that was a bit of a conversation stopper. "Do you have any kids?"

"Yes, one. He's close to your age, I think. He's a professor, ecology and wildlife biology. Lives in Australia now, in Melbourne. He married an Australian woman, and I guess they plan to stay there. No grandkids yet."

"It's funny, that grandparent thing," Natasha said. "My father keeps hinting about them. I used to just tell him,

'Dad, I'm gay, all right?' but now Mari and I are actually thinking about getting married and having kids. It's all so complicated, though, finding a donor and all that. We haven't really worked it out yet."

"That is a tough one. But someone I worked with had a baby and raised him with her partner, and they were very happy. Don't be discouraged."

"Thanks."

I felt like some kind of indulgent aunt. But it was a feeling I didn't mind having.

"What's our plan of attack for tomorrow?" I asked.

"I've got addresses for Todd's mother and sister and one of his friends the police interviewed—there were four altogether, but one moved away, one died, and one I couldn't find a current address for. Also a girl one of Brittany's teachers said she used to hang out with a lot. I thought maybe I could try her place this evening."

Plans made, we paid our checks and walked back to the hotel.

In the lobby, Natasha asked, "How old was your son when your husband died?"

"Twenty-four."

"Oh. My mom died when I was fifteen. She got some really fast-moving form of lymphoma; she died, like, three months after being diagnosed. I think I can relate to how Brittany must have felt, going through so much loss in such a short time. My dad was devastated; it was like he was in a daze for a couple of years. I felt like I'd lost both my parents.

I was really angry for a long time, raged at everything, mad at my dad for not being there for me. After a year or so, Dad got me to agree to see a counselor, just to have someone to talk it out with. She was great; she helped me understand how I was feeling about my mom and my dad and sort it all out. He and I are really close now."

"Terry's death was rough on my son Gavin, even though he was in his twenties," I said. I hadn't been there for him, either, like Natasha's father; the shock wave of grief moves in more directions than we think about.

"I believe it," she said. "People focus on how losing a parent will affect young kids, and they don't understand how bad it is even when you're older."

"You're right," I said. "And it can be hard to see your kids' grief through your own. Gavin still has a hard time with that."

Robert Louis Stevenson once wrote of his own family, "The children of lovers are orphans." The passage, when I found it late in life, made me think of Gavin. Terry and I hadn't been so much doting lovers as close partners, absorbed in our profession and our shared ideals. And Gavin had been a quiet, self-contained child, who didn't demand much of our attention. He had made it through adolescence with a minimum of angst, had done well in school, and when he chose his career, had shown no interest in following us into law. He loved Terry, whose charisma drew him in, as it had me, and when Terry died, I had been utterly inadequate to support him in his shock and grief. I had fled to Corbin's

Landing, and he to graduate school in Australia. We had mourned separately and largely alone.

In the lobby I wished her good luck in her evening interview and proposed meeting in the breakfast room the next morning at around eight thirty and heading out for our day together from there.

"I have the same address for Todd's mother and sister," Natasha said. "So we may get to meet them both. They live in Beanhollow."

"Oh, right." I remembered the name from when Carey and I had interviewed Harry Wardman. Full of stoners and meth heads, or something like that. I could see Carey's point in sending us out together. Not only was there safety in numbers, but the people we'd be seeing lived in a world where the truth was, one might say, malleable. If they said anything useful, it was good to have a witness.

12

Beanhollow was literally on the wrong side of the tracks, on the far side of a grade crossing at the south end of Harrison.

It was obviously older than the rest of the town. The few commercial buildings in its small business district, near the railroad tracks, were two-story wooden blocks with peeling paint and storefronts with blankly reflecting picture windows. Streets, paved and unpaved, stretched from the far side of the main road, and on them the oldest houses on their quarter-acre lots—the little square wood-sided bungalows, with their generous windows and front porches, old swamp-coolers perched on their roofs—were losing their battle with history. They were too small for modern tastes, with dark kitchens and tiny bedrooms, and their thin walls made them expensive to heat in winter and impossible to keep cool in the baking Central Valley summers. As we passed them I mused that the people who had lived in those houses when they were new—the men who worked the fields in broiling heat, the women who canned vegetables in those kitchens in hundred-degree weather—were a hardier race, along with the children they had raised. Or, more likely, they just sickened and died younger under the stresses of weather and poverty.

Some of the little bungalows, damaged beyond repair by termites and dry rot, had been torn down and replaced with newer, slightly larger houses with stucco siding and slab foundations, or with tinny double-wides. A few of the houses had lovingly maintained front yards, with drought landscapes of dyed wood chips and white or gray rock, borders of creeping rosemary and Mexican sage, and an olive or fig tree in the center. Occasionally an old house sat abandoned, broken windows gaping under sagging roof, on a lot overgrown with weeds and the feral descendants of landscape plants popular a hundred years ago. Of those that were still being lived in, some were owned by men and women who had grown old in them and who lived behind drawn blinds while the neighborhood disintegrated around them, the houses they could no longer afford to maintain or leave falling gradually into disrepair and their yards, unwatered, growing tangled gardens of dry grass stalks and rank weeds. Many of the rest were rental properties, minimally upgraded and maintained, and occupied by Mexican workers' families and poor people like Todd Betts's family and his friends.

Natasha and I walked slowly along the edge of an unpaved street, from my parked car to the old house, painted light green with white trim, that supposedly belonged to Todd's mother and sister. Natasha was wearing a summery blue skirt and print blouse in a style that recalled the 1950s. I had on a white short-sleeved knit top and dark blue pants of some synthetic fabric, in which I was already feeling sticky in the mid-morning heat. Coming here, we'd passed fences and abandoned houses sprayed with extravagant graffiti, some of it in Spanish slang; junk cars half dismantled in their parking places; and old pickup trucks with bumper stickers for Republican candidates and the National Rifle Association and Confederate flag decals on their rear windows. It didn't seem to be a friendly environment for an aging defense attorney and a lesbian investigator.

A worn picket fence that had once been white separated the front yard of the Betts's house from the street. In its center, in an opening for a long-gone gate, a brick walkway led toward the front steps of the little bungalow. The left side of the porch had been replaced by a wheelchair ramp of dark green painted wood that crossed the front of the house like a scar, from the middle of the porch to the driveway on the left. The yard was a patch of thinning Bermuda grass lawn, its winter green almost gone in the month or two since the last rains.

We walked down the uneven blacktop driveway, past an aging brown van. Incongruously, in a long brick-lined bed between the driveway and the yard, a row of roses was flourishing, needing pruning, but in full bloom, white, pink, peach, and red. Their scent hovered sleepily in the warm air. Our steps echoed on the plywood surface of the ramp, and I heard a dog start barking inside, along with the faint sound of a television. At the back of the porch, closed drapes covered the front windows.

The doorbell seemed ancient, so I knocked on the front door. The dog inside barked wildly—a little dog, from the sound. After half a minute I heard shuffling, and the sound of a lock being turned on the door. It opened a foot or so, and the woman standing there stared at us skeptically and asked, "Can I help you?" The dog was still barking from behind a door somewhere.

"I hope so," I said. "Are you Kim Grandison?"

"Yeah," she said. She opened the door a little wider. She was a big woman, tall and heavy. Her face was round and unhealthily pale, and her brown hair was skinned back from it into a ponytail. A whiff of air, a little cooler than outside, came from inside the house, carrying a faint smell of old frying grease.

I began what felt like a spiel. "I'm an attorney representing Sunny Ferrante, and this is my investigator. We're hoping we can talk with you and your mother about Sunny's case."

For a second, Kim looked blank, then puzzled. "You mean that rich woman, the one that killed her husband?"

"Yes."

"That's still going on?"

"Yes; it's up on appeal." I left it at that, for now.

"So you're here to ask about Todd."

"Yes."

She drew in a breath, then exhaled it in a sigh, her face stern. "Everybody thought he killed that guy." She shook her head. "You may as well come in." She opened the door wider, stepping aside, and Natasha and I sidled into the house.

The door opened directly into a small living room, with a sofa and two armchairs, none of which matched, arranged in a semicircle around an oval coffee table and, beyond it, a widescreen television on a low stand. The TV, which was playing some kind of morning show with a panel of women chatting in shrill voices, dominated the room. Dwarfed by the television and half-invisible in the dimness of the room, a small gray-haired woman in a nightgown, pink chenille bathrobe, and slippers, reclined halfway in one of the armchairs, watching the show. She peered up, mildly curious, as Kim led us in.

"Have a seat," Kim said. She nodded toward the woman in the chair. "This is my mom, Lynn."

"Hi," I said. "I'm Janet Moodie."

"Natasha Levin," Natasha said.

Lynn looked up at us, without much interest. "Hi," she said, her gaze shifting toward the couch. "Sit wherever you can."

We chose the couch and sat there, side by side.

"I've got to let Muffin out of the bathroom, or she'll bark all morning," Kim said. "Can I get you something to drink? Coffee? Water?"

"Water would be great," I said.

Kim walked heavily away, and a few seconds later a fluffy white dog exploded into the living room, barked a few times, and then stood staring at us with black button eyes. I reached out a hand, and she came over and let me scratch her in the tangle of curly hair behind her ears.

"Muffin?" I said. She wagged her tail.

Kim came back, with four glasses of water expertly balanced in her hands. Natasha jumped up and took a couple to help her set them down on the coffee table. Kim was wearing a loose tank top and leggings that stopped at her knees, and I could see multicolored tattoos on her arms and lower legs. "Muffin behaving herself?" she asked.

"She's fine," I said. "I have a dog at home."

Kim turned to Lynn and handed her a glass about a third full of water. "Here, Mom," she said. "Have this."

Lynn thanked her and took the glass and set it on an end table beside her, alongside a couple of neatly stacked pill boxes. She turned her head to survey us, but did not sit up. Kim took the other armchair, sitting toward the edge of the seat and leaning a little forward. She picked up a remote from the coffee table in front of Lynn and muted the television. The women on the screen continued their animated chat in silence.

"The police told us years ago Todd confessed the murder to Uncle Steve," Kim said. "They came and asked a lot of questions, searched the house for Todd's .22."

"He didn't kill anyone," Lynn said suddenly, and with surprising firmness. "He didn't have nothin' to do with it, I don't care what they say."

Kim glanced sideways at Lynn and said, as if she wasn't there, "Mom never got over losing Todd. He was her youngest, and her only boy."

"I'm so sorry," I said. "It's a terrible thing for a family to go through. And when you come down to it, the evidence against him was kind of thin."

"You can say that again," Lynn said. She glared at us from the depths of her chair. "Steve was the only one accused him. He lied to save his own skin and stay out of prison. That's what he's always done, take care of himself and to heck with everyone else. He's been that way since he was a kid. He's my little brother, so I should know."

"In all honesty," I said, "I don't know who killed Mr. Ferrante. But whoever it was, we don't think Mrs. Ferrante had anything to do with it, and we're trying to prove that."

Kim spoke up. "So you think the man who killed the guy may not have been Todd?"

"I really don't know, but we certainly don't think Mrs. Ferrante hired Todd to kill her husband. And I don't know of any reason Todd would have had to kill him. Do you?"

Kim shook her head. "Not that we could see. Todd was working for the man's brothers and I guess seeing his daughter. He was crazy about that girl, and he was like one of the family at the ranch. The idea that he'd kill his girlfriend's father just didn't make any sense to us. And besides—if you knew Todd—"

A movement from Lynn caught my eye. She had bent her head and put a hand up to her face. After a moment she raised her head again and reached for a tissue from a box on the table next to her. Her eyes, magnified by her glasses, were full of tears. "People say you get over it," she said thickly, "but I never have."

"I'm sorry," I said. "We won't stay too long. Just a couple more things we need to ask. Did Todd ever say anything that might suggest he knew who might have done the murder?"

Kim glanced at Lynn. "No," she said. "Nothing I can think of."

"And do you know where Steve Eason is?" Natasha asked.

Lynn and Kim both shook their heads. "We haven't heard from him in a while," Kim said. "We decided we were done with him when Lynn caught him stealing from her. He took some of her jewelry and a Civil War cavalry sword that had belonged to Ralph, Mom's last husband. Mom said she was going to call the cops. Haven't seen him since."

A cellphone rang, and Kim looked around and found it on the table next to Lynn's chair. She talked for a minute or two, then ended the call and said to us, "I can't talk long, I'm going to have to start getting Mom ready for her dialysis appointment. Is there anything else you want to ask us?"

"We were wondering if any of Todd's friends are still around. We'd like to talk with them, if we can."

"Well, I was just on the phone with Mom's sister, my aunt Rita. She has a son close in age to Todd, Aaron, who still lives in town; they were tight. Then there's Flaco—Jeff Brackett. He's around; I think he's a janitor at the grade school. Todd's best friend then was—let me think—Devin—that's Devin with an 'I'—Schneider. They were housemates when Todd died. Devin was living with his mother for a long time after he got out of the military, but I haven't seen him in a while; I don't know if he's still in the area. The only other one I can think of is Ian; I can't remember his last name. He's not around anymore: I don't know where he ended up. Rory Ebersole—they called him Smurf—was another friend of Todd's, but he passed away."

"Was Todd close to his father?" Natasha asked.

Kim shook her head. "Todd hardly knew him. Mom married him after she and my father split up, I think because she was pregnant. He took off when Todd was really little."

"Did he have any role in Todd's life?"

"No. He was from Missouri, and I believe he moved back there after he and Mom divorced. We never saw him after that. He was an alcoholic; I don't know what happened to him."

"Do you remember his first name?"

"Stanley, maybe. My father was Alan Grandison. He died a few years ago in a car accident."

"Did Todd have a stepfather he was close to?"

"Well, we all liked Ralph Teasdale. Mom married him after she divorced Ron Euler. Todd definitely didn't like Ron. Ron seemed to have some competitive thing going on with Todd; he went out of his way to treat him bad. Ralph was a nice guy, though. He married Mom around 1997, if I remember. Took care of us, bought this house. But he had a heart attack and died in 2001—not that long before Todd, as it turned out. His life insurance paid off the mortgage. If it weren't for that and her part of his pension, I don't know how Mom could have gotten along till now. Poor Mom! She's had a tough life."

"Sounds like it." We thanked her and each gave her one of our business cards. "We won't keep you longer," I said. "If you remember anything you think might be helpful, please call or email us."

"Sure," Kim said. "Here, let me call my aunt Rita and let her know you'd like to see her." She picked up her phone and had another abbreviated conversation, then turned back to us. "Aaron's last name is Oliveira. He lives on the other side of Harrison." Kim gave us Rita's phone number and an address and phone number for Aaron as well. "She says Aaron's probably at work and isn't usually home before six. Hope that helps," she said.

As we turned to leave, Lynn called out a faint goodbye, and we returned it. Muffin rolled to her feet from where she'd been lying on the floor in front of Lynn and skipped after us to the door, where I stooped again to give her a pat on the head.

Kim held Muffin's collar as we slid out the door. "Sorry," she said. "If she gets out, she'll run." She gave Muffin a push away from the door, stepped outside, and closed it quickly behind her.

Hot air settled on us as we stood on the ramp. Kim straightened up and pulled the bottom of her tank top over her hips. "Sorry," she said. "I wanted to say something where Mom couldn't hear it."

I nodded. She was silent for a few seconds, as if organizing her thoughts, before speaking again.

As she gazed into the distance, I noticed that her eyes

were a hazel brown, and I wondered, irrelevantly, what color Todd's eyes had been.

"Back when all this happened, I wasn't living with Mom. I had my own place, an apartment, and my boyfriend at the time worked for the local radio station, and he could get us tickets and free admission to shows and stuff. Todd came by a lot with Brittany, and we all sometimes went out together. She seemed like a nice enough kid, kind of young, though. I used to wonder what Todd saw in her, but she and Todd really liked each other. Todd was always young for his age, too. I remember Brittany said a few things about her stepfather—the guy who was killed. I don't think she liked him.

"Then this other guy started showing up with them. He was a little older, and, like, her cousin or something. He was this total snotty rich kid; I always had the feeling he was slumming when he came over, like we were all beneath him. He'd bring weed, and I didn't like it, because he and Todd and Brittany and Jason, my boyfriend, would all get high and stupid and sit around the living room all evening eating junk food. I can't do it; I have asthma, and I wasn't much interested anyway. I'd end up in the bedroom watching videos. This guy was always running down his family and talking about all these schemes he had to make money. He tried to get Jason to sell weed for him, but Jason turned him down.

"After Brittany's stepfather was murdered, things really changed with Todd and her. I remember Todd came over by himself once right afterward, and I said something about

it, and asked him how Brittany was holding up. And he got
all shaky and said he didn't want to talk about it. He and
Brittany and Jason and I went to a movie together once
around then, and Todd just… well, he had a dark cloud over
his head. Brittany was trying to cheer him up, but he was
in a world of his own. That was the last time I saw them
together. Todd and Brittany and that cousin of hers stopped
coming over; Todd was spending all his time with his friends
and Uncle Steve, probably because they could all smoke
weed together without anyone bothering them about it. But
when I'd see him, like at Mom's house, he looked terrible.
I remember I asked him once where Brittany was, and he
said she was away somewhere with her mother. He must
have started using heroin around then; he looked different,
messed up. But I didn't know that at the time, and it was an
awful shock when he OD'd. Anyhow, all that has made me
wonder if he wasn't more mixed up in what happened than
Mom thinks. And maybe Brittany and that other guy, too;
I don't know."

I was nodding, and I could see Natasha was, also. "It
could be," I said. "There's an awful lot we don't know. Would
you mind if I asked you one more thing?"

"Sure, go ahead."

"Did Todd ever say anything about Mrs. Ferrante?"

"No—well, maybe just in passing; she was Brittany's
mother, so he may have mentioned her."

"Nothing to indicate he had any kind of separate
friendship with her?"

"Oh, no."

"Did he say anything about getting a check from Mrs. Ferrante?"

"Not to me. I know when he died he had a bunch of money in his checking account, over four thousand dollars, and I wondered where he'd got that kind of money. Then later the police told us Mrs. Ferrante wrote Todd a check for five thousand dollars, asked us if we knew anything about it. I guessed that's where the money came from, but more than that I don't know." She stopped—unwilling, I thought, to connect the last of the dots between the check and the murder. "That's it; that's all I can remember."

"Thank you for telling us all this," Natasha said. "The more we know about what happened, the better."

"I don't know where it gets you," Kim said, "but if that lady, Mrs. Ferrante, isn't guilty, maybe you can find out who is. Todd's gone now; he can't be hurt by it." Kim stopped talking and bit her lower lip. When she spoke again, her voice was hoarse. "Damn. He was a good kid, really sweet and kind-hearted. He always wanted to help everyone. It's hard for me to believe he'd do something like this. But if he did, there had to be a reason. He'd never do it on his own. Anyhow, I just wanted to say that. I'd better go inside and get Mom ready."

I thanked her again, and then, because I felt strange about leaving the conversation where it was, I added, "I noticed your roses on the way in. They're lovely."

"They're Mom's," Kim said. "She planted them after Todd

died, and she takes care of them. She doesn't have energy to do much of anything these days, but she goes out when she can and keeps them weeded and such. It makes her feel a little better." She turned away, toward the door.

I didn't feel much like talking as we walked down the ramp and the driveway toward my car, and I don't think Natasha did, either. A cold case like Sunny's is full of melancholy. The painful memories, vivid as they are, are mixed with the events of a world that has moved on; the fires of anger, even if still smoldering, are banked. The neighborhood was quiet; I could hear the humming of bees in the still air. Behind us somewhere, a mockingbird sang, running through its repertoire of borrowed melodies.

13

We crossed back over the railroad tracks and stopped for lunch at a Thai restaurant in a strip mall.

"Did Kim tell the police what she told us?" Natasha asked, as we drank Thai iced tea and picked at our rice plates. "I don't recall seeing anything like that from her in the police reports."

"Me neither. I'll read them again, to make sure. But I think once the police had Eason's statement, they didn't do that much besides look for the gun and maybe someone else Todd might have confessed to. And his family were mad enough at the police for pinning the murder on him; it doesn't sound as if they were interested in helping them."

Over our food, we talked about seeing Todd's cousin Aaron and the friends Kim had told us about. Natasha had her notebook computer out and was scrolling down it for the information she had gathered about Todd's circle of acquaintances.

"Kim gave us a couple of new names—we didn't have Aaron Oliveira or Jeff Brackett—but there are police reports and defense interviews of Ian Nestor, Devin Schneider and Rory Ebersole." I found myself admiring how quickly she had absorbed the volumes of documents in the case. "I ran locates on everyone we knew of. Rory died—let's see—in 2006. Devin is still around; his address is here in Beanhollow. I can probably locate Jeff fairly quickly; and we could even go ask at the school. Those are all the friends of his we know of who are still in the area. There were two more, but they've moved away. I've talked to Ian Nestor; he's living in Riverside County. And there's one in Texas. I'll probably fly out to interview him later in the summer."

"What did Ian say?"

"He said he was kind of shocked by the whole thing. He wasn't that close to Todd. They went to school together, and he knew him socially, like they were in a group of guys who sometimes shot baskets together in the park, played computer games at each other's houses, like that. Todd seemed to have it together; he had a good job and all. Ian thought having a girlfriend who was a minor was a little sketchy, but it wasn't his business. He met Brittany at the park once or twice; didn't remember much about her, except that Todd seemed very serious about her. He didn't remember meeting Braden. He remembered the murder because it was Brittany's father or stepfather who was killed, so it had a connection to them. He didn't recall anything about Todd's reaction. He was really shocked when he heard Todd had died of a drug overdose, because he'd never heard that Todd used drugs. He was also surprised when the police questioned him and everyone else and were saying Todd had killed Brittany's dad; he didn't think Todd would ever do something like that. I asked him about Todd's uncle Steve, and he said Steve hung around them sometimes, but not much because he was older. Steve might have been a user, because he was kind of a lowlife in general; he'd been in and out of jail. But Ian didn't know that for a fact. He gave us a couple of names of guys in their circle, but they were people we already knew about."

"What about Kim's ex?"

"Jason? There's a police interview of him in the file, too, and I tracked him down to Hood River, Oregon. I'll probably see him this summer, too."

After lunch, we hunted down a Starbuck's, where Natasha used the wireless to do some searches on her notebook. "Got 'im!" she whispered triumphantly, after a few minutes.

"Who?"

"Jeff Brackett. It looks like a good address, right nearby; he shows up as living at it for at least the last five years. Shall we try him and Devin?"

Devin Schneider's address was down a dirt road behind a row of mailboxes, in a rat's nest of old bungalows and travel trailers covered in brush and vines. The shades of the houses were drawn, and their yards overgrown with ivy, old roses, and hedges that hadn't been trimmed in decades. Some of the trailers appeared to be occupied and others abandoned, but it was sometimes hard to tell them apart. As we walked, already sweating only minutes after leaving the car, down beaten dirt paths through the maze, a skinny, grizzled man, smoking a cigarette on the steps of his trailer, called out, "You lookin' for someone?"

"Devin Schneider?" Natasha asked.

"You're not from probation, are you?"

"Nuh-uh," we both said, shaking our heads.

"Church ladies?"

"Not exactly."

He shrugged. "Whatever. He lives in that blue trailer over there. Not sure if he's there, but you can try."

With an uncomfortable sense that people, and not just the skinny man, were watching us, we walked, single file, down a narrow path overgrown on both sides by tangles of grass and weeds. The rotting steps to the trailer's door creaked and bent alarmingly under my feet as I walked up them and knocked on the door. There was no answer, and no sound from inside. I knocked again, waited, listening, and then descended the steps back to Natasha. "Nothing," I said.

"He may be asleep," the smoking man said as we came toward him again. "He sleeps a lot." Sweat was wetting the roots of my hair and running down the middle of my back; I could only imagine what it must be like inside a metal RV at this time of day.

The man went on. "You may be able to catch him later at the soup kitchen down on Gridley. He goes there a lot for dinner."

"Where on Gridley?" I asked.

"Church hall over by the food pantry, not far from the

old Masonic Hall. Can't remember what the cross street is."

"What time do they serve dinner?"

"Five thirty. Need to be there by about quarter after, though, get in line."

We thanked him and found our way back to the street and the car. As I climbed in, something small and sharp poked at my calf, and I looked down to see what it was. "Shit, my pant legs are covered in foxtails," I said. We spent a minute or two picking off random bits of traveling seed pods—I from my pants, and Natasha from the hem of her skirt—before we moved on to Jeff Brackett's place.

Brackett lived in a little stucco house on a paved street full of cracks and potholes. It was one of the nicer streets; the houses on it were all well cared for, and some had big shade trees in their yards. His house and yard were carefully maintained. The little front lawn was green and mowed, and the borders neatly edged. An ornate mailbox on its post stood at the head of the driveway, and the flowering bushes under the front windows were neatly trimmed. The garage door and window trim had been recently painted. *Weekend warrior*, I thought. Over the garage door I spotted a basketball hoop. *With a family*, I added.

There was no car in the driveway, a bad sign, but we walked down it and along the swept concrete path to the doorstep, and rang the bell. I wasn't surprised when no one answered.

"Well, we've really washed out today," I said to Natasha. "What now, do you think?"

"Let's try the school, and see if he's at work."

"Sure." Natasha appeared less concerned about our lack of luck than I was. Maybe it was that she, unlike me, was an actual investigator and had acquired a certain patience with days like this. To me, investigation was frustratingly random and inefficient: no matter how well you thought you'd planned, you could get into the field and have no luck getting anyone to talk to you. It didn't sit well with me. And now I was hot and already tired, even though it was barely the middle of the afternoon.

The Sierra Vista School, which educated the children of Beanhollow, was a single-story maze of offices and classrooms connected by roofed outdoor corridors. It was as downtrodden as the neighborhood around it. The stucco walls were faded and chipped, the wooden door and window frames were covered in multiple layers of paint. The concrete of the roofed walkways between the buildings was cracking. It occurred to me suddenly that the school might be on summer vacation, but it was apparently still in session, though barely. A big sign, the kind with removable block letters, at the front of the driveway, said, with a notable lack of visible emotion, "LAST DAY OF SCHOOL JUNE 9." We found the front office, and I asked the plump, middle-aged woman at the desk if we could speak with Mr. Brackett.

"I'll call him," she said. She picked up the receiver. "Would you go get Jeff? There are a couple of people here to see him."

Jeff Brackett walked into the office a few minutes later.

He was tall and a little stooped, dark-haired, with a thin, serious face, a long jaw, and what was probably a perpetual five o'clock shadow on the lower half of his face. Even in his brown janitor's uniform, he looked lean, like a Dorothea Lange photo of a Depression-era farmer. Flaco, his nickname, means "skinny" in Spanish; I could see how his high-school friends would have tagged him with it. He stood, hesitating, for a few seconds before asking, "Can I help you?"

I realized I hadn't prepared what to say next, so I introduced myself and Natasha and then said, conscious of the presence of the woman at the desk, "We were wondering if we could talk with you a bit about Todd Betts."

His face registered mild surprise. "Oh, wow. Maybe we can talk outside. I'm on a break, though, so I don't have much time."

We filed out the office door, and Jeff led us to a bench. Once we'd all sat, he said, a bit doubtfully, "Todd passed a long time ago."

"I know," I answered. "We're part of a legal team defending Sunny Ferrante, the woman who was accused of hiring Todd to kill her husband."

"Oh, wow," he said again. "That. I remember that case. Police came and talked to some of the guys about Todd. That lady was convicted, though, right?"

"Right," I said. "We're trying to get her a new trial, because we think she didn't actually do it. We'd like to ask you some things about Todd, anything he might have said, other people he was close to and might have talked to—that sort of thing."

"I don't have time now," Jeff said, "but can you meet me after work? I get off at four. I can meet you here at this bench, if that's okay."

"Sure," I said. "Thank you."

He stood up. "See you then. Don't know how much I can help."

We managed to kill an hour by driving to the apartment building, a bleak cube of cream-colored stucco and aluminum-framed windows half-filled with air conditioners, where Todd and Devin had been living at the time of the crime. We knocked on doors and talked to a neighbor or two who happened to be home, but none of them had been living there fifteen years ago, nor did they know of any other tenants who might have been there that long.

At four, we were back at the school, sitting side by side on the bench and gratefully drinking from bottles of cold water we'd bought along the way. A little later Jeff approached down a corridor, and we moved over to make a place for him next to Natasha. I'd bought a bottle of water for him, at Natasha's suggestion, and I offered it to him. He took it and thanked us, opened it and drank about a third of it down in one gulp. "Hot day," he said. "Starting early, this year."

"It is that," I answered. "Are you looking forward to summer vacation?"

"Yeah. Actually, we don't really get the whole summer off, though. Part of it we spend cleaning out lockers, doing maintenance, deep cleaning, other stuff you can't do with kids all over the place."

"All that work in the background we don't think about," Natasha said.

"Yeah," he said again, with a nod, a hint of pride in his face. "Would you excuse me please? I need to make a phone call." He pulled out his phone and hit a couple of keys. "Hi, Ruthie? It's Dad. I've got something at the school after work, so I won't be home right away. Yeah, no problem. Make sure Noah gets started on his homework— thanks. I should be there by the time your mom gets home, but if not, tell her I won't be long. Thanks, kiddo. Call me if you need anything. Bye.

"My kids," he explained. "I'm free to talk now. What is it you wanted to ask?"

"I guess, to start with," Natasha said, "we're trying to get a new trial for Mrs. Ferrante. She was convicted of hiring Todd to kill her husband, but we're trying to establish that she didn't do it. I don't know if you followed the trial, but a man named Steve Eason testified that Todd confessed to him, told him he'd killed Gregory Ferrante and Mrs. Ferrante hired him to do it."

Jeff was shaking his head. "I heard about that," he said. "We were all saying, 'Todd? No way.' We were like, 'Nuh-uh.' Some of the guys said police told them he confessed everything to his uncle Steve, and I said,

'I wouldn't believe that guy if I were you.' Steve was a scammer and a dope fiend."

"So the police didn't interview you?"

"Nah. I was up in the Napa Valley that summer and fall, working in a vineyard. My uncle was managing a big one, and they were shorthanded, needed good workers. Guess the police didn't know where to find me. Heard about it all when I got back."

"And Todd never told you or anyone else you know that he was involved in the murder?"

"Not me, and no one else I know of. But I started to wonder. Not to speak ill of the dead, you know. But there were some things."

"Like what?"

"Well, he was thick with that girl Brittany, the guy's stepdaughter, and this other guy—can't remember his name, but he was the guy's son. Todd used to talk about him a lot; he really admired him. One time he said to me they both hated their dad, and he could relate to that. Todd told me a couple of times about this stepfather he'd had who was really harsh, hitting him and putting him down all the time."

"You didn't know Todd, then, when his mother was married to Ron?"

"Nah. I guess Todd lived here all his life, but I didn't really get to know him till we were in high school. We were on the baseball team together."

"About this guy Todd liked. Was his name Braden?"

Jeff thought for a second or two. "Could have been, I'm not sure."

"Sounds like you didn't care for him."

He nodded. "No, I didn't. He came around with Todd a few times. I thought he was kind of a smartass, a scammer like Todd's uncle. All big plans, no follow-through. And he always had drugs. He brought weed, meth; he said he could get heroin, too. I didn't like any of it. My guess is he was selling them to Todd."

"How did you know?"

"Well, I didn't, really; he never said anything. But he started to change, you know, like talk a little faster. He'd be a bit jittery sometimes. I've known tweakers, and he wasn't that bad. But I was worried. I thought he was heading down a bad road."

"Did you say anything?"

"I tried to, but he wasn't interested. He said he had everything under control, and I didn't need to worry."

"How long was this before Greg Ferrante was killed?"

Jeff thought some more and rubbed the back of his neck with his hand. "I don't know, a month, maybe? Not long."

"Did you see any change in him after the murder?"

"Yeah. But I wasn't spending as much time around him then. I had a job for a while before I left for Napa, working swing shift at a cannery. Didn't see anyone that much because I was at work when everyone was off. I saw him on weekends sometimes, but I was a little weirded out by then, by the people he was hanging with and the drugs. I kind of went my own way. But when I heard he'd overdosed, I guess I wasn't as surprised as some people."

"How did he seem changed when you saw him during that time?"

"He seemed to be high a lot."

"Did he ever mention getting a check from Mrs. Ferrante?"

"Not to me."

"Can you remember who else was close to Todd at that time?"

"Hmm. Ian Nestor; he moved away, though. So did Bob Spitz. Rory's dead—that was Rory Ebersole. You know who'd probably know more than anyone? Devin Schneider. He and Todd were renting an apartment together; the two of them were around each other the whole time. Devin still lives here in Beanhollow—another Beanhollow boy, I guess."

"We were trying to find him today, but he wasn't home."

"Home?" Jeff rolled his eyes. "You mean that crazy old trailer?"

"Yeah."

"You went back there? I admire you. That's one weird place."

"You know it, then?"

"Yeah. Couple of us kind of watch over Devin. He went into the Army, got sent to Iraq, and got a head injury, and he's never been right since. Come back here, lived with his mom, but after she died he was homeless for a while. Julie, my wife, and I busted our asses—pardon my language—

to get him help from the Veterans Administration. Julie's a nurse, an LVN, so she knows something about the system. He lives in that old travel trailer—I don't think it's even got water or sewer hookups—because the guy who owns it lets him stay there for next to nothing, lets him run a power cord to it from his house, use a restroom in his garage. If you want to talk to Devin, I can try to get him for you. We bought him a cellphone, so we could stay in touch with him and he could get hold of us if he ran into trouble."

"That would be terrific—thank you," Natasha said.

"I'll give it a try. Half the time he forgets to put it on the charger and walks around with a dead phone. But we're working on him," he said with a laugh. He pulled his phone out of his pocket and hit a number. After a few rings, I heard it pick up, and a faint voice say, "Hello?"

"Hey, Red, it's Flaco. How you doing?" The other voice went on for half a minute before Jeff could speak again. "Wow, man, sorry to hear it. You should go back to your doctor and tell him. Did you call him? Yeah. Call him tomorrow, tell him what's the matter. Or I can give him a call and have him call you. Hey, man, I have two ladies here who want to talk to you. No, they aren't. No, it's okay. They're lawyers working on that case where Todd's girlfriend's mother was accused of having her husband killed. Yeah, that one. Where's a good place to meet you? Around six? Okay, man, I'll send them over. Yeah, I can give them directions, so they can find the place. Okay. And I'll call Doctor Carrillo in the morning. Don't forget to charge your phone tonight, huh? So I can call you and tell you what he says. You take care of yourself. Have a good dinner. Bye.

"He says he'll meet you around six outside the Daily Bread. That's the soup kitchen in the church downtown, on Gridley Avenue, Gridley and Orange Street. Good luck. He can be hard to talk to; his mind doesn't track so well."

We thanked him.

"No problem," he said. "Is there anything more you need?"

"Just one thing—do you have any idea where Steve Eason might be now?"

"Gee, no. I heard a few years ago that he was in prison again, but nothing recent. I don't think he's lived around here for a long time. Sorry."

"That's okay," Natasha said. "You've been really helpful. You wouldn't mind us getting in touch if we needed to talk with you again, would you?"

"No, that would be fine." He stood up, and we followed. "Gotta get home and start dinner." We shook hands. "Good luck to you," he said. He walked away toward the section of the parking lot reserved for staff.

Natasha yawned and rolled her head and neck, working out the stiffness, then massaged the back of her neck with her hand. I sighed and made a little *moue* of exasperation. We'd landed ourselves yet another hour to kill. "Nice guy," Natasha said. I agreed.

"I hope Devin will help us. He was uncooperative with the detective who went to see him. I don't think the defense got to talk to him because he'd been sent to Iraq by that time."

"Lucky guy. What's that old blues song? 'If it weren't for bad luck, wouldn't have no luck at all'?"

14

Beanhollow had its own park, a square block of patchy green lawn, picnic tables, and barbecue grills shaded by sycamore trees, with a play structure of swings and slides in its center. We decided to wait there until our date with Devin Schneider. The air, a little hazy with the dust of ploughed fields and exhaust fumes, was beginning to cool, and a barely perceptible breeze ruffled the leaves overhead. A few kids who seemed to me a bit old for the playground were shouting and roughhousing on the slides and ladders.

"This would be a perfect time for a cigarette," Natasha remarked, leaning back on the bench and resting her back on the table.

"You smoke?"

"Not anymore. Habit I picked up in high school, but Mari and my dad talked me into stopping."

I decided to dive into the deep end of social interaction. "What do you do when you're not working?" I asked.

"Tool around," Natasha said. "Go to events, concerts. Hike in the mountains. Mari's a freelance writer in her spare time, and she's always going out to see things she might write about. She's good; she's had pieces published in local magazines and the *LA Times*. She keeps hoping someday she can afford to write full time. It could happen."

"What does she do now?"

"Works for a bank. It gives us a steady income and health insurance, and she likes the fact that she can walk away from it at four thirty every day and go home and write." Natasha made a face. "Not like me."

"No, this isn't that kind of job," I said.

"How about you?" she asked. "What do you do in your spare time?"

"I'm an old lady," I said. "I have a dog and a couple of cats, and a garden and an orchard. They keep me busy."

"Cool," she said, more out of good manners, I thought, than belief. "We're hoping we can get a place someday where we can have a dog. You know, Carey has horses and a ranch near Ojai."

"That's a lot of work," I said. "She has a lot more energy than I do."

She nodded. "Definitely not for me. I'm too much of a city girl."

The Daily Bread occupied the community hall of an old gray stone church on a corner of Gridley Avenue, the main drag of Beanhollow. The church appeared to be an active one, if barely, judging by the fact that the old letterboard next to the worn main doors advertised a Sunday service at ten. I looked for a sign saying what denomination of Christianity the church purported to serve, but didn't see one. On the other side of the façade a sign said something in a script I didn't recognize; I wondered if it was Hmong.

The soup kitchen was winding down its operations for the day. Through the open door I could see some people in white shirts and hairnets lifting steam table pans from a long counter and carrying them away, and others wiping tables and putting away folding chairs. The warm air was still heavy with smells of meat and gravy.

I didn't have much idea what Devin looked like, aside from the fact that Jeff had called him "Red," so I scanned the small group of downtrodden men standing around on the sidewalk, hoping to see someone with reddish hair who seemed to be keeping an eye out for us. One of the men, leaning on a cane, caught sight of us and limped over.

"Hi," I said, holding out a hand. "Are you Devin?"

He rubbed his right hand on the thigh of a pair of sagging Levis before reaching up to shake mine. "Yes, ma'am," he said. There was no sarcasm in it; he was like a boy talking to his mother or a teacher. He was fairly tall, and though already round-shouldered, he leaned down a bit to talk to me. His hair, starting to thin, was still a reddish blond, bleached on top by the sun. In a face freckled and aged by too many days spent outside, his eyes, a little unfocused, were as blue as turquoises.

"I'm Janet Moodie, and this is Natasha Levin. Is there

someplace nearby where we can sit and talk?" I asked.

His brows knitted, as if mentally reconnoitering the neighborhood. "Things close up here early, 'cept for the bars. It's not a great place to be at night," he said. "There's a little Mexican place 'bout a block that way, may be open." He indicated the direction with a turn of his head.

"Let's try it, if you don't mind."

"No problem."

Time and progress had left Gridley Avenue stranded in Harrison's past. The street was about as depressing as any I've seen. Dusty air, smelling like fried food and diesel fuel, carried the heat of the day up from the cracked sidewalks. The store windows, when they weren't boarded up or empty except for the hopeless pleas of faded "For Lease" signs, contained a scattering of whatever the store was selling, coated with years of dust, their packaging bleached from the sun. We passed a pawn shop, an appliance repair store, a *joyeria*, closed, with its windows and door barred, a barber shop, also closed for the day, and a bar, from whose dark interior came cool air, smelling like whiskey and beer, and the light and sound of a television playing a sports channel. In front of some of the stores were planters that now contained only dried-out dirt and litter. The Mexican restaurant was open; the planter outside its door contained a dozen dusty plastic geraniums.

Inside, the place seemed to be recently repurposed from a former life as a coffee shop. On the left was a Formica-topped counter with red leatherette stools; on the right a row of smallish booths with tables topped in the same worn Formica and padded benches of the same leatherette as the stools. The walls and the high ceiling were painted a plain cream color that I imagined must be sold by paint stores under some name like "Old Diner." The place was air conditioned, though, and a couple of ceiling fans moved the cool air slowly around us. The walls were bare of decoration; aside from the menu posted on the wall behind the counter and the strong smell of tortilla chips, there was little to tell what kind of food the place sold. A pair of Mexican men dressed in work clothes were eating at a booth in the back. The aproned man behind the counter motioned vaguely toward the booths and said, "Sit where you want."

We drifted, by some unspoken consensus, to one of the booths and sat, Devin on one side, Natasha and me on the other. Devin worked his way into his seat with some effort, using his arms to brace himself and pulling his right leg in with his hand. The man behind the counter came out and brought us menus.

"Would you like anything?" I asked Devin.

"Oh, no thank you. I just ate."

Natasha ordered an iced tea, and I asked for a diet Coke. After the server left, we sat for a half-minute in awkward silence. The man brought our drinks; and after he left, Devin asked, "You wanted to talk to me about Todd?"

Natasha nodded, and I said, "We're working on the case of the woman who was accused of hiring Todd to kill her husband—trying to get her a new trial."

It seemed to take him a few seconds to remember the case

we were talking about. "Huh—that was a long time ago."

"I know," Natasha said. "But we're wondering what you might remember about what was happening with Todd around the time the man was killed."

Devin lowered his eyes, brows knitted, as if Natasha's statement presented him with a lot to process. "I don't know how well I remember all that stuff anymore. I don't know if Flaco—Jeff Brackett—told you, but I got knocked on my ass by an IED in Iraq. They said I was thrown thirty feet. Lost my right leg below the knee and had some brain damage. My memory isn't so good. My mind wanders sometimes."

"I'm so sorry," Natasha said, and I nodded in sympathy.

"Jeff did say you were injured over there," I added.

He sighed. "Yeah. Well, it is what it is. I have good friends. Flaco and Julie—his wife—have been like family to me. Take me to the doctor, got me my benefits. But—sorry—you wanted to know about Todd."

"That's okay," I said.

"Todd and me, we knew each other most of our lives. We're Beanholler boys, both of us. Went to grade school, high school together, graduated the same year. We were like brothers. You don't know how much I still miss him." He closed his eyes tightly and bent his head and massaged his forehead with a rough hand. When he looked at us again, there were tears in his eyes. "After we got out of school and both got jobs, we got an apartment together. We was both having some trouble at home. Well, actually, I was. Todd just felt he wanted to go out on his own after his stepdad died.

Todd died in our apartment. I found his body—don't know if Flaco told you that."

"No, he didn't," Natasha said.

"I kept telling him he had to stop using; it was just a high road to hell. But it was like talking to a wall. It felt like there was something bothering him, and he was trying to find a way to forget it."

"Did he tell you what it was that was troubling him?" Natasha asked.

Devin shook his head. "He wouldn't talk about it. If I pushed on him, he'd get mad and leave."

"Was it Brittany? Did they break up?"

"I don't think so. He was really serious about her, and she kept calling him. I'd hear his side of some of the conversations, and he didn't seem mad at her or anything."

"What kinds of things would he say?"

"Oh, man, I don't remember. Probably nothing much, just 'how are you,' 'I love you, too,' 'I'm fine, just tired,' stuff like that. After a while, she didn't call so much. Maybe just gave up, I don't know."

"Huh. When did that all happen in relation to Greg Ferrante's murder?"

"That was the guy that was killed? Brittany's stepdad, right?"

"Yeah."

"It was all after that—at least I think so. Man, it's been a long time, and everything is kind of jumbled together."

"You told an investigator Todd was having nightmares."

"Oh yeah. He'd start yelling in the middle of the night, and I'd have to go wake him up and tell him everything was okay and to go back to sleep. I'd ask him when he was awake what was bugging him, but he wouldn't say."

"Did he ever say anything about having done something bad?"

Devin paused for a bit, as though collecting his thoughts. "Maybe—yeah—maybe it was during one of his nightmares. I do remember something about that, but it's all real vague."

"Do you remember a guy named Braden?"

He thought. "Braden. Not sure. Was he the guy from the ranch? Some relative of Brittany's or something?"

"That sounds like him."

"He—if it's the guy I remember—he used to come over sometimes. There were a few times he stayed the night, slept on the living-room couch. Bought us breakfast, if it was the weekend."

"What did he do during the week?"

"I don't know. I think he was supposed to be working at the ranch with Todd, or something. The owners were relatives of his. When he was with us, he mostly got high and talked about the big plans he had. He had a lot of money and said he could get all kinds of drugs, weed, meth, heroin. I thought the guy was full of b.s., but Todd thought he was great. Todd was always kind of like a puppy, needing someone to follow around.

"You know," Devin said, as if a thought had suddenly come to him, "the police came searching for Todd's rifle, but it had disappeared. I wondered if that Braden guy took it. But I don't think so. Todd would have missed it."

"Todd had a rifle at your place?" I asked.

"Yeah. His .22. We used to go target shooting at the quarry, or sometimes go out in the country and shoot squirrels and rabbits."

"Was he a good shot?"

"Man, the best. After 9/11 we were talking about joining up, going into the Marines or the Army together. I figured he could've ended up being a sniper or something."

"He was that good, then," I said.

Devin nodded. "That good. Sorry—I was talking about when the police came, right? They came by some time after Todd passed away—I don't recall how long. I'd moved out of the apartment; couldn't stand to live there anymore. Joined the Army. I was in basic training at Fort Leonard Wood when they came to see me. Detective came and asked me questions, wanted to know whether Todd had a .22 and whether it was still around. I told them he'd had his .22 at the apartment, but it was gone. Before I moved out I packed up his things for his sister to take, and the rifle wasn't there. I didn't think much of it at the time; there was too much else going on, you know. But yeah, I told them about the rifle and said I didn't see it when we moved his stuff, don't know what happened to it."

"Did it ever turn up?"

"Not that I know of. I wasn't around much for a long time." He frowned, and those turquoise eyes darkened a shade. "You think Todd shot that man?"

"We don't know," I answered. "But if he did, we don't think Mrs. Ferrante asked him to."

The answer seemed, surprisingly, to relieve him. "Jeez," he said, with a shake of his head. "The cops sure seemed to think he did it. But I couldn't imagine it. He was just so normal—kind of happy-go-lucky, go-with-the-flow. He didn't have a dark side, not like some people. I've known men who might be capable of killing someone in cold blood, but Todd—no way."

"Did Braden keep coming around after Greg Ferrante was killed?" I asked.

"Not as much. He sometimes crashed on the couch, still, but I guess Todd pretty much drove him away, with his moods. He probably lost interest in us. He was just a rich kid, playing a game, 'Oh, look at me, hanging out with the rough kids from Beanhollow.'"

"Did Todd ever mention getting a check from Mrs. Ferrante?"

"Oh," Devin said. "That check. No, he didn't mention it. Police asked me about it. I remember that detective was hostile. He was sure I knew more than I was telling him. He even threatened to arrest me as an accessory or something. I was scared he'd do something that would make the Army kick me out."

"Did you know Todd's uncle, Steve Eason?"

"Ol' Uncle Steve? Yeah, kind of. He was Todd's mother's younger brother—lot younger than her, but older than Todd and the rest of us. He used to try and hang out with us, when he wasn't in jail—mostly to sell weed, I guess." He smiled a little. "I remember we used to call him Uncle Steve, just to piss him off. Haven't seen him in years; I don't know what happened to him."

"Was Todd close to him?"

"Not really, that I could see. I mean he was family and all, but I don't think Todd liked him particularly."

"Did you ever hear that he said Todd confessed the murder to him?"

Devin nodded. "Detective told me."

"What did you think about it?"

"Made me sad. Like I said, that just wasn't the Todd I knew. I'd never thought he'd do something like that."

"Do you think he did?"

Devin gave a long sigh. "I don't know what to think. I wasn't there. Todd never said anything to me, and I was his best friend." He shrugged, and shook his head. "I just don't know, probably never will at this point. It's painful. I don't want to remember my best friend that way." He stopped talking for a moment and squeezed his eyes shut, then opened them again. "I'm sorry," he said. "It still hurts, after all these years."

"I'm sorry, too," I answered. "We should let you get home; it's getting kind of late. Thank you for being willing to talk to us."

Natasha said, "Can we get you something to eat later? Maybe some takeout?"

"Nah, I'm okay."

"We'll give you a lift home," I said.

"Thanks, I'd appreciate that."

In the car, Natasha took the back seat, and Devin sat in front with me. He smelled like stale sweat and oily hair. He was silent, except to point out turns on the way. When we pulled up at the line of mailboxes that marked the little compound of houses and trailers where he lived, he thanked us for the ride and climbed laboriously out, maneuvering his prosthetic leg. As we pulled away, I saw him open the door of one of the mailboxes and close it again, then start down the path to the back.

I was sticky, tired, and hungry when we finally crossed the tracks back into Harrison.

"What have we accomplished?" I said, more or less thinking aloud. "Despite all his friends and family saying he wouldn't have done it, we seem to have turned up more evidence that Todd was the shooter, no?"

"Yeah. The missing rifle; the change in Todd's mood after the murder," Natasha agreed. "And there's no question about that check for five thousand dollars—never was, though. But on the plus side, there's still nothing more solid than that to link Sunny to the killing."

"Well, Eason," I said. "He's still our biggest problem. I'm not sure whether we want declarations from the people we saw today. Let's call Carey in the morning and ask her."

Natasha nodded agreement. "If you want to go back

home tomorrow, I can take care of getting declarations if Carey wants them, and trying to catch up with the other people on her list. Also that friend of Brittany's. She wasn't home last night, either. I'll be fine in Beanhollow. I'm not sure what Carey was so worried about."

"I guess we may as well make one more stop, since we're near," I said. "Aaron Oliveira."

"Oh, right," Natasha said. "I don't know about you, but I'm starving." She opened her backpack and pulled something from its depths. "Would you like half of this?"

"Sure; thanks."

It was some sort of energy bar, a compressed rectangle of nuts and dried fruit, the kind of thing I almost never bought for myself because the number of calories in one bar was more than I should eat in an entire meal. I ate my half as slowly as I could, but it took a lot of effort not to devour it in a couple of bites.

It was enough to take the edge off my appetite, and less distracted by woozy thoughts of bread and ice cream I threaded the back streets of Harrison, following the directions on the car's GPS, until we pulled up at the Oliveiras' rambling house, set back behind a tidy lawn on a street shaded with tall sycamore trees. There was a compact car in the driveway, with one of those metal magnets in the shape of a fish on its rear bumper. This one, to belabor the point of its religious message, had a cross in the middle, a little like the armature of a kite. I sighed.

A dog barked inside when we rang the doorbell, but I

didn't hear any sounds suggesting anyone else was home. It was another wasted detour.

In my room, after a late dinner of Chinese fast food, I felt troubled by what we'd seen that day. Witness interviews, and particularly those that bring up the painful past for the person I'm talking to, leave me disconcerted and sad. It's as though the people I meet have made me some sort of offering of their pain, trusted me with it and with their confidences; and that trust is something I need to somehow take care of, but I don't know how. I can't help them or make anything better for them; I'm just a passer-by who comes into their lives and shares their memories for an hour or two, and then leaves them alone again with the past wounds I've reopened. No matter how often I do it, it leaves me with a slightly bad conscience; and I don't sleep well afterward.

I read until late that night, to keep my thoughts at bay.

15

Natasha emailed me and Carey the results of the rest of the trip. "Brittany's friend didn't remember anything. Aaron was a washout, soulless evangelical, lectured me on why we need the death penalty, no interest in helping Sunny." She ended with an angry-face emoji.

As for me, my life settled again into routine: work on my other cases, exercise classes, my struggling garden, walks with Charlie, the occasional shopping trip to Gualala or Santa Rosa, or happy-hour ale at Vlad's, and the obligatory monthly Skype call from Gavin, my expat son, and his wife Rita, in Melbourne. The big event that summer was the addition of data reception to our little enclave, which meant that I could finally receive text messages from Carey and Natasha. Ed and Harriet took a little while to get on board with it, but within a couple of weeks Ed's nightly checks on my welfare had evolved from ten-second phone calls to instant messages I could answer with a word or a smiley face.

Carey and Natasha seemed to have Sunny's case in hand without much help from me. Carey had retained a psychologist to evaluate Sunny and a mitigation specialist, a combination of investigator and sociologist, to tease out information and patterns in Sunny's background that Craig Newhouse and Joan Simon might have missed presenting in the penalty phase of her trial. Natasha made more trips to find and interview people, at this point, mostly minor characters, who might have something helpful to say about Sunny, her family, or the case.

Carey sent me progress reports and copies of witness declarations as they came in, and I blocked out the habeas corpus petition, doing legal research and rough-drafting claims. It was difficult to get very far, though, with the investigation still going on.

In early September, I made my annual trip to Alaska to visit my sisters, Maggie in Fairbanks and Candace in Anchorage. I was a little afraid to leave my house, even for a week. It was fire season, and the long, rainless summer had been hot, even on the coast. The Santa Ana winds, blowing desert-dry across the mountains, had pulled the last moisture from the ground and the brittle grass and weeds and parched the leaves of the tanoaks in the woods between my house and Ed's. Along my driveway and away from the drip lines in my orchard, the dry grass crunched under my feet, and every step I took raised puffs of pale dust.

I spent the week up north picking berries with Maggie and going camping with her and her husband Pete in Denali Park. We walked from the park road over a hill and pitched our tent in a treeless landscape of valley, river, and mountain that was probably unchanged since the Pleistocene. We made a project of heating water for coffee and instant soup on their tiny backpacker's stove and spent a day walking in the hills and reading in our camp, with a weather eye out for bears foraging for their last bit of fattening before heading to their caves for a winter of sleep. In the evening I dreamily watched planets and stars wink into view in the darkening sky. I didn't sleep well; I was cold in my sleeping bag and kept thinking I heard animals padding and flitting around outside. But I didn't care about the lack of sleep; climbing out of the tent in the twilight of a frosty morning and priming and starting the stove with numb fingers were Zen-like experiences on the vast and silent hillside. And as I sat on a rock, drinking sugary tea and gazing down at the river and over at the mountains on the other side, I was filled with gratitude just to be there.

The next month, it seemed half of California caught fire. Not far from Corbin's Landing, the Santa Anas drove walls of flame across Napa and Sonoma counties, burning grasslands, vineyards, and whole neighborhoods of houses. Everyone knew someone who had been burned out; we upended our homes for towels, blankets, kitchen equipment we could spare for the fire's refugees. Harriet and Bill had friends staying at their house. I had no room for another person, but I took in Pogo while Ed, who was part of our local volunteer fire department, went to fight the fires inland, and I played foster mom to a couple of other dogs until their families could find a new home.

Farther south, more fires scoured the hills and ranches near the coast, burning through parts of Ventura County, where Carey lived. When I called her to ask how she was doing, she told me that her ranch in Ojai had burned. "House, barn, everything. We got the horses and other livestock out," she said, gamely. "But it was a cliff-hanger for a while; we weren't sure we were going to be able to trailer them all out in time."

That month, I lost a client. Howard Henley, whose case I had been working on, died of a heart attack in prison, a few months after a hard-fought hearing in which the judge had ruled he was entitled to a new trial on the question of whether he was innocent of the murder he was convicted of. The trial would never have taken place, because we had found new evidence that exonerated Howard conclusively. Nevertheless, the prosecution had contested the decision, and Howard stayed on death row while the state Supreme Court considered it. He was in his sixties; he had spent almost eighteen years on death row; he had grown old there. That it had taken so much time, and such a long, uphill battle, to vindicate him was bad enough; that he should die before seeing the freedom he'd finally gained made all our work feel pointless. When Sunny's case heated up again, I was glad for the distraction.

Carey called one morning a couple of weeks after the fires. "I'm a little overwhelmed here, with dealing with the ranch," she said. "Can you do some more on Sunny's case?"

"Sure, whatever you need," I said.

"I haven't been asking you for a lot lately because the

judge has gotten kind of stingy with funding. I can cover your expenses, but I don't know if I'll be able to pay you for all your time."

It was the old story. Prosecutors are on salary and work in offices with generous budgets, but criminal defense attorneys, even in death penalty cases, are expected to essentially donate a lot of our time. We receive a small fraction of the rate paid to lawyers in civil law firms, and even that is often cut and whittled down. "No worries," I said bravely.

She thanked me. "I've been going nuts here," she went on. "Not just with the fires, but our psychologist—Marilyn Cannon."

"What's up?"

"She can't find anything wrong with Sunny. She says Sunny is basically a normal, well-adjusted woman for her age and where she is. She does think Sunny was clinically depressed in the period before Greg Ferrante's death. Marilyn didn't have much good to say about Greg and how he treated Sunny. It's her opinion that he broke down Sunny's self-esteem by constantly criticizing and downgrading her. Between that and his unfaithfulness, she says Sunny was psychologically crushed to the point where she doesn't think Sunny could have organized anything like having him murdered. It's what people who study abused women call 'learned helplessness.' Sunny felt that Greg was all-powerful, and believing that left her feeling there wasn't anything she could do to get out of the situation."

"That doesn't seem bad as mitigation," I ventured.

"No, as far as it goes, but so far it's all based on what Sunny told her. I'll get a report from Marilyn about that, at least; it'll help with arguing lingering doubt that she's guilty. I wish it were more, though. And that we had more in general at this point."

"Everything does seem kind of inconclusive," I agreed.

"I know. But there's something else."

"Yes?"

"Marilyn thinks Sunny is covering for Brittany in some way. I guess Sunny told her she felt bad because she couldn't protect Brittany from Greg's meanness and said some things about Brittany and her relationship with Greg that made Marilyn wonder if Brittany wasn't involved in his murder."

"I've wondered about that for a long time," I said. "So did Craig Newhouse, if you remember."

"Yeah. Me too. But Marilyn thinks Sunny thinks so, too."

"Oh, boy."

Oh, boy, indeed. If it was true, then I understood why Sunny had been willing to be convicted of murder rather than put on a defense that might point to Brittany.

"That's the problem Craig Newhouse had to deal with," Carey continued, "threading that needle, trying to convince the jury Sunny was innocent without laying the crime on her daughter. And we're in the same position. I can't imagine Sunny changing her mind.

"It's a mess. Everything that points away from Sunny points toward Brittany or Braden—or both of them. I don't know how to write this petition. We need to talk to Sunny again soon, but I have to think a little about how. I've been waiting to talk to Braden and Brittany until we'd talked to some more of the other witnesses, but it's time. I think it's time to talk to the Ferrantes, too."

"Okay."

"I was hoping you could go with Natasha to see Braden and Brittany. And then come with me to visit the Ferrante family. We should probably both go, as Sunny's attorneys."

I was good with that. "I'll get in touch with Natasha. Let me know when you have time to go see the family."

"Thank you so much. Everything is so crazy right now. I'm still in shock over the ranch, and we have to deal with cleaning up and rebuilding and the poor horses. I keep reminding myself that it was just our vacation place; I can only imagine what people are going through who've lost their homes. What a strange case this is. I didn't know what I was getting into."

When I called Natasha to discuss planning visits to Braden and Brittany, she said, "I've finally located Steve Eason."

"Where did you find him?"

"Inmate locator website. I've been checking it from time to time since I've been working on this case. This is the first time his name came up."

"Where do you suppose he was before?"

"Don't know—jail, out on the streets. He doesn't seem to have had a permanent address in a while."

"What prison is he in now?"

"Salinas Valley."

"We should go see him together."

"I'm for that."

An informant like Eason was likely to say one thing to an interviewer and something else on the witness stand. Having a pair of people speak with him made it harder for him to successfully claim that the interviewer had misheard or lied about what he said.

"They'll want to do a background check before we go in," I said. "It's going to take a couple of weeks."

"Let's get started right away. You know, Braden's at the Men's Colony in San Luis Obispo. Maybe we can see them both in one trip."

"How wonderful—the prison tour of coastal California."

16

The parking lot of Salinas Valley State Prison was windy and cold. The prison itself was modern and devoid of landscaping, a treeless sprawl of gray cellblocks and gun towers, fenced with razor wire and spread over some of what had once been the delta of an ice-age river. More recently, it had probably been fields of lettuce, spinach or cauliflower, like the ones that still surrounded it. As I surveyed it from the parking lot I felt a vague moral discomfort that productive earth had been buried under something like this.

Natasha was wearing a bulky black cardigan over her white shirt and long black skirt. She shivered and pulled it closed around her as we stood in the prison parking lot.

"Hardly looks like *East of Eden*, does it?" I said.

She gave me a questioning glance.

"John Steinbeck. This—well, not this, but the whole area—is what he wrote about."

"Oh, right. I've never read it. We read *Grapes of Wrath* in high school. I always thought all his books were about the Central Valley."

"No, he lived here—Salinas and Monterey. He was writing about what he saw."

"Oh, right. Makes sense now I think about it. There's all that Steinbeck stuff around Monterey, Cannery Row…"

We went through the routine for legal visitors without incident and were given our badges. A civilian employee, a brown-haired baby-faced man who was probably about the same age as Natasha, was assigned to be our Virgil through this particular purgatory.

He led us down a wide concrete sidewalk edged with beds of gravel in which not even a weed was visible and stopped at a heavy double door with a window of glass reinforced with wire mesh. He unlocked the door with a key from a large bunch at his belt. "There's a conference room in here you can use," he said.

Inside the building, everything seemed to be white and gray—polished gray floors, white walls with a scuff mark here and there, gray-painted doors. Our guide opened a door. "This is where you'll be." He held it as Natasha and I walked through. "They'll be bringing your guy here. Probably take a few minutes."

"Thank you," we said.

"No problem." The door closed, and he was gone.

The white and gray theme repeated itself in the conference room. The long table was some sort of brushed metal; the steel chairs were upholstered with gray plastic. A counter at one end held an empty drip coffee pot. Above it, white shelves held the only touch of color in the room, a few binders of what appeared to be official reports. Two closed windows of mesh-reinforced glass let in light and a blurred view of the outside, and overhead fluorescents lit the room with a shadowless impersonality. The room felt a little warmer than the outdoors, but not much.

"I hope this isn't an exercise in futility," I said, without much hope. Natasha nodded in agreement, and we sat for a while in the echoing silence. I found myself thinking that it was November already, well over halfway through the one year we had to finish and file Sunny's habeas petition, and we had precious little to show for all our work.

I heard a door open and shut and voices in the hallway. "Sounds like they're here," Natasha said.

They were. We stood and watched as the door to our room opened, and a uniformed guard, his leather belt clanking with keys, handcuffs, and other apparatus, appeared in the doorway next to another, shorter man dressed in the prison inmate's uniform of jeans and a loose blue shirt.

"This is Eason," the guard said. "He your visit?"

"Yes," I said.

From the police reports, I knew Steve Eason had been twenty-eight years old when he made his statement accusing Sunny. He would now be in his early forties. His face was broad, with close-set eyes and a day's growth of pale stubble on his cheeks and chin. His sand-colored hair, shaved in a buzz cut that was starting to grow out, was receding from his forehead back along the top of his head. Under his loose blue prison-issue shirt I could see the neck and long sleeves of a white thermal undershirt, dingy with age. If he had any prison tattoos, they were invisible under its long sleeves.

He assessed me suspiciously from under sand-colored eyebrows.

The guard herded Eason to a spot near one of the chairs at the table. "I'll be out in the hall," he said. "Just let me know when you're finished."

I thanked him, and he left, closing the door behind him.

Eason looked from me to Natasha, obviously trying to figure out who we were and why we'd come to see him. I introduced us with as much formality as the occasion allowed.

"I'm Janet Moodie, and this is Natasha Levin. I'm one of the attorneys for Sunny Ferrante, and Natasha is an investigator." I reached a hand across the table to shake his; he hesitated a second or two and then raised his and took mine. His palm was warm and moist.

"Sunny Ferrante," he said, as if retrieving the name from the depths of his memory, before releasing my hand.

He was wearing prison-issue shoes of cheap canvas with thin rubber soles, and the cuffs of his undershirt, I noticed, were starting to fray. Thermal underwear is not issued by the prisons; inmates usually get that and other comforts, such as decent-quality tennis shoes, ramen, cookies, and candy, from their families, in the care packages they're allowed once a quarter. Judging from the state of his thermals, Eason had probably gotten them used from another inmate—I guessed he wasn't getting much family support.

"Why don't we sit down?" I said, and we did. "Unusual place for a visit," I went on, with a glance around the room. "If there were any vending machines, I'd buy you something to eat or drink."

Something like a slight smile creased the muscles of his face. "That would have been good," he said. "Better than the food here." His smile faded, and he looked from one of us to the other. "Sunny Ferrante," he repeated. "That was a long time ago."

"Yeah," I said. "We're working on her habeas corpus case."

"Um," he said. "She got sent to death row."

"She did."

He shook his head, almost sadly. "Man, no one saw that coming."

That surprised me. "Really?" I asked. "Why?"

"It just didn't seem like that kind of case. Husbands kill their wives; bitches kill their old men. It's like crimes of passion, you know. I mean, I didn't know her, but it's not like she was a serial killer."

"Maybe, but the prosecutor asked for the death penalty, and they got it."

Another shake of his head, and something like a shiver. "Yeah, but I don't think anybody thought the jury would do it. I didn't."

"Just bad luck then."

He let out a brief laugh that was more of a grunt. "Yeah, the worst." His chin tilted up, and he gave me a stare that was almost a challenge. "So, what did you want to talk to me about?"

"You testified at Sunny's trial," I said.

"Yes?" The word, as he said it, was a question.

"And you said Todd Betts told you he killed Gregory Ferrante."

He nodded. "Right."

"And that he said Sunny Ferrante paid him to do it."

This time he didn't nod. "That was a long time ago."

We sat in silence for a long moment, while he thought something through.

"Yeah," he said, finally. "Did that fucking cop a favor, and ended up here."

"You mean in prison?"

"Yeah."

"What happened?"

"They set me up, is what happened."

"What did they do?"

"Shit, what didn't they do? I did my time, got out on parole. Moved to Fresno, 'cause I wasn't exactly welcome in Beanhollow after what I said about Todd. That was okay, I got along in Fresno, not much trouble. Picked up a beef or two, managed to get out with just jail time. Then I got charged with robbery and assault with a deadly weapon, of all the fucking travesties; that's what I'm in here for. And they put me in a module in the jail with some guy who knew that punk Braden Ferrante. He figures out who I am. Stupid blabbermouth tells some buddy of his that I'm the

guy who got Ferrante's stepmother put away for killing his
father. Next thing you know, I'm attacked by three guys—
stabbed, almost thrown over the tier rail. I almost died, they
nicked my liver, collapsed one lung. Just missed my heart,
doctors said. And after I get out of the hospital, they put
me on the PC yard. Protective custody," he said, his tone of
voice turning the phrase into an expletive. "First in the jail,
now here. It was a setup; I know it."

"Aren't you safer here?" Natasha asked.

He glared in her direction. "Are you kidding? This is a
death sentence. I'm looking over my shoulder every day.
Some guy out to make his bones could rush me, guards
wouldn't give a fuck. I almost didn't come out today, except
that I was curious to find out who wanted to see me."

"Why do you think you were set up?" I asked.

"Hansen," Eason said. "*Detective* Joe Hansen. He was
pissed off at me."

"Why?"

"'Cause I wrote him a letter. I kept trying to call him
after I picked up this last charge, trying to get a little help,
but he was never around. So I wrote to him. Reminded
him how I'd helped him put away your Mrs. Ferrante, and
maybe he could lift a fucking finger and help me get a
deal in the case I had. It was after that I was moved to the
high-security module with Braden's old buddy. It had to be
Hansen behind it."

His theory didn't hold together, but I decided not to
probe him about it. "I'm sorry to hear that," I said.

"Yeah, you and me both. So what are you here for about Mrs. Ferrante?"

"We're trying to get her a new trial."

"Really." His tone was skeptical, but interested. "It's been a long time; I thought her case would be over and done with by now."

"No, still going on."

"Huh. Okay." Eason had been a con long enough that he didn't need an explanation.

While waiting for our clearance, I'd reread the police reports and the transcript of his statement to the detectives, as well as his testimony at Sunny's trial. I was about to begin questioning him about details, probing for inconsistencies and any evidence we could find that he had been lying, when he said, suddenly, "You know, that shit I told the cops wasn't true." The words came out quickly, as if he'd made the decision to speak after some kind of inward struggle. He stopped and watched me for a reaction.

Out of the corner of my eye, I could see Natasha start writing on her legal pad.

"What part of it?" I asked, conscious of trying to do so lightly and gently. *Just the facts, ma'am, no judgment.*

He seemed to understand that I knew what was in the police reports and his testimony. "Most of it was," he said. "Just not the part about Todd and Mrs. Ferrante."

"Okay," I said. "What was and wasn't true?" I was speaking quietly, trying to keep my voice neutral and encouraging, trying to channel what I'd seen cops in videos do with a suspect on the brink of confessing. *You're safe here, we're all friends, I'm so glad you're ready to tell the truth, it will set your conscience free.*

Eason seemed to relax a little, and his voice became more conversational, even confiding. "Well, some of it Todd told me, and some I guessed at. The part about us smoking weed together and talking about what he did, that's true. More or less—he never actually said who he killed. But I put two and two together. I mean, who else could it have been? That guy Ferrante had just been shot dead, and Todd worked for the family and was banging his daughter."

"What got him talking about it?"

"He came over to my place. I'm his uncle, I guess you know that; I've known him since he was a little kid. Anyhow, he came over to my place one night and said he was feeling really shitty about something. And I asked him if he wanted to talk about it, and he said no, he just wanted to get high. I had some beer in the fridge and some weed, so I said, why don't we have a beer and a toke; maybe you'll feel better. So we drank some beers, smoked some, and then he began crying, and saying stuff about how he'd killed someone he knew and was having nightmares and feeling all this guilt."

"Can you remember what exactly he said?"

"You know, it's been a long time; I don't remember his exact words. I was kind of high myself. But I was feeling, like, real uncomfortable with what he was saying. I remember telling him he shouldn't be talking about it, and he said he wasn't, just to me 'cause I was family. He was crying and going on about the guy may not have been great, but he didn't deserve to die, and how there wasn't anyone he could tell how bad he felt."

"Just that, nothing more?"

"Yeah."

"Nothing about anyone else being involved?"

"No." Eason looked a little ashamed of himself, like a kid caught in a lie.

"And you didn't ask why he killed the guy?"

He shook his head. "No. I really didn't want to know about it."

"But you guessed that he was talking about Greg Ferrante?"

"Yeah, like I said. I figured it out. I seen it on the news about that Ferrante guy. And I didn't know of anyone else who'd been killed around then. It just seemed logical."

"Did you tell anyone what Todd had told you?"

"Well, the cops."

"Anyone before then?"

"No. No way."

"Why did you decide to tell the police the story you did?"

He took a breath and blew out a sigh that held a whiff of decaying teeth. "Shit," he said. "Desperation; fear. I'd picked up a beef. Got in a fight with my girlfriend, and they wanted to charge me with assault with intent to commit rape. It would have been a second strike, a lot of prison time. I knew by then the police thought Ferrante's wife was behind the murder."

"How did you know?"

"It was in the papers, on the TV. I guess I paid attention because of Todd. Someone interviewed Hansen on TV, and he said he suspected her, but he couldn't prove anything. So I went to the sergeant on my tier in the jail and said I had information about the murder. By that time Todd had already passed, so I couldn't hurt him by talking about it. Hansen came to talk to me, and I told him I needed some help with my case. And he said he'd see what they could do, talk with the DA. He came back later and said they couldn't make any promises, but the DA would see what he could do if I had information that was useful to them. So I told them what Todd told me—plus a few other things."

"You told them Mrs. Ferrante had paid Todd five thousand dollars, but Todd never told you that, right?"

"Yeah. I got that from the TV news, too."

"And what happened to your case?"

"Well, they kept saying they couldn't promise me anything. But the DA in my case let me plead guilty to simple assault. They held off sentencing me until after my testimony, and then they recommended dropping the strike. I served a year in county jail, no prison time, because of my cooperation." He said the last phrase with a hint of sarcasm.

"Not a bad deal."

"Yeah, it was sweet. But now I'm here."

"And you think it was Hansen's fault?"

"Damn straight."

"Is that why you're telling us you lied to him? Because he let you down?"

"Yeah," he said, sullenly. "And because it's the truth. I don't care what they do. I don't owe those s.o.b.s anything."

Now for the sixty-four-thousand-dollar question. "Would you be willing to sign a declaration about what you told us?"

He thought for a second or two, brows knitted, then said, "Yeah. Shit, what are they going to do? Charge me with perjury? You know, I'm serving twenty-five to life. Third strike, no deals. That's what you get for helping the cops. No good deed goes unpunished." His face was tense, and he was absently bouncing one knee and tapping the forefinger of one hand on the table. "I wish there was some water here," he said.

"We'll try to finish up soon," I said. "Would you mind waiting a little while we write out the declaration for you to sign?"

Eason shrugged. "Yeah, I guess; I got all the time in the world."

He had apparently said all he wanted to say, because he sat silent, staring at the wall or tapping his finger on the table, while Natasha and I talked in low voices about what to say in the declaration, and she printed it on her legal pad in a small, clear hand. When she was finished, I gave it to Eason. "Read it carefully, and make sure we haven't gotten something wrong." He read through it slowly, sometimes silently forming the words with his lips. Natasha asked him to initial each page, and he did. At the end, he signed it firmly and handed it to her. "Are we done?" he asked.

"One more thing," Natasha said. "Would you mind signing a release for your prison file?"

I waited for Eason to bristle, but to my surprise, he took the form from Natasha.

"Can't see why not," he said. He signed it with a flourish and slid it back to her. "Is that it?" He was shifting a little in his chair; I wondered if he needed to pee.

"Just about," I said. "I have just one more question."

"Sure."

"I'm curious. If you didn't know Sunny hired Todd, why did you tell the police she did? You knew she'd get charged with murder, didn't you?"

"Like I told you, I had a serious beef, and I needed something to get me out from under it." He thought for a moment, rubbing his chin, before answering without meeting my eyes. "I guess I figured she probably did do it, so it didn't really matter. I mean, she did, didn't she?" He met my eyes for a second, as if hoping to find his answer in my reaction, then turned his gaze toward the door, with longing, I thought.

"I'll call the guard," I said. "Thanks for talking with us."

"Yeah, no problem," he said abstractedly.

I opened the conference room door, and the guard, who was sitting on a straight-backed chair a discreet distance away, glanced over and stood up. It occurred to me how much boredom there was in the job of guarding prisoners. "Ready?" he said.

I nodded.

"You'll need an escort, then." He pulled out his radio and spoke into it. "It'll be five or ten minutes." I moved aside so he could come into the room. "You ready, Eason?" he asked.

"Sure am," Eason said.

"Let's do it." Eason stood and, with the guard behind him, walked out of the room.

17

Natasha and I said almost nothing to each other—I felt afraid to reveal what had just happened in anyone else's hearing—until we were in the parking lot. As we walked toward our cars, she was clutching her manila folder as if it were a briefcase full of cash.

"Well!" I said. "That was a surprise."

"It's huge. I mean, this guy was the star witness against her."

"True," I said, bringing my misgivings into the open. "But I don't trust him."

"Yeah." Natasha was a little deflated by that. "You're probably right. But we have a declaration."

"Right. I'm amazed he signed it."

She nodded agreement. "Jeez, it's cold out here," she said, shivering.

Suddenly, it seemed, the good-cop façade I'd held up during the interview with Eason fell apart around me. As the evangelicals say in their Bible quoting, it was as if the scales fell from my eyes. "God damn it," I said, to no one in particular. "Fifteen fucking years." Without meaning to, I found I'd made a fist of the hand that wasn't holding my plastic prison visit bag. Fifteen years in which Steve Eason had swanned around town beating up his girlfriends, stealing from his family, and putting other men in jail with lies. While Sunny counted out the days between gray walls, watching herself grow old, waiting uncomplaining through the legal process that would decide whether she lived or died, knowing that her family and the world outside were moving on without her. And she was the person labeled by society as the worst of the worst. "Fifteen years," I said again. "He left her there all that time. God fucking damn it."

Natasha was silent as we hurried to the cars. Once in mine, I realized that I was shivering, too. I was grateful when the heat in my old Subaru kicked in.

18

I knew Eason's declaration wasn't the rock-solid evidence it seemed. Snitches are notorious for moving with the prevailing breeze, and changing their stories under pressure. I'd known of cases where informants tried to repudiate declarations they'd signed, claiming they'd been pressured or even that the signature wasn't theirs. Eason was pissed off at the system right now, but that was likely to last only until some detective or DA came to see him and tell him the error of his ways.

In our favor, we had Eason's signature on not just the declaration but the records release, making it that much harder for him to deny. And the evidence that he'd told a different story in a sworn declaration from the one he'd testified to at Sunny's trial would badly damage him as a witness if the prosecution tried to use him again. Old and cynical as I normally felt, I had to admit this was a breakthrough.

We had another appointment that afternoon, to see Braden at the California Men's Colony state prison, a couple of hours' drive away. There was just enough time to meet in the nearest town to grab coffee and premade sandwiches before we flew down the freeway, eating lunch as we drove.

As with Steve Eason, I hadn't written Braden Ferrante beforehand to let him know we were coming, because I didn't want to make it easy for him to refuse to see us. Instead, I relied on the likelihood that natural curiosity and the tedium of prison life would make him interested in the prospect of a visit, even without knowing who his visitor was. Braden didn't disappoint me; he walked almost jauntily into the attorney visiting room and took a seat across from Natasha and me. I offered to get him something to eat or drink before the guard locked the door on us, but he shook his head, saying, "I'm good."

Braden was tall, slim, and handsome, and clearly well aware of that fact, with dark brown hair slicked back from his forehead. His thin face, with its somewhat sharp features, reminded me a little of my son Gavin's, though Braden's eyes were brown, rather than blue-gray. But where Gavin's expression was open and candid, Braden's was coolly speculative. He appraised each of us in a second: I was an old woman who would have been invisible but for the fact that I was a possible authority figure of some sort. Natasha, his contemporary, wasn't hot, his passing glance said, and was therefore of no interest.

I introduced us and told him we were representing Sunny in her habeas corpus case. On hearing that Natasha was an investigator, he regarded her with a bit more respect, but then sat back in his chair and stared at both of us through narrowed eyes. "I don't think I can help you," he said. "I didn't have anything to do with my father's death."

"I understand that," I lied. "We're interested in speaking to you as someone who was close to Todd Betts around the time your father was killed—"

"I wasn't close to Todd Betts," he broke in. "We worked at the ranch at the same time, that's all. Maybe socialized a little. And I didn't know my stepmother at all. We saw each other rarely, at family get-togethers; that was it. I'm telling you, the police asked me all this stuff, and they cleared me. I don't want to get into it again, okay?" While talking, he moved until he was sitting up in his chair, and his tone was irritated and defensive.

"We really don't have much to ask."

He shook his head. "I have an appeal going from the case I'm in here for. I don't want to get hauled back into this stuff about my father." He got up, walked over to the door and pushed the button next to it that summoned the guard. "Sorry," he said. Clearly he wasn't. He stood in silence, looking out the reinforced glass window, until the guard appeared and opened the door.

We got up too. "I want to go back now," Braden told the guard.

"Right," the guard said. He glanced at us apologetically as he put handcuffs on Braden and followed him out of the cell.

"Well," Natasha said. "Short, but not sweet. What a creep!"

Win some, lose some, I thought. "It's been a pretty good day, all things considered."

The next leg of our epic journey was from the Men's Colony to Wofford Heights, where Brittany lived.

The route crossed the middle of the state on a series of two-lane highways. The area was enormous and empty, mile after mile of hills and valleys covered in dried summer grass, not yet greened up by winter storms—range land without enough water for farms or towns. It often amazed me that a state as populated as California could contain so much empty space.

Because Natasha had driven from Los Angeles to meet me, we were each in our own cars, so I was left to my thoughts as I contemplated the almost meditative landscape of hills and valleys and hills beyond to the pale sky. I was surprised by how few I had and how prosaic they were. Whether the tanker truck four cars ahead of me would ever turn off so we could move faster. What Natasha and I would say to Brittany when we saw her. Whether the families of the dogs I was caring for (and who were currently living, along with Charlie, at Ed's) would ever be able to have them back. How it would feel to have to give your dog away because your house had burned down. The fact that anything you have can be taken from you in an instant—by a fire, a crash of glass and metal, a doctor's words, a phone call. When my thoughts turned again to the country I was crossing, I noticed that the color and shape of the little clouds in the sky around and above me, the color of the sky itself, were those of autumn, carrying imaginary scents of apples and fallen leaves and the real promise of rain.

Eventually I reached one of the arterial freeways that connect the north and south of the state, like concrete rivers down the Central Valley, and drove for an hour or so past a succession of industrial parks and weed-filled lots. After turning off and driving some more, through suburbs of new subdivisions and then more range land, I suddenly entered a long desert canyon, miles of winding two-lane road next to high sandstone cliffs and a rapidly flowing river. When I emerged, just as suddenly, onto a larger highway, it was in a long, wide valley dotted with ranches and stands of mountain pine trees. At its end lay a large lake, a reservoir with a dam at its near end. Wofford Heights was across the highway from the lake, a hillside full of houses facing the view across the valley. I pulled off the highway into the dirt parking lot of a white-painted Quonset hut with a carved wood sign over the door reading "Antiques" and another of cardboard on the door saying "Closed for the Season." The place was utterly deserted; the fitful rush of wind from the valley seemed only to intensify the silence.

I phoned Natasha. She had pulled off a little down the road, and I drove to meet her.

"Dang, this place is remote!" I said, as we stood next to our cars.

"Actually, it used to be kind of famous," she told me.

"Hollywood studios made a lot of westerns around here. It's still a pretty popular place for people to have a little vacation home up in the mountains. When I was in college I had some friends in LA who used to come up here on river rafting trips. I went with them a couple of times."

I had never been on a rafting trip, even in Alaska. "How did you like it?"

"It was fun, not too scary; I'd do it again."

In phone calls and again over lunch after our abortive visit with Braden, we'd compared notes about what we wanted to ask Brittany. I felt as prepared as I ever would be for this meeting. I took a deep breath and said, "Well, are we ready to go?"

"Yep," Natasha said.

We drove up in my car, leaving Natasha's parked off the road. The sun had dropped below the mountains, and we climbed the narrow roads that wound up the hill in gray twilight, searching for signs for the streets my GPS was telling us to follow. Most of the houses along them were manufactured homes; Brittany's was a white double-wide in a small yard prettily landscaped with desert plants. A fall-themed garland with yellow and orange oak leaves and red berries hung on the front door, and three pumpkins were arranged at one side of the small front stoop. The evening was growing chilly, and a faint scent of wood smoke from stoves and fireplaces gave the air around us the cozy feeling of a winter night. I felt a twinge of longing for my own home and stove.

As we reached the door, I could smell food cooking and hear children playing inside, and then a single bark from a large-sounding dog. We rang the bell, and a few seconds later the door was answered by a tall, muscular man in a dark shirt with a Cal Fire logo. His face was ruddy, broad, and boyish, and his reddish-blond hair, cut short, bristled on his head and at his temples. He looked surprised, but friendly. Next to him and a little behind, a Belgian Malinois dog—the breed used by the police and military—eyed us watchfully. Behind him, in the living room, I glimpsed a small boy and girl watching us with silent curiosity.

"Hi," the man said. "Can I help you?"

"Is Brittany Ecker here?"

"She is. Can I tell her who's calling?"

"I'm Janet Moodie, and this is Natasha Levin. We're from her mother's legal team."

"Oh!" he said. "Come on in and have a seat. I'll get Britt for you. I'm Rick, her husband, by the way."

He led us to the sofa, a Scandinavian-type with marine blue upholstery and light wood arms, and went on toward the back of the house. The younger of the children, a little blond-haired girl, was standing and watching us shyly; as we sat she moved closer to the older child, a boy, who was sitting in an armchair watching something on an iPad and glancing up at us every few seconds. Natasha smiled at her, and she smiled back shyly.

A minute later, Brittany, dressed in jeans and a violet Shaker-knit sweater with a print chef's apron over them, came out from the back of the house, followed by Rick. Brittany was bigger and heavier-boned than Sunny. Her broad, pale face was pleasant, but not especially pretty; a few old acne scars pitted the skin on her forehead and chin. Her straight, reddish-brown hair was swept back and casually pinned up with a big barrette.

"Hi!" she said cheerfully, as we stood up to greet her. "Mom said you'd be coming to see me at some point, but she didn't know when." She looked from one of us to the other. "What were your names again?"

We told her, and she nodded. "I wish I'd known you were coming," she said. "I don't have *any* time to talk right now. I have a planning meeting at my church—we're organizing relief for Puerto Rico—and I can't skip it because I'm the chair. I'm just running around right now trying to get the kids fed before I go." Her voice was high and youthful, with a bit of Harrison drawl in it; she sounded younger than Natasha, even though they were close to the same age. "I hate to ask you, but could we talk tomorrow morning? Will you be here overnight?"

"Yes," I said, nodding. Natasha might be able to make it back to LA tonight, but I'd have to wait till morning to start for home anyway.

"Oh, good. When would you like to come over tomorrow?"

"Whatever works for you."

"Nine would be good."

"Okay," I said. "I guess we'd better go and let you get everything done."

She gave us a grateful smile, and we turned and let ourselves out.

"I hope you don't mind spending the night here," I said to Natasha as we drove back to her car.

"Nah. I was thinking we should even if we did the interview tonight. I wouldn't want to drive back down that canyon in the dark."

"Any idea where we might stay?" I asked her.

"There's a cute town up the road a bit. It's where the kayak and raft tours used to take off. There are some motels up there. We used to camp, though, so I don't know much about them."

We registered at the first motel we found in the town, a rustic-themed place with a lobby decorated like a small hunting lodge—wood-paneled walls, prints of forest and hunting scenes, and a big fireplace with a tame, but warm, gas fire. A vague attempt had been made to replicate the rustic theme in my room, but the result was a melancholy shoe box, with tan walls, dark wood furniture, a spruce green bedspread, and one window at the end, shut off from the outside with red, brown, and green plaid curtains. After dinner with Natasha at a diner nearby, I scrolled through the stations on the TV, turned it off, and read myself to sleep over an Ellis Peters mystery I'd packed in the bottom of my overnight bag in case of emergencies, of which this was surely one.

In the morning, frost covered the ground and the windows of our cars, and the air seemed to glitter in the slanting sun.

After breakfast at the same diner we made our way back to Wofford Heights and Brittany's house. She seemed more at ease when she greeted us. "Come and sit down," she said. "Would you like some coffee? I just made a fresh pot."

"No thanks, we just ate breakfast," we said, almost in unison.

"I hope you don't mind if I finish mine," she said. She picked up a cup from the coffee table and carried it to an end table next to an armchair, while we took places on the sofa and opened our notebooks. In the morning sunshine her living room was bright and homey, with creamy white walls, maple laminate floors, and accents of bright colors in the print of the curtains and the cushions on the couch and chairs. The kids' toys had been put away. In the corner stood an old-fashioned wood stove, with a protective screen around it and a dog rug in front of it; a fire was glowing in its window, warming the room. The walls displayed an assortment of family photos and a trio of framed cross-stitch panels of bouquets of flowers. "My mom made those," Brittany said, noticing that they caught my eye. The air smelled faintly of last night's dinner, woodsmoke, coffee, and dog. The dog, after sizing us up, had settled for a nap in front of the stove, with one eye partly open.

Brittany leaned toward us, confidingly. "I'm glad you could come this morning," she said, her voice lowered. "I feel a lot more comfortable talking without Rick here."

I nodded sympathetically, though I wasn't sure why she felt that way.

"The kids are in preschool until noon," she went on, "so I'm free till then." She sat up, reached for her coffee cup, took a drink, and put the cup down. I found myself wishing I'd asked for something to drink after all, if only to have something to do during the silence. "What do you think my mom's chances are?" she asked, looking from one of us to the other.

"I honestly don't know," I said. "Her appeal is still going on, and we're going to file a habeas corpus petition for her. It all depends on what a court decides."

"Will they let her go?"

"If we have strong enough evidence, they may send the case back for another trial."

"Oh." Brittany sounded a little deflated. "Mom won't talk to me about how she thinks things are going," she said, a faint note of frustration in her voice. "She always says everything is fine and tells funny stories, and says not to worry. I know she's trying to protect me, but—" She stopped and shook her head, and said, in a voice that for a few seconds seemed suddenly childlike and unguarded, "I just can't believe this all happened, and she's there." I got the impression that Brittany was hungry for someone she could talk to freely about Sunny's plight and her own feelings. "It's like a constant weight—I feel so helpless." She sighed, opened her hands, then clasped them together. "If there's anything I can say or do, please tell me."

I glanced over at Natasha, who picked up the cue. "Maybe we can start with how things were with your family—you and your mother and Greg Ferrante. Like from the beginning."

Brittany nodded. "Okay. Wow, from the beginning. I was only around two when Mom and Greg got married, so basically all I remember as my family is the three of us. Mom always loved me, and so did Nana—my great-grandmother. And Linda and Pete were cool—Linda is my grandmother, Mom's mother—she never wanted to be called Grandma," she said with a smile and a little eye-roll. "But Greg always seemed kind of distant, kind of abrupt. I never called him Daddy or Dad, always Greg."

"What about his family?"

"We used to visit the ranch quite a bit—Thanksgiving, Christmas, barbecues in the summer. They were nice to us, most of them."

"Did you make friends with any of your step-cousins?"

"Not when I was a kid. They were all older or younger; there wasn't anyone my age."

"What about your biological father?"

"He wasn't really in the picture. He got married again and had a couple of kids. He'd send, like, Christmas cards and some money on my birthday, but that was about it. Once he and his wife invited me to visit them for a week, but I don't think his wife liked me, or something, and they didn't ask again. Greg would bitch about him to my mom because he thought he wasn't paying enough child support."

"How did Greg behave to you? Did he yell at you, or was he abusive to you or your mom?"

"Not physically. He'd get mad, but it was all words."

"So was he abusive in other ways?"

"Kind of," she said slowly, as if uncertain. "He was mean—always putting us down, criticizing something. It seemed as if Mom and I could never do anything quite right. Like what we did was never up to his standards."

"What kinds of things was he critical of?"

She sighed. "Oh, Lord, everything. He'd say stuff about the clothes Mom bought for her and me, or my hair, or how I behaved around company or his family. When I was younger, he blamed Mom for everything he didn't like about me. But when I got older, he started ragging on me about all sorts of things: my weight, my grades, my music and clothes and friends. He never said anything kind or helpful. That's really wrong to do to a teenage kid. I had little enough confidence as it was, and he just crushed me. Mom used to say not to let it bother me, that I was pretty and smart. But you can't help it; it gets under your skin. When I was old enough to see how much he hurt her, too, I really started to hate him." Brittany said the last part in a rush of words, and then stopped. "I didn't know what to think of it then," she went on, more thoughtfully, "but now I know what he was doing was, like, he was always gaslighting us—Mom even more than me."

"Did Greg and your mom argue?"

"Not that much in the beginning. More toward the end. But Mom wasn't any match for him. He was really overbearing, and at some point, she'd just stop talking. She'd just shut down."

"Were you aware that he was unfaithful to your mother?"

"When I got old enough. Mom didn't talk to me about it. But I overheard things they said sometimes. And I knew Mom was hurt. She always tried to be cheerful around me, but it was like—I don't know—the atmosphere at home was always tense. Greg was pissed off all the time, Mom was trying to avoid him. I couldn't stand to be there. I'd call Todd, and he'd come get me in his truck, and we'd go out to the ranch or to his sister's place. Just get away."

"Did you know about the rumors that Greg was planning to leave your mom?"

She hesitated. "I—I don't think I heard about that until after—after he was killed." I remembered that Sunny had told me the opposite, but decided not to confront her at that point. "I did see that Greg wasn't around as much, and Mom was even more depressed than usual just before he died. I figured he was having another affair."

"More depressed? Does that mean she'd been depressed for a while?"

"Yeah. She just… ran out of steam or something. She did the stuff she usually did—took care of the house, visited, played tennis—but she got more and more quiet. I was so used to Mom being perky and upbeat—that's why they call her Sunny, I guess—that I really saw the change. I heard her tell Nana that she was trying an antidepressant and was taking something so she could sleep."

"Did she confide in Nana about her troubles?"

"She tried not to. But Nana saw she was hurting. Nana

could tell I was unhappy, too. Nana told Mom she ought to
leave Greg, but Mom said she didn't know what she'd do;
she said the support he was supposed to pay her under the
prenuptial agreement would only go so far, and she didn't
think she could find a job because her skills were all out of
date. She said that if she stayed with Greg he'd give me a
better life than she could on her own, pay for me to go to
college. That is one thing I have to say about Greg, he was
never stingy with money. It was all about appearances, but
he always gave Mom plenty of money for clothes and the
house and stuff. He wanted us all to look good because that
made him look good."

"Right," I said. "The prosecution said that her motive for
killing him was to get his money."

Brittany shook her head. "She didn't want his money. I
don't even think she really wanted to leave him. She didn't
hate him. It's like he'd convinced her that all the things he
did were her fault, because she wasn't the wife he wanted her
to be. All she wanted was for things to be okay." Her eyes
met mine. "She didn't kill him. Or pay for him to be killed.
She'd never do that."

Natasha and I both nodded. "I know," I said. "We'll
definitely get to that."

Brittany nodded and waited for the next question.

"What happened right after Greg was killed?" Natasha
went on. "Starting when you got home from visiting Nana?"

She shivered. "Ugh. Let me think. We got home, went
upstairs to put away some stuff—clothes we'd bought. Mom

went back down, and then I did. She was in the kitchen, and I went out back over by the pool, and that's where I found Greg." She paused for a second, biting her lip. "Man, this is so hard, even after all this time."

"I'm sorry," Natasha said. "It has to be tough to remember all that."

Brittany nodded. "Yeah."

"Do you remember why you went out to the pool?" Natasha asked. "Was it to swim?"

"I don't remember anymore; I just did. And saw him lying there; and I screamed and ran back into the house and called for Mom."

"Did you see the blood?"

I saw her tense, and she nodded. "Yes. Kind of pooled behind his head. And his face…" She closed her eyes for a couple of seconds as if to push the memory away. "You'd think I'd be inured to all that now. But it's different when it's someone you know."

"Anything else catch your eye?"

"I don't remember anything."

"What happened after that?"

"I told my mom that Greg was lying on the patio, and she ran out after me. She knelt down next to him; I think she was trying to see if he was breathing or anything. She just kept saying, 'Greg, oh my God, oh my God.' Then she got up and ran back into the house and called 911."

"And then what happened?"

"Paramedics came, and then the police. It was just mass

confusion. And they told Mom at some point that he was dead and that he'd been shot in the back of the head."

"How did your mom react?"

"She was, like, in shock. I remember her just sitting there in a chair in the living room and crying while people kept asking her questions."

"What about you?"

"I went and sat by her until they took us away."

"Where did they take you?"

"The police took us to the station. They put us in different cars. I was freaking out because I wanted to be with Mom."

"What happened after that?"

"They put me in a room, and a lady detective came and asked me a lot of questions. And then she left, and they left me alone for a long time in the room. Then they told me I could go. And I went out, and my mom was there, and her friend Carol. Carol took us to her house for the night, and we stayed with her until we could go back home."

"You were seeing Todd then; did you talk with him after Greg's death?"

"I called him from Carol's and told him what happened."

"Did you and he see one another after that?"

"He came over the next day."

"How about from then on?"

She looked uncomfortable. "I don't know. Not so much. I guess I was in shock. Then right after school let out Mom and I went out to the house on the coast, just to get some peace and quiet. And because we didn't really want to be in the house in Harrison after what happened."

"At some point, you actually did move out, right?"

"Yeah. Mom rented a condo, and we moved there. It was a few weeks after."

"What happened to the house?"

"It was put up for sale."

"Did you go anywhere else that summer?"

"Mom took Nana and me on a cruise up to Alaska after the life insurance money came in. That was after Todd died. She was trying to help me deal with it, with everything that had happened. She thought going away someplace beautiful might help."

"Did it?"

"Not really. I don't even remember that much about the cruise. All I could think about was Todd and how our whole life had become so weird. After we got home Mom got me into counseling; and that helped a little. But then she got arrested."

"How did that happen?"

"They just came early one evening, knocked on the door, Detective Hansen and a couple of cops in uniform, and a social worker. They came in and took her away in handcuffs. The social worker took me to a home, but I was allowed to go live with Nana after a week or two."

"How was that for you?"

"I was really grateful. I had to transfer to high school in Sparksville, which was rinky-dink, but at least no one was whispering about me all the time because my mom was in jail. Half the kids there had been in the same boat at one time or another," she said with a rueful smile. "And I was actually glad to be able to help Nana out. Mom had been helping her, visiting, buying groceries, making sure she got to appointments and stuff, and I kind of took over. Mom told me when I visited her in jail that she'd worried a lot about what was going to happen to Nana and how happy she was that I was living with her. And it took my mind off my own troubles. I don't know what would have happened to me without Nana."

"How did you get around?"

"I had my permit and Mom's car, so I could get groceries and drive Nana to doctor's appointments during the day. And then I got my license, so I could drive at night."

"At some point, though, you moved down south with Linda and Pete."

"Yeah," Brittany sighed. "Poor Nana had a stroke the summer after I graduated high school, and I couldn't care for her anymore. Linda and Pete had to move her into a nursing home down near them, and they sold her house. So I moved down there, too, and stayed with them till I turned eighteen. I had some life insurance money from Greg that was in trust for me till my eighteenth birthday, and I used it to pay for community college and rent an apartment with a couple of other students. And I got a job; that helped."

"What were your plans?"

"I thought about being a nurse. I studied physiology in community college, and then decided I wanted to be an

EMT, so I trained and studied for the certification. Did that until I was pregnant with Kyle. I loved it. That's how I met Rick."

"Where did you work?"

"LA, Orange County."

"How did you come to move here?"

"We both wanted to live somewhere outside the city. Neither of us are really city people. Rick grew up on a farm in Monterey County. He's a firefighter, and after Kyle was born, he applied to Cal Fire, and got hired here. It was a good move for him. They really like him here; he's been promoted a couple of times."

"How is it for you?"

"Quiet. Restful, in some ways, even though I seem to be busy all the time. I'm staying home while the kids are little. I volunteer at the preschool one day a week, and I do some work at our church. Once the kids are in school, I'm thinking of going back to school to study nursing. I'd have to go to Bakersfield, which is a long commute, but we can make it work."

"You've done well," I said. "I know your mom is proud of you."

She looked shy for a minute. "I really want her to be. It's all I can give her, really." She gave a sudden, ragged sigh and blinked back tears, then hunched her shoulders and squeezed her fists against the lower part of her face. After a couple of deep breaths, she sat upright. "I'm sorry; sometimes it just catches me off guard. Are you sure you wouldn't like some coffee or tea? I'd like to get up and stretch for a minute."

"Actually, coffee sounds good after all," Natasha said, and I agreed. Brittany disappeared into the kitchen and returned with three mugs and spoons, then made a second trip for a sugar bowl and a cream pitcher and a couple of paper napkins. She must have guests a lot, I figured; I didn't even own a cream pitcher.

She sat in the armchair, then put a heaping spoonful of sugar into her coffee, added milk, stirred it, and then put the spoon onto a napkin. "Rick laughs at the way I drink coffee," she said, confidingly. "Like a kid. He says I really like it to taste like coffee ice cream."

We all doctored our coffee according to our tastes and had a contemplative sip or two before I asked the next question. "You're convinced your mom is innocent. Can you tell me why?"

Brittany's gaze shifted to her right, then down, then back to me. "Because I know what happened," she said.

"Is it true that Todd shot him?"

She hesitated for a second, then nodded. "Yeah." She shut her eyes for a moment and bit her lower lip. Giving up her old boyfriend, even dead, was not something she wanted to do.

"How do you know?"

"Well, for one thing I heard them talking about it."

"Who was 'them'?"

"Him and Braden." Out of the corner of my eye, I could see Natasha watching her intently.

"What did you hear them say?"

"Braden talked about it a lot. He'd say, like, how he hated his father and wished he were dead, so he could get his inheritance and start investing it in some of his business schemes. Todd didn't like Greg already because of the way he treated me and Mom."

"Did you hear them actually planning the murder?"

"Not directly, just hints. Laughing and joking—Braden, mostly."

"Then how did you know they did it together?"

"Todd told me afterward. He said Braden put him up to it."

"Did you know ahead of time when Todd was going to kill him?"

"No. He told me later he had to wait for a day when all of us but Greg would be out."

"So you didn't tell him Greg would be home that Saturday?"

Her eyes were downcast when she answered. "Yeah, I did tell him that." She looked up again, from me to Natasha, as if begging us to believe her. "But I didn't know he was going to do what he did. I just happened to tell him what we were doing that day."

"So Todd told you he'd committed the murder."

"Yes." She stared at her hands in her lap, and her voice was almost a whisper.

"When did he tell you?"

A small hesitation while she seemed to try to remember,

her head half raised. "Really soon after. I don't remember exactly when."

"Did he describe how he did it?"

"Yeah."

"Can you tell me what he said?"

She shivered and went on, not looking directly at either of us. "He said he parked his truck on the other side of the golf course and snuck around through the woods and climbed the fence into the back of our yard. He thought Greg would be inside the house, and he was kind of surprised that he was out by the pool. But Greg didn't see him because he was busy with the water blaster and his back was to him. Todd said he kind of snuck up behind some bushes until he was close enough to take aim, and then he fired, just one shot. Greg fell—he just went down—and Todd panicked. He didn't even go see if Greg was dead; he just ran away, climbed over the fence, and took off. He told me he hardly remembered getting back to his truck, he was so freaked out."

"Todd had a difficult time with it, didn't he?"

She nodded, head still down. "Yeah. He felt really bad. I don't think he really understood what it would be like to kill someone."

"What did he do?"

"Oh, God—well, he cried, a lot. He got rid of his rifle; he told me he drove somewhere and threw it into a canal. And he started smoking a lot more weed and got into heroin. Braden was getting it for him. And he started kind of avoiding me. We'd talk on the phone, and he'd tell me he loved me, but when I wanted to see him, he'd say he didn't think it would be a good idea."

"Had Todd been into drugs before the killing?"

"Not heavy, or at least I don't think so. We all smoked weed, and Braden sometimes had some meth. He and Todd and Jason, Kim's boyfriend, all snorted it when Braden brought it around."

"Did Braden pay Todd for the murder?"

"I don't think so. I don't think Todd wanted money." She stopped, and her gaze drifted, turned inwards, retrieving a memory that had never actually gone away. "He told me he didn't do it just for Braden."

"Then why did he?"

"He said he did it for me," she said, almost in a whisper. "Dear God—everything changed when he pulled that trigger."

"Why didn't you tell anyone what happened?"

She took a deep breath and exhaled. "I didn't want to get Todd in trouble. And I thought I might get arrested for knowing about it and not telling anyone. I was sixteen, I didn't know anything about the law or who to ask." She paused a second or two. "I kept thinking that if I just didn't tell anyone it would blow over, go away. I mean, the police were questioning us, but they didn't seem to have any evidence."

"What about after Todd died?"

Her eyes grew wide. "That's when it got really scary. After Todd overdosed, Braden called me and asked me how I was doing. And I said not good. And he said he was sorry to hear that, but that I'd better be quiet about what happened, or I could end up like Todd."

"What did you think he meant by that?"

"I thought he meant that he'd killed Todd."

"Were you using heroin then?"

She shifted uncomfortably. "No. I didn't like the whole needle thing; it was too icky."

"But you thought Braden could slip you something and kill you?"

"Well, yeah. I thought he could make it look like I was using and OD'd, just like Todd." She made an almost apologetic gesture with her hands. "I don't know if it made sense or not," she said. "I was sixteen, I was stupid. I was panicking, with everything that happened—Todd killing Greg and then dying, and the police acting as if we were criminals—it was really awful, and I was afraid to turn to anyone."

"After your mom was arrested—you didn't tell anyone then?"

She returned her gaze to her hands. "No. I was scared. I kept thinking Mom would be okay, that the jury would see she was innocent."

"What about after she was convicted?"

"I still thought Braden would have me killed if I told. But I did tell Mom after she went to prison. I could never talk to her about anything on the jail phones because they were monitored. But when I saw her in prison, and we had some privacy, I told her everything."

"What did she say?"

"She said not to worry, and that I shouldn't say anything to anyone."

"Did you ever talk about this to anyone else?"

"No. Not even Rick."

"Not the police, obviously."

"No."

"Not your mom's lawyer?"

"No."

"But you're telling us now. Did something change?"

She nodded.

"What?"

"My mom told me in a phone call that Braden is doing life in prison for trying to murder someone else. I guess one of you guys must have written to her about it. I don't think he can hurt me anymore." She smiled wanly. "I hope I'm right."

"I think you're safe," I said, reassuringly.

She gave me a look of gratitude and relief. "I'm so glad I can finally talk about it. I've carried it around for so long; it's been this huge secret."

"Do you think Sunny would be okay with your telling us?"

She shook her head. "I don't know. After I told her, she was afraid something might happen to me. But I figure now that Braden is locked up, she doesn't have to be anymore."

"Good point," I said.

"Is it too late to tell the judge?"

"No, actually. We're going to file a petition for habeas

corpus, where we'll be able to present new evidence. We can include a declaration from you about what you told us. You'll have to sign it under penalty of perjury. Do you feel you can do that?"

Again, she hesitated for a beat before answering. "Yes. Yes, I can do that."

"I have one quick question," Natasha said. "There was that check Sunny wrote to Todd. Do you know why she did that?"

"Oh, yes," Brittany said, almost brightly. "That was my idea. I thought it might cheer Todd up, give him something to distract him, if he had money to fix up his truck. I told him Mom was loaning it to him because she was scared to think of me riding in that old thing, with the brakes and the clutch all shot. That was all true; that's how I convinced Mom to loan him the money."

Natasha nodded. "Thanks. Can we type up a declaration and bring it to you in an hour or two?"

"Yeah. I have to pick up the kids at noon, but I'll be home in the afternoon. Can you get here before Rick comes home? He's doing days this week, so he gets home around five thirty."

"No problem," I said. I stood up, and Natasha and Brittany followed. "Is there anything like a copy service around here?"

"There's a shopping center in Allenville, about twenty minutes away. An office supply store there does printing and copying."

"Great. We'll write up a declaration and come back this afternoon."

"Okay." She nodded, wide-eyed, in a way that made me feel as though she were a child and I were her mother or a teacher.

She went ahead of us to the door and let us out. "See you later," she said, and we smiled and waved back as we started down the path.

"Do you believe her?" Natasha asked me in a low voice, as soon as we were sure we were out of earshot.

I shook my head.

"Me neither," she said. "It's like something you'd see on TV."

"Yeah," I said. "A little far-fetched, and so was her reaction. Hard to believe she'd be so afraid that she'd let her mother go to prison without saying anything."

"I think one part of it's true," Natasha said.

"What part was that?"

"Where she said Todd killed Greg for her. Did you see her face? She's been carrying that guilt around with her all these years."

Natasha called Carey while I drove us to the shopping center with the office supply store. Her secretary said she was in court. Natasha called her cellphone and left a voicemail telling her we urgently needed to talk.

"We may as well write up the declaration," I said, "in case Carey says to go ahead and get it signed." So we found a booth at the back of a diner, ordered drinks, and settled down with Natasha's notebook computer to type up what Brittany had told us. We had just finished, and were contemplating ordering something for lunch, when Carey called back.

"Let me tell you our dilemma," I said, and laid it out. "We have to get a declaration from her," I concluded, "but there are risks, and I wanted your say on it before we go ahead."

Carey was silent on the line for a moment before answering. "Right," she said, finally. "I guess the problem is that we're concerned Brittany may be committing perjury if she signs on to what she told you. On the other hand, her statement exonerates Sunny. I don't see how we can justify not using it just because we aren't sure we believe her."

"That's it," I said. "But I worry about getting her into trouble if she signs this, and it's somehow disproven. It would hurt our credibility, too."

It was another few seconds before Carey responded. "Here's how I see it," she said. "This is a statement Brittany is willing to swear to. We haven't disproved it; we have no way of telling it isn't true. I think we have to use it."

When the declaration was finished, we took it on a flash drive to the office supply store and printed a couple of self-service copies, then hurried back to Brittany's house.

"You came at the perfect time," she said. "Brianna just went down for her nap. Kyle, honey," she added to her son, who was sitting on the floor with a picture book, "would you please go play in your room for a few minutes, while Mommy talks with our friends here?"

Kyle picked up the book and left, giving us a curious look over his shoulder. "I'll take you guys to the park later, when Bri is awake," Brittany called after him.

We took our places on the sofa, and Natasha opened a binder and pulled out two copies of the statement we'd printed. "Here's a declaration we wrote up," she said to Brittany, "with what you told us this morning. If you could read it and initial each page, and then sign it at the end, if what's in there is correct. It's under penalty of perjury, so it's important to make sure it's the truth as you remember it." Brittany nodded, her expression sober. "If you see anything that's incorrect, let us know. If it's minor, you can just correct it on the page and initial your correction. If it's bigger, we'll prepare a new declaration fixing it."

"Okay," she said. "How will you use it?"

"We'll attach it to the habeas corpus petition we file for your mom," I said. "It will be like sworn testimony, to let the judge know what evidence we have. If the judge thinks we have enough, we hope he'll order a hearing, and if that happens, you'll testify in person."

"Oh. I see."

She reached for the declaration, took it from Natasha, and began reading. After the first page, she asked, "Where do I put my initials?"

"At the lower right," Natasha said, and handed her a pen. Brittany put the declaration down on the end table next to her and wrote her initials. A couple of pages in, she found a typo and asked what she should do. "Print the correction over the top and then initial it." She did, and continued. When she had read the last page, she put the paper down on the end table again and filled in the date and signed her name, then handed it back to Natasha. "I hope it helps Mom," she said.

We thanked her and stood up. Natasha gave her the second copy. "This one is for you to keep," she said.

Brittany took it and folded it in thirds.

"When will you know if Mom will get a trial?" Brittany asked, as we made our way toward the door.

"We'll file the petition in February," I said. "After that, we have to wait for the judge to decide."

"Oh," she said, a little sadly. "That long? Well, I'll pray for a good decision."

She watched us from the door as we drove away, biting her lower lip and turning the paper over and over again in her hands.

19

Thanksgiving gave me a breather from Sunny's case. Harriet talked me once again into volunteering for her church's holiday dinner. "We need more people than ever," she said. "We'll probably have a lot of people who lost their homes in the fires." Bill couldn't go this year, she said. He was under doctor's orders to stay out near the ocean and rest, because he had emphysema and had struggled with the smoke from the fires in the fall. That summer, he'd had a heart episode that resulted in his being taken by helicopter ambulance to the emergency room.

Around Corbin's Landing, everyone who could afford it paid an annual premium for helicopter insurance, since the area was over an hour's drive on winding, narrow roads from the nearest emergency room. The noise of the motors overhead was like sirens in a more populated place; it meant a car accident, a medical emergency, or a fire. When we heard them, the curious went outside and watched the sky overhead, straining to see where the 'copter was circling and whose lives had suddenly been upended.

Harriet hated to talk about health issues. "It's all some old people do," she groused now and then; "I don't want to be like that." Her brief description of Bill's condition before we left for the dinner was the longest report by far I'd ever received from her. Bill himself didn't say much more. "Growing old sucks," was all he added to what Harriet told me. I was dimly aware that they had skipped their annual visit to Harriet's hometown in the Sierra foothills to visit the graves of her first husband and son, who had died long ago in a truck accident, but it hadn't occurred to me before to ask her why they'd changed their plans.

Harriet's church was not far from one of the neighborhoods that had burned, and dozens of volunteers had gathered to cook and serve food and socialize. I was assigned to the kitchen, where I filled in wherever I was needed: filling and emptying dishwashers, peeling potatoes, cutting pieces of pumpkin pie and dotting them with dollops of whipped cream from a can. Except for Harriet, the men and women there were strangers to me or, at best, people I saw once a year when we volunteered together.

I listened to them talk with each other about children, grandchildren, houses, health issues, politics, and the ongoing misery caused by the fires. I felt like an eavesdropper on their lives, and I didn't say a lot myself, but nothing was asked of me except to be a smooth link in the network of well-meaning people getting dinner for the crowds in the rec hall.

Back home afterward, there wasn't a lot to do except

continue my work on Sunny's petition and my other cases. It was too cold to plant in the garden and too early to prune the orchard. I ate stored apples and winter pears, and a lot of chard and bok choy because they were the survivors from the cold-weather vegetables I'd bravely planted at the end of summer.

The two dogs I had been caring for had been reduced by one, after one of them, Peggy, went home to her family. The other, a little copper-colored cocker spaniel named Lizzie, I had ended up adopting after her owners, an elderly couple, decided they needed to go into assisted living instead of trying to find another house. When I took Peggy to the shelter to go home, I got to meet one of her family, a woman in her forties who was almost as ebullient as Peggy herself at their reunion, and who thanked me effusively for caring for her and easing their minds about her well-being while they dealt with the loss of so much else. I never met Lizzie's owners; it was a woman from the shelter who called and told me they had decided to put Lizzie up for adoption and asked if I wanted to keep her. She gave me as much information as they had about her; she was three years old, and as far as the couple knew, her health was good, and her shots were up to date, but both their house and their vet's office had burned in the fire, and all her paperwork from before the fire was lost. Lizzie came to me like a refugee, undocumented; and thus we started our new life together.

Our investigation in Sunny's case was winding down. Natasha was going to Harrison in early December to interview the trial jurors, at least those she'd been able to find alive after a decade and a half. Carey had called before Thanksgiving and suggested we go at around the same time to see the Ferrante family and pay another visit to Sunny.

For defense attorneys, meeting the family of the person your client was convicted of killing is, to say the least, fraught. In the adversary system we have, the police and prosecutors are the first representatives of the justice system to speak to crime victims, or if the victim is dead, for his or her family; and they quickly position themselves as their advocates. They befriend the outraged victim or the bereaved parents, wives, children, and impart their views about the suspect, until they are seen as the champions who will fight to get justice for the victim by ensuring that the defendant is convicted and punished as much as the law will allow. Almost inevitably, the defense attorney, who comes into the picture later, is viewed as an enemy, a hired gun whose goal is to subvert the judicial process for the benefit of his guilty client and rob the family and society of the just result they deserve. How strong the family's feelings are depends a lot on the intensity of their grief and their susceptibility to persuasive propaganda, and how good a job the prosecutor and the police detectives have done at cultivating them.

As Carey and I prepared to shake the web of the Ferrante family, we knew a few facts, some more helpful than others. Greg's mother, Costanza Ferrante, had been, by all accounts, obsessed with avenging Greg's death and certain that Sunny was guilty. As Craig Newhouse had said, she had used her family's political clout and enlisted the backing of victims' rights groups to push the prosecution to seek the death penalty and reject a plea bargain for a more lenient sentence.

Costanza and Robert Ferrante, Greg's father, had testified at Sunny's trial as so-called "victim impact" witnesses: people close to the victim, such as family, coworkers, and friends, whom the prosecution presents at death penalty trials to paint a sympathetic portrait of the person killed and show how much pain his murder caused to those around him. Mrs. Ferrante had broken down in tears on the witness stand, and when the district attorney had offered her a tissue, she had thanked her, using her first name.

We also knew that no one else in Greg's family, including his brothers and sister, his ex-wife, and his children, had been called to testify. All of them had been interviewed by police detectives before Sunny's trial, but the family had declined to talk with anyone from the defense.

Greg's father and mother were both dead now, but his brothers were still working in the family business, along with a couple of their children. Carey had called and talked with Robert's oldest son, Robert Ferrante, Jr., and set up a time to meet with him.

The ranch was a few miles out of town, down a two-lane highway. The land here was gently rolling, rather than flat. Some of it was planted in stone fruit orchards, their branches bare of leaves this time of year, in citrus with bright yellow or orange fruit hanging among dark green foliage, or in orderly rows of wine grapes on their cordons, still bearing their withered red leaves, giving the landscape a feeling of lingering autumn. The rest was pasture, just turning green after the first rains, on which cattle—dark Angus or black-and-white Holsteins—were grazing or lying under oak and pepper trees. On both sides, an occasional private road led to a farmhouse, with its outbuildings and long, low cattle barns.

Bob Ferrante had told Carey to watch for the orchard of olive trees just before the driveway. Nevertheless, we almost missed the discreet wood sign reading "Ferrante Ranch" that marked the long blacktop lane to our left. Beyond the stand of gnarled olives, the lane went up a slight rise, from which we could see an expanse of hillside planted in grapevines and another, much larger stand of olives. The road here forked, and a sign said "Store and Office/Tours," with an arrow pointing left.

We turned, and after a few minutes' drive found ourselves at the entrance to a small parking lot. To its right, down a short path, stood a single-story Victorian ranch house, freshly painted pale yellow with white trim. Steps led up to a front porch that ran the length of the house and a generous front door. Behind the house I glimpsed a complex of gray wood and metal sheds and outbuildings, the working heart of the ranch, and behind them on a rise, a couple of cattle barns, some dark green water tanks, and a glimpse of a pasture dotted with white cattle. It had an air of settled prosperity that made me briefly envy farm life.

We walked up the steps into the house. An old-fashioned

bell above the door tinkled as we opened it. The front of the house was fitted out as a retail store, its walls painted off-white, with the windows framed in a warm light wood. A few old painted tables held patterned plates, mugs, glasses, tablecloths, and napkins for sale, along with seasonal decorations for Christmas and Hanukkah. Along the walls, hutches and shelves and a glass-doored refrigerator displayed jarred olives, bottles of olive oil, and vinegar, all with the Ferrante Ranch label, and other products such as crackers, cheese, candy, and local honey. A counter at the back held small labeled bowls of olives and oil, with toothpicks and small pieces of bread for sampling. The large old windows at the front of the house were trimmed with dark green and white checked curtains; in one of them stood a lighted and decorated Christmas tree. At the end of the room, the old fireplace had been converted with a gas-burning insert that gently warmed the shop.

A man came out from the depths of the house and greeted us from behind the counter. "Can I help you?" he asked, and then checked himself as if he had just realized something. "Are you Ms. Bergmann and Ms. Moodie?" he asked.

We nodded. "Yes, we are," Carey said.

"Bob Ferrante," he said, coming around the counter and extending a rough, tanned hand. He was tall and weatherbeaten, and slightly stooped; his hair, black streaked with iron gray, was coarse and thick, cut short. "Come on in. I hope you don't mind, but I told my brother Tony you were visiting, and he and my son John wanted to meet you, too.

Rob—my oldest—is at a growers' conference out of town."

He led us around the end of the counter and into the back part of the house, to an office on the right. It was a plain room, not very big, and there were two other men in it; they stood as we came in, and shook hands with us, introducing themselves in turn. "Tony and I are mostly retired at this point," Bob said. "John and Rob run the ranch, and Tony's daughter Melissa handles the business end."

The Ferrante genes must have been unusually strong, because the family resemblance was visible in all three men, and I was struck by the similarity between them and the photos I'd seen of Greg. That said, there were noticeable differences among them. All of them were tall, with similar dark eyes and dark, stiff, wavy hair—Bob's and Tony's black and iron gray, and John's silver-flecked dark brown. Bob was lean and craggy, the picture of an old-time rancher from his madras plaid shirt and Lee jeans to his well-worn cowboy boots. Tony also wore jeans and boots, with a long-sleeved polo and a fleece vest. He was wider in the face and broader in the shoulders, with a paunch that made him look a bit like a pigeon. John was a younger version of Bob, but with his jeans he wore a dress shirt in a tattersall pattern, without a tie, and a dark-colored quilted vest. The five of us crowded the office. Bob had placed a couple of extra chairs out before we came, and we sat in a circle of sorts, with John behind the desk.

"I'd have found us somewhere more comfortable," Bob said, "but Alison is taking a group on a tour, and I said I'd stay here in case anyone comes into the store."

If Carey was awed by this crowd of big men, she didn't show it. She gave a spiel, of sorts—that we were representing Sunny to file a habeas corpus petition for her, to revisit her conviction and sentence, and that we wanted to talk with Greg Ferrante's family, to see if they could help us gain some insight into what had happened. Bob nodded, and Tony and John followed her talk attentively. Bob spoke first.

"Well, I guess the whole thing was a real shock, to all of us," he said. "First, losing Greg like that, and then Sunny getting accused of killing him. I mean, murder's a horrible crime, and when someone in your own family does it—" He stopped, failing to find the words for how it felt.

Tony and John nodded agreement, and Tony said, "It was like losing two family members at once. Sunny—she was family, too. And we all liked Todd. We didn't know what to think."

"At first," Bob said, "none of us wanted to believe she'd do something like that. But then the district attorney told us Todd had confessed the whole thing to some relative of his before he died. You couldn't shrug that off."

"Not to speak ill of the dead," John said. "But I sometimes thought that if Sunny did it, she had her reasons."

"Why is that?" I asked.

"Uncle Greg never treated her well, that I saw," he answered, and Tony nodded agreement.

"He was always kind of abrupt with her. He'd tell her to be quiet or say she didn't know what she was talking about, in public, in front of everybody. I'd never talk to my wife like that. You had to wonder what things were like at home."

"It was the cold-bloodedness of it," Bob said. "I mean, we all knew what Greg was like. If she'd shot him during an argument, I wouldn't condone it, but at least I'd have understood, okay, he finally pushed her too far. But to plan and premeditate like that, and to get a nice kid like Todd to do the actual deed—her own daughter's boyfriend, no less—that was just cold. Todd was no killer. I don't know what she told him to get him to do something like that."

"It never made sense to me," Tony said. "I couldn't see the Sunny I knew doing that."

"So you have doubts about whether she was guilty," I said to Tony.

He hedged. "Yeah, a little. I still wonder."

"Any particular reason?"

He shrugged. "Not really. I just always thought I was a good judge of character, and I didn't see Sunny for a minute as someone who'd do something that awful, not in a million years. Nor Todd, either. But the DA must have had something, because the jury convicted her and gave her the death penalty."

"Well, there was the other woman," Bob said. "I guess you probably know," he said to Carey and me. "Greg fooled around on Sunny. We all knew it; I'm sure she did, too. I saw something in the paper about how he was planning to leave her for some other girlfriend when he was killed."

"I heard that, too," Tony said. "I don't know what they

said about it at her trial. I didn't go. Mama did, though. Every day."

"Yeah, Grandma was obsessed," John said. "She said she wouldn't rest until that horrible woman—that's what she always called her—was dead."

Bob spoke up. "You have to understand her," he said. "Greg was her baby." He turned to Carey and me. "Mama had a baby girl after Tony. She was born with something wrong with her heart, and they knew she wouldn't live long. I was a little kid myself then, but I remember. It was hard for Mama. My dad was away in the Navy, and he didn't get to come back until after the war ended, so she was by herself with us kids when everything happened with Rosie. I remember she was sad all the time, and she was always fussing over Rosie. Even as a parent, I can't imagine what that must be like, taking care of a baby you know is dying. After Rosie died, it seemed Mama never really got over it. When I was older, I heard the doctor had told her she couldn't have any more children because of something that happened when Rosie was born. Then my dad came home, and she had Greg. So he was like the miracle baby. My dad said she was convinced God sent Greg to her to comfort her. So Greg was more than just her youngest; he was her gift from God."

"She spoiled him something awful," Tony said. "I don't know about you," he said to Bob, "but there were times when I really hated him, growing up."

"Yeah, he was kind of a pill," Bob said, with a smile. "He got away with everything."

"Kind of explains how he turned out," Tony said.

"What was he like?" I asked.

"As a kid?" Tony responded, and went on. "He knew he could get away with almost anything with my mom, and he took advantage of that. He'd steal stuff—toys, bats, baseball mitts, swimming equipment—from me and Bob, use them and break them, and then deny it. And Mama would believe him, or if it was clear he was lying, she'd forgive him because he was so much younger than us. He learned he could play Mama and get away with all kinds of sh—, sorry, bad behavior. It got to be kind of a habit with him, cheating, seeing what he could get away with."

"Yeah," Bob agreed. "Greg was kind of a master manipulator."

"Sounds like he stayed that way as an adult, too," I hazarded.

"Yep," Tony said. "Always trying to get something for nothing, put one over on you."

"Come on," said Bob. "You're still pissed about the timeshare deal he got you into. I don't think he knew it would go south."

"Maybe not," Tony said. "But he made his money on it before it did, and left me high and dry. And he kept badgering us to sell part of the ranch land for a housing subdivision, said we'd all get rich off it. Almost convinced Dad to do it. I know who'd have gotten rich, and it wasn't us."

Bob sighed. "Well, he's long gone now. Anyhow, that's why Mama was so bent on getting Sunny convicted. Greg was almost everything to her; it made her crazy when he was killed. And she felt betrayed by Sunny, just flabbergasted— she treated Sunny like a daughter, and the idea she'd do this to her own husband and his family just outraged her."

"Yeah," Tony said. "You couldn't talk to her about it. It was like if anyone said anything to contradict her, you were the enemy. Her best friends were the district attorney and that detective, Hansen. She'd say they were the only people who really supported her through the trial. It tore the family apart, is what it did."

"So you didn't always agree with her?"

"I thought it was ridiculous to give Sunny the death penalty," John said.

"I could never believe in my heart that Sunny did it," Tony said, "even after that guy said Todd confessed. But I stopped saying anything around Mama because she'd go ballistic."

"Did you have a theory about who might have?"

"No—that was the trouble. I mean, I imagine Greg made some enemies over the course of his life, given how he treated people. But if it really was Todd who killed him, then it seemed like it had to be someone in the family who put him up to it."

"He wouldn't have done it on his own?"

"Todd? I can't imagine why. Like Bob said, he was no killer. He was just a happy-go-lucky kid. He was like a puppy, liked everyone, liked working here."

"No reason why he'd personally resent Greg?"

"None that I ever saw. I don't think they knew one another that well. I never saw them exchange a word when they were both here."

"What was Brittany like?" I asked.

The three of them thought for a moment. John spoke first. "As far as I could tell, a typical high school kid. A little rebellious, but not beyond normal, that I saw. Greg treated her as bad as he did Sunny. That probably didn't help with her behavior. She and Todd seemed to be really tight; she was out here at the ranch a lot after school and on weekends. I wondered how her parents felt about her dating Todd. I mean, he was a nice enough kid and all that, but he was twenty or so, and probably wasn't going to amount to a lot."

"When Braden was here," Bob said, "the three of them spent a lot of time together."

"That was probably because they were about the same age," Tony said. "They didn't have much in common with the rest of us in the older generation."

"I always wondered if Braden didn't have something to do with it," John said.

"You've said that before," Bob said, "but I don't know what reason he'd have to kill his father, and besides, wasn't he out of town that weekend?"

"That wouldn't matter if he hired Todd," John said. "He'd probably want to arrange it that way, to make sure he had an alibi."

"Yeah, I know," Bob said.

"Well now he's in prison for, what, trying to have some

guy killed he was in business with? I didn't trust him when he was here, you know that."

The bell on the shop door began a steady ringing, and we heard voices and footsteps. "Sounds like Alison's back," Bob said.

"Would you all like to come to the house?" said Bob. "It's just up the hill; we can walk from here. We can talk more without being so crowded."

Bob pulled his phone out of a jeans pocket and made a call. "Alison? How'd it go? Great! Do you think you'll be all right there by yourself? We have some company, and I'd like to go up to the house. Thanks, hon. Good luck!" He then made a second call. "Honey? I have those lawyers here I told you about; can we all come up to the house to talk? Okay. See you in a few.

"We're all set," he said. "We can go out the back." We stood, and Carey and I walked with them toward the back of the store. We passed through a long room, almost like a wide corridor, with windows along the sides. I recognized it as something common to many early ranch houses, the big dining room which separated the front of the house from the kitchen, where the family and the hands had all eaten meals together at one long table. Now it seemed to be a file room and storage area. Behind that was the old kitchen, converted into a mail room, with a copier and printer, stacks of packaging materials, a work table, and a couple of desks. Two women were working at the table; they looked up and smiled as we passed and exchanged hellos with the Ferrantes.

"We do a pretty good business with online sales, particularly during the holidays," John remarked to us, as he stood aside for Carey and me at the back door.

Robert Ferrante's house was along the right fork of the private road, the farthest of three houses in a semicircle behind a vineyard. "The big house is my son Rob's now," Bob told us. "Marlene and I moved to the little house here a few years ago." As we walked down the road, Carey and Bob talked livestock. "Charolais cattle," he was saying. "Excellent beef cattle. We sell to restaurants in LA and the Bay Area. My granddaughter, Melissa, has some Jerseys here, too; she's started making cheese, gouda and lately cheddar. It's good, too; we've got some for sale in the store."

The house that was now Rob's was the central one of the three. It was fairly large, but not ostentatious, a comfortable split level that reclined gracefully across the top of a small rise. Shade trees around it, now bare of their summer leaves, probably kept it somewhat cool in the heat of summer. The front lawn between it and the vineyard had recently, it appeared, been conscientiously converted to a low-water landscape, with lavender and succulents and a winding dry creek of rounded rocks.

"Marlene and I built that house in 1974, 1975," Bob said, as we walked past it. "Tony's place is the first one that we passed. Tony and Greg and I were raised in the old house—the one that's now the store and offices. That's the third house our family built on the ranch, in 1890. The first one was just a shack, an adobe my great-great-grandfather built and lived in while he got the ranch going. He was Swiss-Italian, came here from Europe. Went by ship to Panama, crossed the isthmus, and then sailed up to San Francisco; ended up out here. Worked for a rancher, then bought this ranch right after the big drought, when the land was cheap. Once he got established he went back home and married a girl from the old country, my great-great-grandmother Giovanna, brought her back here. They built a real house in the 1870s. My great-grandfather built the next one. Our dad said the adobe and the first house were still standing when he was a kid. The old house burned in the thirties, and the adobe was pulled down to build the current hay barn. There's an old photo of the two of them on the wall of the store." He talked casually, but with a certain proprietary pride, about the history of his family on the ranch. I wondered how it must feel to have such ties to a place.

After passing Rob's house, we turned up a gravel driveway and walked around the side of the third house. It was a one-story post-war ranch-type house, flanked, like the bigger house, with old shade trees, and with a deck around its front and sides. "This is where Marlene and I started out," Bob said, "and we're back here now. It's a good size for the two of us, less work for her."

He walked us around to the back, where we entered through a mudroom into a big, bright kitchen. Three women, two with gray hair and one with honey blond highlights, were cutting vegetables for a salad at the counters; they turned to meet us as we came in. Bob made introductions:

"My wife, Marlene, my sister-in-law Cindy, and my daughter-in-law Barbara. These are the attorneys come to see us about Greg's case—" He stopped, unsure of our names, and we introduced ourselves, to nods and smiles from the women. All of them were wearing blue or black jeans and sweaters of different colors—Marlene, tall and slender like Bob, in ice blue, Cindy, stocky and solid, in bright green with an applique of poinsettias on the front, and Barbara, middle-aged and fit, in off-white, with a silver and turquoise necklace and earrings.

"I'll get everyone settled inside," Bob said, "and come back, okay?"

"Why don't you all sit at the table?" Marlene said. "We're fixing lunch right now."

The dining room was just past the kitchen. There were enough seats for all of us around the long table. Through a wide archway I could see into the living room, where a generously decorated Christmas tree stood silhouetted in front of a picture window, partly obscuring a view across the valley.

Carey and I glanced at one another, thinking, I suspected, the same thing. This was not how I'd expected the family of the man our client supposedly murdered to respond to us.

We sat together near the far end of the table, and Tony sat across from us. John and Bob returned to the kitchen. "Cindy says I get in the way in the kitchen," Tony said. "She'd just chase me out, so I'll stay here and keep you girls company. Where did you come here from?"

We told him. "I don't know the north part of the state too well," he said. "Been to San Francisco and the wine country, made a road trip in the motor home once to see the redwoods, but that's about it. But I know the area around Ventura, Santa Barbara. Dad and Mama used to take us camping by the beaches around there in the summer. We'd take this little old travel trailer we had, pitch a tent, and stay for a week or so. When Cindy and I had kids, we used to do the same thing every summer. We loved it—still do."

Bob came back in with place mats, plates, and silverware, and we helped distribute them around the table. A moment later, John showed up with glasses and a pitcher of ice water; and the women followed him with a bowl of salad, plates of sliced bread, cheese and cold cuts, and jars of mustard and ketchup. "We're doing kind of a deli thing," Marlene said. "Everyone making their own sandwiches." We nodded and set to work. When we all had sandwiches and salad, Marlene said to us, "So I understand you're here for Sunny."

Carey nodded. "We're her lawyers for her habeas corpus case. We're reinvestigating it and filing a petition arguing for her release."

"Hmm," Marlene said. "I'm not sure what to say. We all liked Sunny, but if she did what they say, she deserves to be in prison. It was horrible, we were all in shock. You don't expect murder to touch your family."

"I'm not so sure about the death penalty, though," Cindy said. "I mean, I believe in it, even though I'm Catholic, but for people a lot worse than her. I just wish I knew what happened. We all loved her, she was such a sweet little thing. It was like a double loss, losing Greg and then poor Todd. And then finding out that someone you'd loved like your own family had committed such a horrible crime... It was a terrible time. We didn't know what to think."

"Except Mama," Marlene said. "She was convinced Sunny killed Greg. She completely turned on her. You could not say a word around her in Sunny's defense. We all stopped talking about it while she was alive, to keep peace in the family."

"Yeah, even with each other," John said. "It became, like, this awful family secret."

There was a murmur of *yeahs* and *uh-huhs* around the table.

"So have you found anything?" Barbara asked.

I didn't want to talk about Brittany, so I said, "The man who claimed that Todd confessed to him has just signed a sworn declaration saying he lied about it all."

Everyone's eyes were on us. "No way!" a couple of people said.

"You mean he said Sunny never hired Todd to kill Greg?" Tony asked.

"He said he didn't know; he just made it up."

"Jesus—why?" Bob asked.

"He was in legal trouble himself. He was Todd's uncle, so he knew about Todd's connection to your family, and he knew the police were investigating Sunny. He figured he could get leniency in his own case by concocting a story about Todd confessing."

"That's awful," Cindy said. "So Sunny may have been innocent this whole time?"

"Yes," Carey said, "but we still have to look at the whole case."

"Okay," a couple of them said—a little unsure, I guessed, at why.

"What can you tell us about Greg and Sunny's relationship?" Carey asked.

"Whew," Cindy said. "Where to begin? Well, you know that before Greg married Sunny he was married to Pat for—what, twelve years?"

Marlene nodded.

"She left him when she found out he was seeing Sunny," Cindy said. "I don't think it was the first time he'd fooled around on her, but it was kind of the last straw. We liked Pat. It took a while for the family to warm up to Sunny."

"We saw her as a trophy wife," Marlene said, "and of course we blamed her for breaking up Greg and Pat's marriage. She really was beautiful, but young, just a kid, and not too bright. Pat is sharp and funny. She and I were good friends; Bob and I are her daughter Emily's godparents. We're still close, in spite of the divorce. But Sunny—I mean, she was young enough to be my daughter."

"Greg treated her like a trophy wife, too," Cindy said.

"How was that?" Carey asked.

"Like a possession," Cindy said. "Like something he'd brought along to show off to his friends. He never really seemed to treat her like a person. They'd come here, and he'd ignore her most of the time, except when he wanted to sort of flash her like a fancy piece of jewelry he'd bought."

Barbara nodded agreement. "I was just appalled sometimes at how he talked to her. He'd just order her around—tell her to go fix her hair or makeup or get him a drink. And he'd criticize her in front of everyone. I remember once when he told her a top she was wearing made her look like trailer trash. I saw her sometimes go into a corner somewhere and cry after he embarrassed her in public like that."

"We felt sorry for her over time, in spite of everything," Marlene said. "She obviously didn't marry into any bed of roses with Greg."

"She was really sweet and helpful and good with the little children," Cindy said. "And you could see she loved Brittany."

"She never had an unkind word to say about anyone," Marlene said. "Even Greg."

"Did she ever confide in you about her life?"

Cindy shook her head, and Barbara said, "No. She kept it to herself, never complained. She always tried to put the best face on it, stay upbeat about everything. She'd talk about trips they'd taken, things like that, always the good things."

Marlene added, "We were Greg's family, after all. I don't think she wanted to say anything bad about him to us."

"Did anything seem different just before Greg was killed?"

The women shook their heads; then Bob said, "He was a little troubled the last time or two I saw him. Asked me if I could loan him some money—a bridge loan till he could find permanent financing on some property of his. It didn't seem like a big deal, just a liquidity issue."

"Did you loan him the money?"

"I was going to, but he died before we finalized it. I hate to say this, but I was probably lucky. My accountant knew his, and he advised me against making the loan; told me in confidence that Greg was on the verge of bankruptcy. He was right: I was Greg's executor, and his estate was used up paying off creditors. Sunny got nothing from the sale of any of the properties. My guess is he overextended himself and got caught short by the recession that year."

"He never said anything to me," Tony said.

"He was probably too proud," Bob said.

"Or too devious."

"Did Braden and Brittany get anything out of the estate?" I asked.

"Let me think," Bob said. "Not much, because there was really nothing left after all the creditors were paid. Greg had life insurance policies that paid something to Braden and Emily, maybe fifty thousand dollars each, and about the same to Brittany. But that was it, as far as I can remember."

"Did you notice anything going on with Todd around the time Greg was killed? Or Braden?" I asked.

There was a momentary silence as the women shook their heads, and the men seemed to be trying to recall what they might have seen. "I liked Todd," John said, finally. "He was a good worker. Handy, willing. Dad was training him to work with the cattle. But then he got all caught up with Braden and his little schemes."

"What was Braden doing on the ranch, anyway?" I asked. "I've asked a couple of people who knew Todd, and they didn't seem to know."

John made a face. "Interning, I guess you'd call it. He was having trouble finding work out of college, and Mom and Dad did Pat a favor by offering to let him work in the family business, see if he liked it, or if not, it'd be something he could put on his résumé. He lived in the granny unit and ate with the family. It was a sweet deal for him."

"Did it work out?"

"Nah. Braden had an allergy to work."

"Oh, John, isn't that a little harsh?" Marlene said.

"Mom, you weren't with him all day. I was supposed to be mentoring him, showing him how the ranch was run, particularly the vineyards. We grow premium wine grapes, and we sell to some of the best winemakers on the Central Coast. It takes skill and good management. I'm proud of what we do. Braden wasn't interested in any of it; all he talked about was stuff like flipping houses or getting some job in banking or finance that would make him a big killing in five years. And poor Todd started hanging around with him in his off hours. I don't know what Braden saw in him; maybe he was bored and wanted someone else young to hang out and smoke weed with. And there was Brittany in the middle of it, because Todd would bring her to the ranch to visit."

"Did you know he was smoking marijuana?" Carey asked.

"Absolutely. I could smell it. And personally I suspected he was using other drugs, too, and getting Todd into them, though I couldn't prove it."

"What made you think that?"

"Experience. I had friends when I was young who got into meth or heroin; and we've had workers here who were using. I know what it looks like. Todd got flaky, started being late to work, kind of scattered, sometimes hyper and working extra hard, and sometimes just not focused. He wasn't himself."

"What about after Greg was killed?"

"It got worse. I was on the point of letting him go when he died. When I heard it was an overdose, I wasn't surprised—just guilty that I hadn't confronted him and had it out when I first saw what was happening. Damn, he and Uncle Greg might both still be alive."

"How is that?" Bob asked.

"Well, assuming he actually was the guy who killed Uncle Greg, I don't think he'd have done something like that if he hadn't been under the influence in some way. You knew him, the Todd we knew wouldn't have hurt a soul."

"Do you think Brittany was using?"

"I don't know," John said. "I didn't know her well. She didn't have much to say for herself; she was just kind of around some of the times when Todd and Braden were together."

"Where did Braden go after Greg was killed?" I asked.

"He stayed a little longer, couple of months, then went back to Fresno, not long after Todd died. Pat wanted him back home after everything that happened; I don't blame her. He said he was going on a trip to Europe with Pat and her husband and then starting an MBA program somewhere back east, in the fall. I was glad to see him go."

Smart woman, I thought, *getting him out of the way of the investigation.* I wondered if Brittany was telling the truth after all.

After lunch, Carey and I helped clear the table, and then thanked the Ferrantes for their hospitality and for taking the time to talk with us. "You know the way down the hill from here?" asked Tony.

"I'll walk down with you," John said. "I have some stuff I need to do in the office."

The puffy white clouds in the morning sky had thickened to billows of light and darker gray. "Looks like it's about to rain," John said. I nodded.

As we turned onto the road back to the store, John said, "I tagged along because I wanted to say a couple of things I wasn't sure I should mention with the rest of the family there."

"Thanks," I said. "What's up?"

"Well," he said, apparently trying to find words to begin, "this whole thing with Greg shook up the family real bad. I know Aunt Marlene and Aunt Cindy said something about it back there. But it was worse than they let on. That whole crusade of Grandma's against Sunny almost split up the business. Uncle Tony was so disgusted that he and Aunt Cindy moved away, got a place in town. He almost quit, which would have been awful, because he and his son Ken were the people who really knew about growing wine grapes; they were teaching me. Even so, we lost Ken. He went up to Napa to work at a winery there; he didn't want anything to do with the atmosphere here."

"I'm so sorry," I said. "I hope we haven't stirred anything up."

"Oh, no," he said. "Not in a bad way. It's just that we all fell into the habit of not talking about it, even after Grandma died. I'm just now starting to see that we've all had our thoughts about the situation over the years. Personally, I don't know if Sunny was guilty or not, but I sure didn't think it was right for the prosecutor to push for the death penalty. And listening to my dad and my uncle and aunts, they probably feel more or less the same. But I'm not sure any of us knows each other's thinking for sure. I hope you can get to the bottom of what happened with Greg's murder, and I'd like to help you if I can. I'm sure Barbara would agree with me. But I can't speak for anyone else. I guess the bottom line is, it's still a sensitive subject, and we're all kind of tiptoeing around each other right now, because we don't want another blowup."

"Thank you," I said.

"I'm sure this is very difficult for your family," Carey added. "We're grateful that you were willing to talk with us."

"No problem," John said. "Are you heading back home from here today?"

"Yeah," we both said.

"How long a drive is it?"

"About three hours for me," said Carey.

"Closer to seven for me," I said.

"Whew," John said. "Hope the weather doesn't get bad."

"Thank you," Carey said. "And thank you all for meeting with us. We really appreciate your hospitality."

"No problem."

Alison came to the counter as we entered the store. "It's just us," John said. "I'll go on back now." He turned to Carey and me. "Nice to meet you. Have a safe trip home. Wait just a second." He walked over to one of the shelves and took down a couple of bottles. "Our premium olive oil," he said. "Arbequiña, this year's pressing. We've won medals with it in a bunch of competitions."

We both thanked him. "I hope you like it," he said, and he shook hands with each of us and disappeared into the back.

As we walked to our cars, Carey said, "That thing about Braden being hauled off to Europe and then sent to school back east."

"Yeah?"

"That sounds like his family suspected something and wanted to get him out of the way."

"It sure does," I said. "It also makes Brittany's story about being afraid of him even more sketchy."

"It does, doesn't it? He couldn't be all that much of a threat if he was three thousand miles away. But then I guess she could say she knew he'd be back. God, what a mess. I don't see any way around using her declaration. She may be telling the truth; I don't feel in a position to judge."

"We need to talk to Sunny first," I said.

"You're probably right. I'm so busy right now; do you think you can do it?"

I certainly had time, and I said so.

"Thanks. I'll go back to town and check in with Natasha, see how she's doing with the jurors. I imagine you want to get on the road as soon as possible. I can fill you in on what she says."

I thanked her. I was looking forward to hearing what Natasha found out from the trial jurors, but not enough to stay an extra day in Harrison.

20

Back home, I continued writing Sunny's habeas petition, sending draft arguments to Carey and revising as she edited them. It was the last big rush; in a couple of months we'd have to file the petition with whatever we'd been able to find to help Sunny's case. We were both tense about the deadline and worried that we didn't have more—more documents, more witness declarations—to convince the judge that Sunny should get a new trial. The way the law works, we were required to proffer all our evidence and arguments in that one petition; if you find something new later, it's damned near impossible to get a do-over. I was anticipating that I'd spend the rest of the holiday season working on it, when I got a phone call from Toni Jackson, the state defender lawyer who had taken over Sunny's appeal when I'd left the office.

"Sunny Ferrante's appeal has been set for oral argument on January 8th," she said, after a minimum of initial formalities. Although I had a lot of respect for Toni and was pleased that she'd been picked to take over Sunny's case, she and I had never gotten to know one another well at the state defender. We'd moved in different circles: she was ambitious to advance in the office, while I just wanted to do my work and be left alone.

"Interesting timing," I said. "Her habeas petition is due at the end of February."

"Probably just coincidence," she said. "Anyhow, I'm wondering if you have time to come down and help with a moot court. You know the case better than anyone else I can think of."

I said I'd be happy to.

"We're thinking of the Thursday or Friday before. Would either of those work?"

Both days were clear on my calendar. "Could you make it in the late morning or early afternoon, though?" I asked. "It's kind of a long drive down there."

"No problem. I'll get back to you when I find a day that works for all the volunteers. How are you, by the way?"

"Fine. Busy getting Sunny's petition together."

"How's that going? Any breakthroughs since Eason recanted?"

I felt uncomfortable telling her about Brittany's story until I was less doubtful of it myself.

"Not much. Our investigator talked to eight of the jurors, and four or five remembered the evangelical guy and confirmed that he'd quoted Scripture and argued that Sunny should get death basically for insubordination. The rest didn't remember."

"Petty treason, isn't that what they used to call it?"

"The crime of a wife killing her husband. Yep. Guess the guy wanted his patriarchy back."

She gave a short laugh. "And the trial judge refused to hold a hearing."

"I know. The jurors she interviewed wouldn't go so far as to say it affected how they voted. One of them said she thought he was a nut."

"Only one?"

"Well, it's Harrison. Some of them probably agreed with him, but were too embarrassed to say so. Anyhow, the man himself died ten years ago."

"Pity; that's the trouble with cold cases. It might have been interesting to hear what he had to say for himself. You're going to argue the misconduct in your habeas petition, right?"

"Absolutely."

"Anything else happening?"

"Carey and I had a very interesting meeting earlier this month with a bunch of Greg's relatives. They were amazingly friendly. At least some of them have doubts about whether Sunny is guilty."

"Huh. Let's see where that goes. Well, good luck. Have a good holiday, see you next month."

A moot court is basically a practice oral argument, where the lawyer makes the presentation she has planned for the court in front of a group of other lawyers and receives feedback and critiques. Toni emailed me the briefs in the case and the list of topics she hoped to cover in the forty-five minutes the state Supreme Court gave her to make her legal arguments before them. I decided to wait to see Sunny until after the argument, so I could tell her any news there might be about how it went. In the meantime, I kept working.

A lot of businesses not directly involved in selling holiday merchandise seem to go on something like hiatus as Christmas approaches; little work gets done from about the third week in December until after New Year's Day. The courts are an exception; they operate like clockwork, winter and summer. Filing deadlines don't change, and trials continue to be held; I've worked on two appeals, one of them a capital murder, where the trial jury handed in its verdict on Christmas Eve.

As for me, as I grow older and more ambivalent about the holidays, my preparations for Christmas have become minimal. I'd sent presents to Gavin and Rita in October to save the expense of airmail postage to Australia. Aside from them there were very few people in my life any more to whom I gave gifts: Ed, Harriet, and Bill, a jar of jam to Zoe, my aerobics teacher—that was about it. We all had enough stuff anyway, and they weren't that interested in acquiring another white elephant in the form of a present; they wanted things they'd consume, like food and candles. I'd bought an artificial tree small enough to sit on my coffee table without obstructing my view of the TV, and trimmed it with miniature ornaments, a chain of popcorn, and a couple of strings of tiny lights. I strung some multicolored lights over the living room windows and along the roof line outside and called it good.

In the middle of the month I made the trek to San Quentin, on a foggy morning, for holiday visits to my client Arturo and some other inmates I still kept in touch with. We spent the time in small talk about Christmases past and how our families were doing, reminiscing about our favorite holiday meals. I left with promises to send quarterly food packages and books of stamps and a sense of duty done for another few months.

My few friends left town for Christmas—Harriet and Bill took the train to Reno to spend Christmas with Bill's son and his family, and Ed ran off to meet his son for a week of fishing in Baja California. Gavin and Rita skyped me from Australia on Christmas Eve, panning their laptop around their apartment to show the tree and window decorations, and told me it was eighty degrees and sunny there, and they were on their way to a barbecue at Rita's parents' house. I spent Christmas Day at home, eating cookies and drinking home-made eggnog and binge-watching *The Lord of the Rings*.

On Boxing Day, I settled back into working on my cases. In addition to Sunny's petition, I was writing an opening brief in another murder case, fortunately one not involving the death penalty, that had to be filed in mid-January. With Ed, Harriet, and Bill gone, New Year's was as quiet as Christmas. Vlad's had a party going, but I wasn't interested in sitting around drinking and waiting for midnight among a bunch of strangers, so I stayed home and went to bed early.

A few days before the moot court, I settled down to rereading the briefs in Sunny's appeal, admiring the job

I'd done on the opening brief—had I really ever been that smart?—and making notes of questions I'd ask Toni if I were a particularly hostile and devious judge, in the hope it would help prepare her for any question, however strange, that might be lobbed to her from the bench.

Naturally, it was raining when I had to make the drive to the state defender's office in San Francisco. After feeling my way gingerly along the curves of Highway One and meeting the inevitable traffic jam, courtesy of a car that managed to slide onto the rear bumper of another on the freeway, I left my car in the parking garage I remembered as the least outrageously expensive of a bad lot and trekked damply into the lobby and onto the elevator to the suite of offices that housed my old employer.

Everything was the same, except the young African-American woman at the reception desk, who was new to me. The metal and plastic upholstered chairs in the waiting area, the magazines on the side tables (surely they were different, though I couldn't tell), the track lighting, off-white walls, and business-blue carpet. The place even smelled as I remembered it, like a forest of copy paper and toner, with just a whiff of coffee. I had expected something like a rush of painful sense memory from the worst few months of my life, but I didn't feel anything except mild relief that I didn't work here anymore.

The receptionist was on the phone; from her end of the conversation, I could tell she was speaking with a prisoner unhappy that the lawyer he wanted to speak to was out of the office. When she hung up the phone and turned to me, her expression was one of not-quite-exhausted patience. "I'm sorry," she said; it seemed to be more of a general observation about the state of the universe than an apology meant for me. "Can I help you?"

I smiled. "Rough morning?" I asked, and by way of explanation, added, "I used to work here, years ago."

"Yeah," she said. "I just can't seem to get off the phone today." As if to confirm what she'd said, it started ringing again. She picked it up and asked the person on the other end to hold. "I'm here for the Ferrante moot court," I said, to spare her having to ask. "Janet Moodie."

"Oh. I'll get Ms. Jackson." She made a call, said, "Toni, Janet Moodie's here for the moot court," hung up, and returned to the call on hold. I moved away from the desk toward the chairs and leafed through a magazine—a fairly new issue of the State Bar monthly journal—while I waited.

Toni came through the door to the offices. Tall and dark-skinned, she had always had a lot of presence; now, a little heavier in the face and body, she also had that regal bearing that some African-American women seem to acquire with middle age. The long red shirt of heavy silk she wore over dark slacks enhanced the impression. She smiled and shook my hand. "I'm so glad you could help. How was the drive here?"

I gave her a bowdlerized version, and she commiserated. "Traffic just gets worse and worse."

She walked ahead of me to the conference room, where

two other former colleagues, Joe Scott and Marty Silverman, stood and greeted me, Marty with a hug. "Congratulations on the Henley decision," Marty said.

I thanked him. "I wish he'd lived to see it."

"A real shame," he said, soberly. "I heard you did great work on the hearing."

"We had good luck," I demurred. "Most of the credit should go to Mike Barry. But it's always a crapshoot. When I think of all the cases we've all deserved to win and didn't—"

"Don't I know it," Marty said. "Nice when your hard work finally pays off, though. If it was luck, I hope some of it rubs off on Sunny." I didn't have time to say anything more before the last of the participants came in. "Jill Epstein," she said, shaking my hand. I didn't know her; I assumed she'd been hired after I left.

"Right, let's get down to business," Toni said. A podium had been moved to one end of the table, and Toni took up her position behind it. We anointed Joe as chief justice and time-keeper, and Toni began her prepared remarks. As she went through her arguments, we peppered her with questions, each of which she answered articulately and concisely; she was definitely ready for the hearing. *Death penalty lawyers may be quixotic by the standards of most of the profession,* I thought, *but we're no dummies.* But as I listened a little tensely to the dialogue, I realized that I was feeling a proprietary interest in how a work that was at least partly mine was being presented to the court.

The morning of the hearing itself, I sat at my desk at

home, a cup of milky coffee before me, its handle to my hand, watching a live stream of the oral argument over the state's Internet channel and marveling at the technology that allowed me to be in the audience of a hearing in Los Angeles without leaving my house. My connection left something to be desired, and I spent a few frustrating moments waiting while something or other buffered. But all in all it was a lot cheaper and less time-consuming than traveling five hundred miles. The argument went well, as those things go; the justices asked Toni many of the same questions we had in the moot court, and they seemed interested in the case, though without sending any real signal about which way they were leaning.

My appointment with Sunny was two days later.

"You're here early," Sunny remarked, as we sat across from one another over coffee and cookies in the attorney visiting room.

"I drove up yesterday," I said, "so I wouldn't be so tired when I got here."

"I guess that's good for me. I'm a morning person."

"How is your knee?"

"Pretty good. They did the surgery not too long after you were here last. Took me to an outside hospital. You know how the security works here; sometimes they just wake you up early and take you to the hospital with no warning. I had a day's notice because I had to fast before the operation. But it feels so much better now! I'm still using a cane, but I won't need to for much longer. How have you been? How was your Christmas?"

"Quiet. I'm pretty much alone; my son and his wife live in Australia."

"Wow—that's a long way away! Do you get to see them?"

"We talk on Skype."

"Skype?"

"It lets you talk to people over the Internet and see them at the same time."

"That's amazing—so much has changed since I was on the outside. I wish they had that here; it would be fun to get to see Kyle and Brianna more often. It was quiet here, too. But we had a nice dinner, with ice cream for dessert. There was eggnog in the vending machines. Carol visited, and Brittany and her family, and we drank eggnog both times. I was happy as can be to see them again; the kids are so much bigger than the last time they were here, and Brianna is smart as a whip." Sunny was trying to sound upbeat, as usual, but something behind her eyes showed the hurt she felt at seeing them so seldom. "Britt says she can read some of her books already, and she's only three! Britt said you came to see her, by the way."

"Yes, Natasha and I went. We had a good visit. Got to meet Rick and the kids."

"Does she seem happy?"

"Yes, very much so. She's an impressive young woman."

"Yes. She really turned around after that awful summer. I didn't know what would happen with her after I was arrested; she'd been so wild, and then she was really depressed after Todd died. I can't tell you how relieved and proud I was when she said she wanted to go live with Nana because she was worried about what Nana would do without me to help her. Britt was always good-hearted, just immature. But all the things that happened made her grow up fast," she added sadly.

"A couple of big things have happened in your case," I said.

"Oh—what?" Sunny watched me with the polite interest of someone who had learned to be afraid to hope too much.

"We saw Steve Eason." She made a face. "He told us he lied when he said Todd confessed to him. He said it never happened."

Sunny's eyes widened in surprise. "You mean he admitted it?" She was shaking her head. "I knew someone was lying. I didn't know if it was him or Todd. Oh, God, I can't believe he would do that to anyone. Why?" She seemed on the verge of tears.

"He was charged with a crime and wanted to stay out of prison."

Sunny was overcome. "Oh my God," she repeated. "And he did what he did, for that?" She was shaking. "I'm sorry," she said. "I'm just in shock."

I reached a hand to take hers. "You have every right to be. But this will probably get you a new trial."

She was still shaking her head. "After all this time."

"Yeah, I know. And something else happened, too."

She roused herself. "What was that?"

"Brittany told us about Greg's murder."

Sunny grew still. After a second or two, she asked, in an unsuccessful attempt at casualness, "Oh? What did she say?"

"She said Todd killed Greg."

"Okay." Sunny nodded; that was something she'd apparently accepted as fact.

"And that he and Braden planned it." I could see her relax, and she nodded her head at the news.

"She never said anything," I went on, "because she was afraid of Braden. She said Braden hinted to her that he had killed Todd and that she'd be next if she talked."

Sunny was nodding, as if this had been her theory all along. "Okay," she said again. I could tell she was still shaken by the revelation about Steve Eason.

"She said she'd been afraid to come forward because of Braden's threat. But now that he's serving life in prison, I guess she thinks it's safe for her to talk about it. She signed a declaration for us saying that's what happened." I didn't mention that Brittany had told us she'd told Sunny the same story; and Sunny didn't, either.

"So she really wasn't part of it?" Sunny said, tentatively. I felt she was probing us for confirmation.

"That's what she's saying. She said they kept her out of it. And Todd told her afterward."

Sunny had resumed nodding.

"We want to file Brittany's declaration with the habeas petition, but we wanted you to know what was in it ahead of time, so you wouldn't be surprised."

"Right. It won't get Brittany in trouble, will it?"

"We don't see how, unless someone can show she's lying."

Brows knitted, Sunny thought for a few seconds before speaking again. "I see. What about Braden? What does he say?"

"He won't talk to us, so I don't know. I can't imagine he'll admit that he conspired with Todd to murder Greg."

"No," Sunny said, shaking her head more or less automatically in agreement. "I can't imagine that."

"I'll show you the declaration, and you can see what it says."

I gave her a copy, and she read it over several minutes, studying each page. When she had finished, she gave it back to me.

"Are you all right with our filing it?"

She nodded, caught between hope and worry. "You're really sure this won't hurt Brittany?"

I struggled for the right words to reassure her, but somehow it all sounded like legalese. "On the basis of what she says, I don't think she can be charged with anything now. She says she wasn't part of the plot to kill Greg, so she isn't admitting she was involved in the murder, and personally, unless something changes, I don't see that they'd have any basis for charging her. The DA might try to say she was an accessory for not reporting it, but I don't think they'd get far; the statute of limitations has expired for that kind of charge. The only way it could hurt her is if some evidence came out that she lied in her declaration. We don't know of any such evidence; do you?"

"No—no." She shook her head.

"If that's the case, I think we can go ahead and file it, all right?"

"I guess. You're sure, right?"

"I can't absolutely guarantee anything. But based on what we know, I can't see any way it can hurt Brittany to go ahead with it. And Brittany signed it because she wants us to use it to help you."

Sunny took a deep breath and held it for a couple of seconds, then nodded and said, "Okay, then."

"I think with that plus Steve Eason's declaration, the court will have to give you a new trial."

"Oh." She sounded exhausted, and it occurred to me that a new trial, with all the stress that entailed, and the risk of another death sentence, wasn't necessarily the good news I'd assumed it would be.

"If they grant you a new trial," I added, "there's a good chance the district attorney will agree to some plea bargain that will let you out of prison."

She seemed to brighten a little. "So I may get out."

"Hopefully. I think there's a good chance of that happening."

"Thank you," she said. I could hear a note of relief in her voice.

"I have one other question," I said, suddenly remembering. "Were you aware that Greg's business was in financial trouble before he died?"

Sunny nodded. "Kind of. Greg didn't say anything—

he wouldn't, not to me. But Carol told me he asked her husband for a loan to cover some kind of balloon payment that was coming due. I remember she said I shouldn't worry about Greg divorcing me; he probably couldn't afford to."

"Would Brittany have known anything about this?"

She shook her head. "I don't see how. I didn't say anything about it to anyone, for fear it might get back to Greg."

"Thanks," I said. "That was a question that came up. Now I'll tell you how the oral argument went." I took a swig of my vending machine mocha and then summarized for her what Toni had argued, and what the justices' reactions seemed to be. "Toni did a terrific job, and the justices seemed interested in the case, but I wouldn't want to bet on where they're going with it."

"Well, it's nice to know they were interested."

"That's true," I said. "And on that note, we're done with business, unless you have any more questions."

She managed a small smile. "I can't think of a single one. My brain is overloaded."

We spent the rest of the visit exchanging pleasantries about how our lives had been going. I told her about Lizzie. "I just love cocker spaniels," she said. "We always had a dog and cats when I was a kid, but Greg didn't like pets. If I get out, I'm definitely getting a cat, at least." She told me more about the holiday visits from Brittany and her family and Carol, and the antics of the children, and shared a few funny stories about life on the row. Somehow, we found ourselves comparing favorite Christmas cookie recipes. We were both surprised when the guard knocked on the door and said our time was up.

"We'll send you a copy of the habeas petition when it's filed," I said. "And the court's opinion in your appeal should come out some time in March. They ought to mail you a copy, but I'll send one anyway."

As I made my way out of the prison, the copy of Brittany's declaration tucked inside my manila folder of papers, I thought about how easily Sunny had accepted both Brittany's story and her excuse for not having come forward with it when she might have been able to save her mother from a murder conviction and death sentence. I knew already that Brittany's account, or at least the major part of it, was not a surprise to her. Yet she had never even hinted at it to me or anyone else I'd talked to on her various defense teams. It left me feeling off-balance and apprehensive. We were about to file a habeas corpus petition advancing what we'd thought was a new theory and new evidence of Sunny's innocence, when an important piece of it wasn't new at all to the person it most affected. It made me wonder, anxiously, what else Sunny wasn't telling us.

21

Carey and I agreed we should file Brittany's declaration with the habeas petition, though Sunny's reaction left us both befuddled.

Carey had also enlisted a couple of friends, an accountant and a probate attorney, to review the files Craig Newhouse had received from Greg's business and the probate of his estate. Their reports concurred that Greg's business had been in deep trouble at the time of his death. "They say he really was on the verge of bankruptcy," Carey told me. "He'd borrowed a lot, and bought a lot of properties at the wrong time, so a lot of them were underwater. Max, the accountant, didn't think Greg could have raised enough money to keep going." We added an argument to the habeas petition, that Craig had provided ineffective assistance of counsel for not presenting this evidence at Sunny's trial.

With Eason's declaration and Brittany's, I felt, for the first time, optimistic that the court might grant our request for a hearing to take evidence on whether Sunny should get a new trial. Sometimes, as I work on a case, I can grow to believe in it, to nurture a feeling, however delusional, that we might just win. In my more realistic moments I realized that some of that was happening now, and that even with the case we had, we'd probably still lose. The petition was just the opening salvo in a long battle. Eason might return to his original story with some excuse for why he lied to us; and we had no idea what Braden would say when he learned of Brittany's accusation. We might get a judge who just thought that the best we had wasn't enough in his or her mind to deserve retrying the case. None of that mattered for the moment, though. We were on the home stretch, with the filing deadline looming ahead of us, Carey and I writing and then editing each other's drafts, and Natasha gathering the last records and witness declarations we'd need for the exhibits.

The little spare time I had was consumed by walks with the dogs and trips to town with Harriet for grocery shopping and garden supplies. I kept going to exercise classes for the sake of my mental health; and I took a few precious hours to winter-prune my apples, pears, and plums and plant last year's grafted trees.

Emulating a Jewish tradition a friend had told me about, I'd burned a candle to Terry on each anniversary of his death, in February. As I lit it this year, I spent less time resenting that cold gray day when my life had collapsed like a house of cards, and more time surveying my complicated, but gradually mellowing feelings of anger, betrayal, loss, and love.

Over time, as I'd worked through my shock and grief at
Terry's suicide, I was coming to remember why I had been
happily married to him for almost thirty years. Terry was
brilliant and intellectually curious, with a dry sense of humor.
We never ran out of things to talk or laugh about. He was
unsparing of dishonesty or willful ignorance, but generous
and compassionate to underdogs of all persuasions. When
we first worked together, I was awed and charmed by him;
and when we started dating and then became serious, I felt a
certain surprise that out of all the women in the world he had
chosen me. As a couple, there was always a comfortable give
and take between us; we shared laughs and private jokes, and
we brainstormed with each other over our cases and traded
ideas and inspirations. I owed a lot to him, professionally
as well as personally. Even though Terry always seemed to
keep a certain part of himself walled off from everyone in
the world, including me, he probably confided more of his
feelings to me than to anyone else. I felt easy with him in a
way I never had with most people, even though I always felt
overmatched by his effortless intelligence; one of the many
things that hurt in losing him was how alone I felt without
him. And I missed him a lot, though I'd spent years refusing
to admit it.

After lighting the candle that day, I sent Gavin a text,
"Remembering your dad," with a photo of it shining on my
stove top, and Gavin texted back, "Thanks, Mom; I miss
him, too."

By the middle of February, the petition was nearly

finished, and I had time for a conference for attorneys and other people who worked on defending death penalty cases. It was an annual event, three intense days of workshops and lectures, and it always felt like a reunion of old acquaintances bound by our common calling. Terry had been a celebrity in that tribe and had lectured or been on panels at every conference as long as I knew him. After his death, I had sworn off capital work and stayed away from the conferences. But for the last few years I'd started going again, and it had actually felt comforting to be back among people I'd known.

Carey and Natasha were both there, and after running into one another at various workshops, we met one evening for drinks and dinner. I got to meet Carey's husband, David, a quiet corporate lawyer, who seemed in awe of Carey's tough idealism, and Natasha's partner Mari, who was as petite and unflappable as Natasha was stout and brash. And I had lunch there with my old friend Dave Rothstein. Dave was an investigator who'd worked on cases with both Terry and me; it was Dave who'd first told me the news of Terry's death. He and his new wife, Sue, had traveled to Argentina and Patagonia since we last talked, and they showed me photos on his phone of the two of them hiking through a magnificent, uncompromising landscape of rocks, mountains, and immense blue skies. "You should go," he said.

"I'm a hopeless stick-in-the mud," I replied sadly.

Dave obviously felt he needed to explain why I hadn't been invited to their wedding. "We didn't invite anyone," he said. "We dithered for a long time about where to get married and when and who to ask; and then one day we said to hell with it, went to the courthouse and got a license and then went back a week later, got married by a judge."

"We eloped," Sue said, proudly.

Not long after returning home I had a phone call from my client Arturo Villegas. He was worried and upset; his father had been picked up and detained by the immigration authorities and was likely to be deported. His sister called me, tearfully, the next day, and I promised her I'd try to get names of some good immigration lawyers in Los Angeles. It took a few phone calls, but I was able to call her back a couple of days later and give her some recommendations. The arrest had upended Arturo's family: his mother was hiding in a friend's house, afraid to try to work; his sister, who was American-born and in college, was afraid she'd have to drop out of school to support the family; and his younger brother, angry and out of control, had taken up with a local gang.

I made a visit to San Quentin to see Arturo, and give him a chance to talk through his anxiety and feelings of helplessness at being in prison and unable to help his family. His little brother, he told me, had gotten involved with the gang out of anger at how the government was treating Mexican families in the United States and a desire to strike back in some way. It was a stupid choice, and Arturo, who had been a gang member himself, said he'd tried to tell his brother, through letters and phone calls, not to take that path. "Now he'll end up in prison like me," he said, despairingly. "He thinks he's making some kind of stand, but he's just being hard-headed and stupid." I agreed. Arturo was learning a bitter lesson in the hurt his own bad decisions had caused the people he loved.

Back home again, I grafted a few more trees for next year, and Carey and I put the last touches on the habeas petition; she filed it in the court in Harrison and emailed me a copy. We settled back to wait—and then a miracle occurred.

22

When I first started out as a lawyer, appellate court decisions were announced to the world by putting a couple of paper copies of opinions in an outbox on the clerk's counter for members of the public to read and take away with them. If you were one of the attorneys in the case, a copy was mailed to you, and unless you could get to the clerk's office to pick one up sooner, you got it when you got it. On a couple of occasions I learned of a decision in a case of mine when a reporter from the local legal paper called after seeing the opinion at the counter. The courts have changed with the times, and now anyone can sign up for email notifications about developments in an appeal. The courts still mail paper copies to the parties, but now when a court issues an opinion anyone can download it in seconds.

When the opinion in Sunny's appeal was filed, I got an automated email from the court the day before, telling me it would be on the state Supreme Court's website at ten o'clock the following morning. I wasn't expecting much; few death penalty judgments are reversed on appeal, and of those, most are reversals only of the death sentence, not of the guilty verdict. But, as Terry used to say, we live in hope, and by a minute past ten I had downloaded and opened the file.

I had to read a half page of summary information about the charges against Sunny, her conviction, and her sentence, before I reached the part that read, "Because the trial court erred prejudicially in excluding evidence of other instances in which the informer provided questionable information to the police, appellant's conviction for murder and the special circumstances must be reversed."

For a moment I just sat, staring at the screen, my hands over my mouth. When it seemed my heart had started beating again, I scrolled down the page and continued reading, half believing that I had misread that sentence, that it was just a typo, and that it would all be taken away somewhere later in the opinion. But it wasn't. The opinion was fairly short— no need to discuss most of what we'd argued in the appeal, since most of it didn't matter anymore. The state Supreme Court wrote that the trial judge had made a mistake when he refused to let Craig Newhouse present evidence that Steve Eason made a practice of giving information about other inmates, including their making surprising confessions to him, in exchange for lenient treatment in his own cases, and that in at least one instance he'd been shown to have lied.

Given that the other evidence tying appellant to the victim's murder was circumstantial and hardly

compelling, we cannot say that the error in keeping
the informant's history from the jury, and depriving
jurors of the opportunity to assess his credibility on a
complete record, was harmless.

This was my win, I thought proudly, as well as Toni's; that
argument was in the opening brief I'd written while I was
still Sunny's appellate lawyer.

When I found my voice, I called Carey, who was in
court, and left her a voice mail, and then called Natasha's
cellphone. She wasn't answering, either, so I sent her a text
saying Sunny had won on her appeal and would be getting a
new trial. Then I called Toni to congratulate her. We had no
way to get the word to Sunny herself that day, but the court
would mail her a copy of the opinion, and so would I, so
she'd know in a couple of days.

After finishing my calls, I still felt too agitated to do
any work. By this time, the dogs had picked up on my
excitement and were milling around my chair, watching me
closely for some sign of what it all might mean. What it
meant for them was that I pulled on a sweater and found
a hat and bundled them into the car for a ride down to the
bluffs above the ocean. There we walked the trails for an
hour or so, while I periodically whooped and skipped like
a nine-year-old. When I'd calmed down some, we picked
up our mail at the real estate office, and I treated myself to
a lunch of baked macaroni and cheese and a pumpkin ale at
Vlad's, followed by a double chocolate brownie which I took

with me back up the hill to the house. By then, I'd gotten a return text from Natasha; I called her, and we chattered breathlessly about what had happened. At one point, she asked, "What happens to the habeas petition?"

"It's moot, I guess," I said. "Sunny's getting a whole new trial, so what we asked for has been granted already, just on different grounds."

"Dang," she said. "All that work."

"It's going to be useful for the new trial," I said, "or for negotiating. With Steve Eason admitting he lied, and Brittany's declaration, and the evidence that Greg was broke, the prosecution case will be a lot weaker. They could decide not to bother to try it again."

"I hope so," she said. "Maybe we did some good after all."

We had. But I realized, as I thought it, that I wouldn't be part of what happened from here. I'd been appointed for the habeas corpus proceeding, and now that the petition would certainly be dismissed as moot, my role in Sunny's case was over. It was a slightly melancholy feeling; if nothing else, it would have been nice to follow through with it. But as it was, we'd be handing it off to someone else and hoping he or she would do a good job for Sunny. Before trying to settle back into something like the day's work, I called Harriet and Ed and invited them to join me for dinner at Vlad's, to celebrate.

Carey called that afternoon, during a court recess. She hadn't had a chance to read the court's opinion, so I summarized it for her. "That's amazing," she said. "They really shouldn't retry her. There's a good chance we can get the charges dismissed."

"But we won't be her lawyers," I reminded her.

"Right," she admitted, and paused for a few seconds. "You know, maybe I'll see if I can get the court to appoint us for the retrial. Would you like to keep working on the case?"

My day suddenly brightened even more. "Sure. I'd like that," I said.

The presiding judge in Harrison had other ideas, though. A few weeks later, Carey called me again. "Well, we got some of what we asked for," she said. "The judge said he'd appoint me, but I'm not allowed to charge for travel to and from Ventura." Stingy, I thought, but not surprising. "But he won't appoint second counsel. His reasoning is that the case is being retried, so it doesn't need as much work as a brand new case. So he doesn't see why I need a second chair. The most he'd do is give me a little money to retain you for specific things, like a motion now and then or a witness interview. I'm sorry; I really tried."

I wasn't as disappointed as I thought I'd be. I'd decided after more sober reflection that agreeing to work on Sunny's retrial hadn't been that good a decision, personally or economically, and the prospect of spending more time in Harrison wasn't inviting. Sunny's case was in good hands with Carey; helping out occasionally would be enough for me.

It wasn't long, though, before I heard from Carey again. "I need your help," she said.

"What's up?"

"Braden Ferrante."

"Him? Really?"

"Yeah. The DA has offered to let Sunny plead to voluntary manslaughter and be released from prison immediately."

"That's not too bad."

"Not good enough. I've been thinking that if I keep at them I can get them to dismiss the charges entirely. Without Eason, they have nothing—just a loan to Todd to fix his truck, which she never tried to hide. But then up comes old Braden and messes everything up."

"How?"

"Joe Hansen, the investigating officer, went to see him in prison. I guess he showed him Brittany's declaration, and it pissed Braden off enough that he talked to Hansen about the murder."

"Oh, dear. He didn't say Sunny was behind it, I hope."

"No, thank God. But what he did say was that it was Brittany. He said she convinced Todd to kill Greg because she hated him and wanted him dead and so she and Sunny could have his money. He says none of them knew Greg was going broke.

"As Braden tells it, Brittany kept badgering Todd about it, until Todd agreed to kill Greg. He said Todd told him before he did it, and he told Todd not to. He didn't really care whether Greg lived or died; he had a trust fund from his grandparents on his mother's side, so he didn't need Greg's money. He absolutely denied threatening Brittany or having anything to do with Todd's overdose—he says she's lying about all of it."

I remembered Brittany's statement, during our visit, that Todd had said he'd killed Greg for her. The genuine pain with which she recounted it—along with the fact that there had been no benefit to her in telling us—had given it a feeling of truth, of a genuine secret held and finally, reluctantly shared. *Braden might actually be telling the truth,* I thought, with a twinge of fear.

"But that doesn't hurt Sunny, does it?" I asked. "It actually seems to help her."

"Yes, it's great. I don't see how they can possibly try her at this point, with so many stories floating around. But Sunny is freaking out about the possibility that Brittany might be prosecuted. She doesn't want to keep fighting for a better deal; she's willing to plead to anything, as long as the DA promises not to prosecute Britt. I've tried to tell her I don't see that happening—I mean, the only evidence against her would be Braden, and he's in prison and frankly as much a suspect as Brittany at this point. But I really need some help talking Sunny down. Someone she trusts more than us."

I worked through everyone I knew connected to the case, trying to think of someone. Sunny's family? There were only Brittany and Linda. Brittany was out, and I didn't think Sunny would feel she could rely on Linda for much of anything. I thought about friends, and realized she had named almost no one. The few she had, from what she'd said about them, were little more than tennis partners or other wives she had met sometimes for lunch or shopping. The only friend who had stayed with her since her arrest was Carol Schiavone. At my last visit, Sunny had said it was Carol who had warned her about Greg's financial troubles. I recalled that she lived in New Mexico, but I didn't recall whether Carey or Natasha had ever gotten in touch with her.

"What about her friend Carol?" I asked. "She seems to be really loyal, if she still comes all the way from New Mexico to visit Sunny. She visited her at Christmas, too."

"I'm willing to try anything," Carey said. "I talked to Carol on the phone last fall. I don't think we got a declaration from her, I think because what she said was basically the same as her testimony at Sunny's trial. Would you be willing to give her a call and find out whether she thinks she can help? I hope she can make it to Harrison; Sunny's been transferred to the jail there for the retrial." She gave me Carol's phone number.

I waited until early evening to call, and a man answered. I asked him if Carol Schiavone was there and gave him my name. "May I tell her what this is about?" he asked.

"It's about Sunny Ferrante."

"Oh. Okay. I'll get her."

When Carol came on the line, I introduced myself.

"So you're the other attorney working with Ms. Bergmann," she said. "Is Sunny all right? I sent her an Easter card, and it was returned."

"That's probably because she's been transferred to the county jail in Harrison."

"Oh. Because they're going to try her again?"

"That, or maybe work out a plea bargain, or maybe even drop the charges."

"And she'll be free again? Right away?"

"We're insisting on it."

"Good. Thank you for all you've done for Sunny. It's such a relief to finally have hope again. But you called me about something."

"Yes," I said again. "I'd like to talk with you about a problem that's come up."

"What is it?"

"The district attorney offered Sunny a plea bargain."

"That's not a bad thing, is it?"

"No. It's not bad, but Carey—Ms. Bergmann—thinks she can do better and get the charges dismissed—"

"But Sunny's worried about Brittany." Apparently sensing my surprise, she added, "I've known her for almost thirty years. She's afraid Britt may be accused of the murder, right?"

"Basically, yes," I said, surprised at how much Carol seemed to know.

"Do you think she will be?"

"No, but we need to convince Sunny."

"Convince her of what?"

"Well, that the district attorney isn't going to go after Brittany for the murder; they don't have any basis to, really. And also that taking the DA's offer won't make it any safer for

Brittany. They could still investigate Brittany for conspiracy even if Sunny takes the plea deal. They won't, but we haven't been able to convince her of that. I think she's too worried to think clearly."

"That sounds about right. So where do I come in?"

"You're someone she trusts, a really good friend."

"Probably her only one," Carol said. "Poor girl."

"It seems that way, doesn't it?" I agreed. "We were wondering if you were planning to see her in the near future."

"You said she's back in Harrison?" Carol was quiet for a second or two, then said, "Just a minute, I'm thinking here— Tom has a conference in San Jose in a couple of weeks. I was trying to decide whether to go with him. If I do, I can make the trip to Harrison from there. We'd have to stay an extra day or two, I think. Let me talk to Tom and call you back."

I thanked her, and we said our goodbyes.

She called back the next morning. "We can do it," she said. "We changed our return flight so we can drive to Harrison and spend the night there. Tom is actually looking forward to it, can you believe it? He can touch base with some old friends. He grew up in the area, kind of misses some of the people we knew. I don't. I'm thrilled to be out of there, never looked back. We should talk before I see her, so I can find out more about what's happening."

I agreed.

"Do you want to meet in Harrison?"

"Actually," I said, "I live in Sonoma County, so San Jose would be better for me."

"Lucky you. I love it up there. Why don't we meet in San Francisco? Easier for you, and I'd love an excuse to spend a day there. I know this really nice dim sum place out in the avenues." She gave me its name and address and a date and time to meet. "There. That's settled," she said. "See you then."

After we hung up, I felt the need to smooth down my hair; talking with Carol had felt like having it ruffled by a brisk breeze.

23

Carol was standing in front of the restaurant, talking on her phone, when I walked up. She was Asian, perhaps around sixty. She was small, even shorter than me, slender and casually but impeccably dressed in dark slacks and a creamy-white silk shirt. A jacket in a coordinating geometric print was draped over her shoulders.

I apologized for being late. "I had trouble finding a place to park."

"No problem," she said. "It gets worse and worse. I've only been here a minute or two." She put on her jacket. "I always forget it's colder here in the city," she said. "Let's get inside."

The restaurant was an old-fashioned dim sum place, a big room full of the cheerful buzz of conversation and the clink of dishes, where servers wheeled carts of little plates and covered bamboo steamers among the many tables. Carol led me to a table off to one side, where the noise of the lunchtime crowd was more muted and we could have some privacy to talk. "I'm afraid it's a bit out of the way for getting food, though," she apologized. Not that I could tell: carts full of wonderful things came around at intervals, and we soon chose enough dumplings, rice in banana leaves, turnip cake, and pork buns to keep us busy and happy. At one point she asked a waiter something in Chinese; he shook his head, and she said something else and turned back to me. "There was a thing I was hoping I could get," she said, "but I'm from Taiwan, and this place is Cantonese. It's not a dish they make.

"So," she said, after we'd taken the edge off our appetites with a couple of shu mai and shrimp balls. "What's happening with Sunny?"

I laid out the story. Carol listened without comment until I'd finished, and then said, "Ah."

"Do you think you can help us convince her Brittany is safe?"

"I can try," she said. "But there are some things you need to know. Sunny probably wouldn't want me to tell you all of them, but I think I should anyway."

"Okay," I said. "I like Sunny, but I've always felt there are things she hasn't been telling me."

"I'm sure there are." She opened a banana leaf and tipped the glossy lump of sticky rice inside it onto the saucer. Cutting it in two with a chopstick, she picked up half and put it on her plate. "Try it," she said, and I took the other half, wiggled a piece from it with my chopsticks, and took a bite. It was delicious, just chewy enough and full of exotic flavors.

"To begin with," she said, "I've known Sunny since she was first married to Greg. Tom was part of an engineering firm in Harrison that Greg was involved with over the years. We knew him back when he was married to Pat. Pat and I were friendly, not that close; we lost touch after she left Greg and moved to Fresno. Try the shrimp and chive dumplings, they're really good." I took one and ate it; she was right. We kept eating and talking between bites.

"Anyhow, to get back to Sunny, it was so clear she was a trophy wife for Greg. She was petite, beautiful—perfect figure, perfect little face. Like a beauty queen. A Disney princess. It was clear that that's what her attraction was for Greg. But they didn't really have anything in common. And Sunny didn't have any of the social graces Greg wanted in a wife. She was just a girl from the country. I mean, she was as sweet as can be, but she couldn't hold up her end of a conversation with Greg's business buddies and their wives, she didn't know how to dress or entertain. Greg was constantly criticizing her and trying to change her into what he wanted. It was like Henry Higgins and Eliza—except that Henry Higgins knew what he was doing. Greg didn't; he just harped. And he kept having affairs with other women—his friends' wives, cocktail waitresses, whatever."

"Ugh," I said.

"Right." She grimaced in distaste. "I felt really sorry for poor Sunny.

"I wasn't happy, either, in Harrison. Tom grew up in the Central Valley, so he knows the culture, and he felt at home there. But I never did. I was so bored. Such limited people. I grew up in Whittier. That was bad enough, but we had LA nearby; I went to college at UCLA. But Harrison— ugh! I guess I ended up taking Sunny on as something like a project. Probably because I didn't have enough to do; I decided to take a break from work while my son, Michael, was small. Tom says I'm a busybody, and he's probably right. Michael was about Brittany's age, and we used to have play dates. Sunny told me about her problems meeting Greg's expectations, and I tried to help her get some polish— maybe just to get Greg off her back, I don't know. Whatever it was, we became close friends. Maybe she saw me as sort of a mother figure, someone she needed because she never had a real mother. I met Linda a few times, and I didn't think much of her.

"Greg didn't like it. He seemed to believe I was interfering, teaching Sunny to stand up for herself—which in a way I probably was, or at least trying to. But he couldn't order Sunny to stop seeing me because he had an ongoing working relationship with Tom and his company. And I'm not easy to push around; you can ask Tom," she said, with a laugh.

"Jeez, would he really have tried to do that?"

"Oh, yes. He often told Sunny who she could and couldn't have as friends. He was kind of a social climber, and he wanted Sunny to learn to cultivate people, like the wives of men who could help him get ahead. She was no good at that. She was so over her head. He played her family against her, too. He did favors for Linda and Pete and Nana,

tried to buy their loyalty, so they'd be on his side in case
Sunny complained about how he was treating her. It worked
on Linda and Pete, but I have to give Nana credit; she saw
through him."

"Poor Sunny! She must have been unhappy a lot of the
time."

"She was. She was like that old cliché, a bird in a gilded
cage. Materially, she had a life she could never have had on
her own. And that mattered to her. Not for herself, but for
Brittany. She wanted Brittany to have the advantages of
growing up well off. But it really was a bad choice. Greg
didn't have much use for Brittany. He just left her for Sunny
to raise. He started to take notice of her when she was in
junior high, but only to criticize, because he didn't think she
reflected well on him. She was too big, too heavy, not pretty
enough. He said she dressed like a slob and hung out with
white trash at the school. I thought when she started dating
Todd, this kid that was just a farmhand on Greg's family's
ranch, that it was like a rebellion—really, a slap in the face to
her stepfather. But Sunny told me later Brittany was really in
love with him; I know she was completely broken up when
he died. And Sunny was caught in the middle, trying to keep
Greg happy and heal what he was doing to Brittany's self-
esteem, all at the same time. I'm surprised Brittany didn't
hate Sunny as much as she did Greg."

"But she didn't, did she?"

"No. She's a good kid, at heart, and she could see what
Greg was doing to her mother. She tried to protect her.

She got into arguments with Greg a few times about how he behaved toward them. Sunny told me she tried to calm Brittany down because she was afraid Greg would throw her out of the house."

"He couldn't do that when she was underage."

"I told her that. But Sunny didn't know that; she thought he could do anything. By then she was just so anxious all the time that she couldn't think."

"So it sounds as though things were bad in the time leading up to the murder."

Carol nodded. "They were very bad."

"And Greg was having an affair with someone, right? This woman Carlene, who said he was going to divorce Sunny and marry her?"

Carol rolled her eyes. "Oh, that. That was never going to happen. I told Sunny Greg was in no position to divorce her. She had a prenup—not that generous, she showed me the paper once—but still it meant Greg would have to give her a settlement if he left her. And he probably couldn't even do that, at that point. He was in a cash flow crunch, Tom said, trying to borrow money wherever he could."

"So that would have been a bad time to kill him for his money?"

She laughed again. "We are so cynical! But yes, for Sunny. There wasn't that much there; as it turned out, his estate all went to pay debts, and his life insurance wouldn't support them for long. If she wanted money, her best bet was to stay with Greg until he was on his feet again. But Brittany didn't know that. Sunny told me she didn't know Greg was in trouble until I told her."

I hesitated before asking the next question. "Are you suggesting Brittany might have been involved in Greg's murder?"

Carol shrugged. "Personally, I don't know. But Sunny is convinced of it. She is Brittany's mother, after all. They lived together; she saw her every day. Heard things between her and Todd. She told me she began to suspect something right away because of how Brittany found Greg's body."

"What was that?"

"Well, she said they came home from shopping with Nana that day, and Brittany went right upstairs to her room. Sunny was putting things away and could hear her talking on the phone—not what she was saying, just her voice. She figured she was talking to Todd, but didn't make anything of it. But then Brittany came downstairs and went right out to the pool, to where Greg's body was. Even at the time, it made no sense. There wasn't any reason for her to go out there. She wasn't going for a swim, she didn't have her suit on. Sunny said she thought afterward that Todd must have told Britt where Greg's body was. And then there were other things: Brittany's worry about Todd, lots of whispered phone calls. The money for the truck. It seemed like a strange thing to ask for. But Sunny was feeling sorry for Brittany, with all the disruption around Greg's death, and the full extent of Greg's debts hadn't really penetrated, so she said she didn't see any harm in loaning Todd some money to fix his truck or get another one."

"Did she tell you about any of this before she was arrested?"

"Yes. I was the only person she dared to confide in about her suspicions. She made me promise not to say anything to anyone else. She was really afraid for Brittany, but there wasn't anything she could do. She wasn't going to tell the police she suspected her own daughter of being involved in the murder. She kept hoping it would somehow blow over. Actually, she was kind of surprised when she realized the police suspected her; she'd been so focused on protecting Britt that she didn't see that coming. And then that guy turned up who said Todd told him Sunny hired him, and she was arrested. Even then, it seemed like such a weak case, we were all hoping she'd be acquitted. The conviction was a real shock, and the death sentence simply floored me. I wanted to say something, but Sunny swore me to silence. We had no way to talk when I visited her in jail; everything was over the telephone, and we knew they were monitored. But we managed to communicate a few things in a kind of code, and she made it clear that she could never do anything that might throw suspicion on Brittany."

"Did you talk with her about it afterward, when she was in prison?"

"Yes. We could talk more there, because we were meeting face to face. She told me, oh, years ago, that Brittany had told her that story you told me, about Braden, during a visit to her in prison. Brittany wanted to go to the police and tell them, but Sunny told her not to. I had to agree with her. It was too late; no one would believe it, and Braden would just say it was all a lie. It would probably just backfire, make both her and Brittany look like liars."

"So now we're back in court facing another trial," I said, "and Sunny is afraid that Brittany is still in jeopardy."

"Definitely. And I'm sure Sunny'll even go back to prison again before she lets anything happen to Britt."

"But she won't have to. Nothing will happen to Brittany; we're sure of it. But she isn't convinced."

"How can you tell nothing will happen?"

I swallowed a bite of a pork bun before answering. "Here's how things stand now. The prosecution already tried the case on the theory that Sunny was behind the murder, and they won it. Now they'd have to go back and say, no, it was actually Brittany. But they have nothing on her, other than that she was Todd's girlfriend, and she didn't like her stepfather. Brittany herself has said that Braden was the person behind the murder. The only witness against her is Braden, who (a) is the other logical suspect and (b) is in prison for soliciting another murder. There's just no case against her."

"What about Sunny?"

"At this point, there's a real lack of credible evidence connecting Sunny to the murder. Steve Eason, the guy who said Todd confessed to him, gave us a sworn declaration saying he was lying. If the prosecution puts him on, either he'll testify, as he told us, that he lied about Todd's confession, or if he doesn't, the defense will impeach him with his sworn declaration, and they'll get to introduce all the evidence about his other snitching that was kept out of his first trial. Eason is completely discredited as a witness. And his testimony and the loan to Todd were about the only solid evidence the prosecution had against Sunny. Everything else was just motive. Bring in Greg's money troubles and the fact that Sunny knew about them, and a lot of that disappears. And now we have Brittany and Braden each saying the other one is responsible, and not Sunny. So I really doubt the DA will retry the case if we stand firm."

"But Sunny wants to take the plea bargain—manslaughter?—if they'll promise not to prosecute Brittany?"

"Right. Call it pride, or politics, or something, but prosecutors hate to dismiss cases after someone has been convicted. The DA wants her to plead guilty to something, and they're offering manslaughter, which would mean she'd be released from prison immediately. We're trying to convince Sunny that it's safe to hold out for a complete dismissal. But we're not having much luck. She wants us to insist that any deal includes a promise not to prosecute Brittany. She doesn't seem to understand that this could make things worse, not better."

"You mean she'll just draw their attention to the possibility that Brittany did it," Carol said.

"Right. I don't think they're taking that possibility seriously at this point, but if she insists, they might take another look."

"Poor Sunny! I'll see what I can do. But it's going to be hard, with those jail phones."

Another cart came by, this one with desserts. "Let's have some custard tarts," Carol said. "Take our mind off fixing Sunny's problem." She pointed to a plate of them and another of sesame balls. "I love these," she said. "I never get them at home." We both ate one of each, enjoying the contrasts between crumbly pie crust and eggy custard, chewy, sesame-crusted shell and the sweet bean paste inside it.

Before we left, Carol paid the check and got boxes for the food we hadn't eaten. She arranged the savories into one and the sweets into another, and gave them to me. "You can take them home," she said. "I can't; we're in a hotel." I thanked her for the wonderful lunch and for taking the time to talk with me.

"It was my pleasure; I feel like we owe you all so much," Carol said. "I'm looking forward to seeing Sunny free. I haven't been so hopeful in years."

24

Carol called me the day after she saw Sunny. "I don't know if I convinced her," she said, "but I think I got her to understand she can trust your judgment and Ms. Bergmann's. Let me know if you need me to go there again. She's still awfully anxious and uncertain—no wonder, really—and she needs a lot of TLC. Whatever happens, please definitely let me know when she's going to be released. I want to be there to meet her."

After that, Sunny's case crept slowly, as these cases so often do, toward some kind of resolution. A lot depended on keeping the case under the radar of the media and people who might use it for political gain. It got a little buzz initially, because it isn't often that anyone on death row gets a new trial, but the case was old and not that sensational, as murders go, so many people no longer remembered it or had never heard of it, and it soon dropped off the local news cycle.

Neither side wanted to try the case again, but the district attorney's office needed a disposition that would save face, either a guilty plea to something or, if they were going to dismiss the charges and leave a murder unsolved, a credible reason why. And when and if that happened, the less visible the case was, the better. So the prosecutor and Carey moved in baby steps—or, rather, the prosecutor did, because Carey stood firm that her offer was dismissal or another trial. The judge was also hoping the case would be resolved without another expensive trial, so he kept moving the date back, on one pretext or another, as spring drifted into summer, and summer into fall.

My life continued on its own set of cycles—records to read, briefs to write, clients to visit, summer pruning, tomato processing, jam making, and occasional treats like music festivals and fairs. The tomatoes were better than usual because the summer this year was hot—exceptionally, miserably hot. All of us around Corbin's Landing, used to summer fog and sweater weather in the height of summer, found ourselves facing global climate change on a personal level.

Santa Ana winds—the ones that had made the previous year's fires east of us so hugely destructive—swept from the hot inland valleys over the mountains and over us, bringing heat waves with hundred-degree temperatures and desert-like humidity and more fires, whose smoke made us cough and tinted the air above the ocean with murky brownish smog. The smaller redwoods were stressed, the tips of their needles browning from lack of water, and our tanoaks were like matchsticks, with the grass and dried weeds underneath them nothing but tinder. Working early in the mornings, we cleared space around our homes to make firebreaks. We lived in constant fear of a stray spark from a power mower, a tourist's forbidden campfire, or a downed power line.

Looking back, though, I believe the end of my idyll in Corbin's Landing began with the rats.

I saw the first of them one morning on my deck. Charlie alerted me by whining at the kitchen door as I was padding around in robe and slippers, preparing to pour coffee beans into the grinder. Curious, I opened the door and saw a half-grown rat next to my compost bucket. It froze and stared at me through bright black eyes. I was touched rather than repulsed by the sight; by its youngness, by the shine of its eyes and its inquisitive face. After a few seconds, it turned and scurried down the steps and out of sight.

I mentioned it to Ed the next time I saw him. "You need to deal with it," he warned. "There's never just one rat. You probably have a family of them somewhere near your house, and if you leave them alone, they'll start coming inside."

Ed was right. I left them alone, and one morning a couple of weeks later, when I lifted the bag of kibble to pour some into Charlie's bowl, I saw that something had eaten a ragged hole in one corner of it.

After that and a couple of evenings punctuated with mysterious scratchings and scrabblings in the wall between the kitchen and my bedroom, I made the drive to the hardware store in Gualala and asked the clerk to recommend some traps. Baits scared me because of the possibility of poisoning the dogs and because I had read that they caused horrible and painful death by internal bleeding. At that point, I wasn't ready to wish such a fate even on a rat.

So I reluctantly trapped a few, rushing to see when I heard the snap and rattle of a trap shutting and the victim's final struggles, or checking them in the mornings and finding, every few days, another rat with its neck crushed. I dug holes in the orchard to bury them and hated picking up the traps, opening them, and dumping the stiff little bodies into their miniature graves.

The scrabblings in the walls became less and less frequent, until I didn't hear them anymore, but the traps still claimed an occasional unwary forager. Ed suggested I get a barn cat, since my house cats, Effie and Nameless, were completely uninterested in rodents large enough to stare them down.

So, for a fee, I adopted a barn cat from a shelter in Santa Rosa which made a minor specialty of rescuing feral cats, spaying or neutering them, and offering them to farm and ranch owners who needed cats with experience in catching furry pests. My new cat was big, rangy, and orange-striped. The young women at the shelter told me he'd been found in Santa Rosa several months after the big fires, wandering the ruins of a burned-out neighborhood. They had named him Dodger because he was so hard to catch. I kept the name, thinking the reference to the Dickens character suited him.

Dodger wouldn't set foot in the house, so I left food and water for him on the deck, hoping it wouldn't have the paradoxical effect of bringing more rats. If it did,

Dodger must have nailed them, because I didn't see any sign that anyone else but he and the other cats were eating his kibble. When I fed him he would sometimes let me scratch his ears for a few seconds. But at the sight of Charlie, Lizzie, or one of the other cats, or any random sound he didn't recognize, he would turn, quickly and silently, and disappear into the brush.

Dead voles, and an occasional young rat, began appearing on the stoop outside my kitchen door in the early mornings, possibly as thank-yous for the cat kibble. Sometimes in my walks into the garden and orchard, I'd see the head—nothing more—of a vole or mouse, lying in the path. Dodger was doing what he'd been hired for, and I was grateful. Nevertheless, I felt a little uneasy because of all the rodent death suddenly occurring around me. Not that I didn't realize, on an intellectual level, that it had been there all along. "Nature, red in tooth and claw" was always around, in the form of hawks, barn owls, foxes, and other feral cats; and I hadn't been above hiring a gopher trapper, who discreetly emptied his traps while I stayed in the house. But I didn't like it when it was made visible to me, and it made me a little depressed when I saw a young rat or mouse dead or dying on my doorstep and realized that this was the trade-off for my living comfortably in my home and harvesting unmolested fruit and vegetables. For all that, I grew fond of Dodger and the fact that he left what he felt were gifts for me, and I tried to cultivate his friendship, partly out of an egotistical desire to win him over, and partly because I wasn't sure how I'd be able to feed and shelter him once the winter rains started. But by the time they began, it no longer mattered.

2 5

Anyone who lives in the forest in California, unless they are in serious denial, must consider the fires that scorch parts of the state every summer and fall and realize that the odds are against them—that someday it will be their turn, and those giant sheets of flame they watch on the news will be sweeping across their ridges, through their wooded canyons, and up their roads.

Our turn came that fall, with a heat wave in the middle of October, just when we thought the dangerous season was almost over. The arid winds that sighed over our heads and around us and shook the branches of summer-dried trees swirled around an abandoned campfire in a state park and transformed it, like a horrific genie rising out of its bottle, into a column and then a wall of flames that ran before the wind too quickly for any fire crew to stop.

Most of my legal files were in storage in Santa Rosa, and as the fire became worrisomely close I made a trip there one morning with a carload of most of the rest. When I didn't hear from Ed, I called him, to see what was up. When he called back, he explained that he and Molly's husband were out fighting the fires. He had taken Pogo to a friend's house out of the danger zone. I'm not religious, but I said a prayer for their well-being.

Back home I loaded one irreplaceable item after another into my car—personal records, the last few boxes of files from the cases I was working on—and I strapped a carrier with some camping equipment onto the top. I piled cat carriers next to my kitchen door. With a hose I watered the roof of my house and a perimeter around it as thoroughly as I had time for, without much hope that it would help much in the bone-dry air, now filling up with smoke and the harsh smell of burning brush and logs. I kept the dogs and the two house cats indoors, in case we had to leave, but Dodger evaded all my blandishments and kept melting into the brush when I tried to catch him. When a sheriff's car came up my driveway, and two kind but firm men said it was time to get out, I packed my computer and pets and made one last run into the back yard calling frantically for Dodger. We had to go now, if ever. I couldn't see the fire from the house, but the air was brown and hot and the smoke so thick it made me cough, while carried on it was an occasional ominous cinder.

We fled north, up the coast highway, toward Sea Ranch and the town of Gualala. As I made the turn onto it, I could see flames from burning trees on the ridge, and on the way I pulled over several times to let fire trucks through. Harriet and Bill had left a couple of weeks earlier to stay with Bill's son in Reno, because Bill's damaged lungs couldn't handle the smoke from another set of fires burning to the north of us.

I camped out for three days on a beach in a county park near Gualala, where the dogs and cats could be with me, the dogs tied up on leashes near my tent and the cats in an old wire dog crate I'd brought along. I texted Ed a couple of times and then figured he'd answer when he had time. When I heard, finally, that we were allowed to go back to check on our houses and land, I packed up and drove back home to see what was left.

The fire wasn't that big, as wildfires go. The land it burned was sparsely settled, mostly forest and pasture and parks. Nobody died, and the number of houses lost to it numbered in the dozens, not the hundreds or, as in the great fires of those years, the thousands. It made the local TV news and papers, but got barely a mention outside northern California. But for us in the middle of it, it took away irreplaceable things—not just possessions, but the beauty around us and our various ways of life.

The road to my house and the driveway were passable, and my house had been saved, along with its old detached garage. Both were dark with soot, and the house stank of stale smoke and damp, but they were still standing, with no serious damage that I could see. My orchard had burned, though, and the apple and pear trees, some of which still had ripening fruit when I left, were now a tangle of bare black branches and blackened trunks. When I saw them, I began to cry. But I was lucky. Ed's house was burned beyond repair, a blackened skeleton cluttered with twisted remains of furniture and appliances, all too visible across the rubble-strewn waste that had once been a forested lot between our properties.

There was no power, and therefore no water, since I couldn't run the pump in my well. With the weather still warm, I spent some time pulling furniture, books, bedding, curtains, and so forth, damp from the water that had saved the house, onto the deck and driveway, in the hope that they would dry out. I drove to Gualala and bought big black garbage bags, dry ice, gasoline for the generator I'd bought after a winter storm and power outage, groceries, and drinking water. Back home, I put the dry ice in my refrigerator and freezer and started up the generator to give them some power, so my food wouldn't spoil and I could charge my phone. Power company trucks were already working out on the highway, so with luck all this wouldn't be necessary for long.

Inside the house, I opened all the windows and started a fire in my stove with the wood in the rack next to it. My wood pile outside had been hosed down by the firefighters, but I scavenged until I found some wood that wasn't too wet and laid it out to dry outside and on the stove.

Every time I went outdoors I called for Dodger, but he never appeared.

When night fell I cooked some frozen thing for dinner and ate it on a paper plate, hardly tasting it. I had no Internet connection, so I spent the evening reading by the light of a camping lamp. Since my sofa, mattress and box spring were out on the deck, I set out a sleeping bag and inflatable mat on the floor and slept there. Before going to bed I put a bowl of kibble and one of water on the deck.

The next morning I took the dogs, my computer, and some files, and drove up to Gualala to find someplace with wifi. Before leaving, I checked the bowl of kibble; it was still full.

I spent the day in the public library, writing notices to several courts that I'd need more time to prepare briefs in appeals before them because I'd be dealing with the damage and disruption from the fire. While I was there, Ed called. Under the watchful eye of the librarian, I raced into the lobby to talk to him. "Ed, how are you?"

"Okay," he said. "Not bad, all things considered." His voice was hoarse.

"Where are you?"

"In Gualala. Staying at a friend's house."

"You don't sound so good," I said. "Are you really all right?"

"Yeah. Sprained my ankle, some smoke inhalation."

"Jeez, what happened? I'm in Gualala today. Would your friend mind if I came over?"

"Laurie's at work, but I'm sure she wouldn't mind."

So Ed had a lady friend, I thought. Good for him.

He gave me the address, and I cleared my things from the library and drove over.

Laurie lived in a neighborhood of little houses and cabins in the redwood forest above town. Her house was shaded by an enormous redwood in her front yard. Under it were an old wooden bench, several arrangements of plants in pots, and curious bits of sculpture and ceramic. A Talavera pottery sun, in bright colors, had been fastened to the tree trunk, and on the ground below it was a half-size statue of St. Francis of Assisi, a stone bird resting on his raised arm. Windchimes, hanging from the eaves, jingled softly in the breeze.

Ed opened the door a minute after I knocked. He was leaning on a cane, and his eyes were bloodshot. His face was tired and pale under its tan. The interior of the house was open plan, with one big room spanning the breadth of its front half. Ed hobbled ahead of me, lowered himself into an armchair and used his hands to raise his ankle onto a straight chair in front of it. "Have a seat," he said. "I can't get you water or anything, I'm afraid; I have to stay off my ankle as much as possible." He coughed, a deep grumble, cleared his throat, and then sat silent for a minute, catching his breath.

"Jeez, what happened to you?" I asked.

"Stupidity," he said. "Bunch of us almost got overtaken by the fire, and I twisted my ankle on a log running away."

"Shit!" I said, unable to help myself.

"Everybody made it," he said. "I was the worst hurt of the group."

"Well, that's good, I guess."

"I heard my house burned down. How's yours? Have you been back?"

"I was there yesterday. It's still standing, not much damage; they saved it." I didn't mention the orchard just then; it was nothing to lose compared to Ed's home. "I owe someone a huge debt of gratitude."

"Glad to hear it," Ed said. "Someone told me a tree fell onto my driveway, and they couldn't get up to the house in time."

"Damn."

"Yeah. I didn't get much stuff out beforehand. Lost most of my record collection."

"Oh, shit, I'm sorry." I looked around. "Where's Pogo?" I asked.

"At work," Ed said, with a laugh and a cough. "I left him with Laurie because I was afraid you might have your hands full if you had to evacuate."

I nodded; he was probably right.

"Laurie takes him and her dog with her to work. She works at a plant nursery, and they're cool with it. She can give them a walk at lunchtime."

"Nice."

An idea had been slowly forming in my mind as I drove from the library. I hadn't been sure of it, but as we talked my intention suddenly clarified itself, surprising me.

"Are you planning to rebuild?" I asked.

He nodded. "Yeah. I've lived there forty years. Figure I'll have enough from the insurance to build a little place big enough for me."

"I'm not sure I want to stay," I said.

Ed looked a question at me, but didn't ask why.

"I don't know what I'm going to do," I went on, "but if

you're going to rebuild your house, maybe you can stay in mine—when you're on your feet again, of course. There's some water damage and a bunch of cleaning up needed on the property—all covered by insurance, I hope. I wondered if you could maybe hire some people to take care of it—I'll pay you for it—and watch over them for me."

Ed nodded. "Sounds like a good idea; we can talk details when we know more. I hope you'll be back. I'd be sorry to lose you; you've been a good neighbor and friend."

"You, too. I don't know exactly why I feel like I do—it just hit me when I saw the place. My orchard burned."

"They come back a lot of the time," Ed said.

"Maybe. But I don't know that I have the will to wait for it."

I asked Ed how it had been fighting the fire, and he told me stories, some funny and others scary or sad. "There was a crew from the county jail," he said. "Young guys. Good men, absolutely fearless. One of them was from up the ridge; his parents' house burned. He was all broken up when he heard about it. Bob Cordero's place came out okay, but half the houses on the way up there burned; the road was so bad the trucks had a hard time reaching them. Bob said his wife was saying it served them right, for not paying to have the road fixed."

I had to smile. "Molly was right," I said.

"All in all," he said, "it was quite an adventure. Wouldn't ever want to do it again—I'm probably too old, anyway."

Before I left I made him some lunch, a sandwich from

cheese and cold cuts in the fridge and a cup of filter coffee. "You want to stay off that foot as much as possible," I told him. "Keep it elevated."

"I know," he said. "You sound like my doctor."

When I left, he said, "I'll get back to you about your house. Think I'll take the offer. I have some thoughts about a crew I could get to help. Have to wait till I can walk again, though."

"Whenever you're ready," I said.

I let myself out the door and drove back to the library. I still wasn't sure I was making the right decision, or how I was going to be able to afford it, but amid the uncertainty, I felt light, as though I'd been released from a tether holding me to the ground. Now I just needed to figure out what I was going to do next.

It was late afternoon when I got back to my house. There was still no electricity, and the weather had finally turned cool; the house, its walls and floors still damp, felt cold inside and clammy. I built a fire in the stove, loaded more dry ice into the freezer, topped up the gas tank of the generator, and headed down to Vlad's, which had power, food, and a good dark ale.

Back at the cabin, with only the glow of the stove and the light from my camping lamp and a couple of candles, I felt apprehensive. The rooms were full of shadows, and the night outside my windows was pitch dark. I was painfully conscious of the burned land around me and the charred frame of Ed's empty house, looming invisibly a few hundred feet away. I felt very alone, and I found myself listening intently for any sounds other than the crackle of the stove, the stirrings of the dogs and cats, and the noise of the generator. The house, which had once seemed so secure and welcoming, felt fragile as a half-burned sheet of paper, a thin and brittle shell between me and the dark shapes hunting blindly in the night.

After Terry died and Gavin moved away, I noticed that I'd stopped feeling that I even had a home. I stopped getting homesick on trips out of town, the way I used to when I had to be away from my family. For a long time, it didn't much matter to me where I lived or stayed. Eventually I'd developed an affection for the house in Corbin's Landing and had made friends there, but the fire had revealed how shallow all that was. In a half-dozen years there I'd learned little about even the people I was closest to—Ed, Bill, and Harriet. Maybe, with the scars of experience on our souls, we defend ourselves from the kinds of all-absorbing friendships we had when we were young. Whatever it was, I was feeling that Corbin's Landing wasn't where I was going to settle, but a way station on a road to somewhere—another destination as yet unknown, or maybe just dusty death.

In September, Harriet and I had gone to Santa Rosa to see a performance of Brahms's German Requiem, and I remembered a passage that had spoken to me at the time: *Denn wir haben hier keine bleibende Stadt.* "We have here no permanent place." Even the melody and the rhythm had suggested the wandering journey of someone who knows he has no real home on this earth. This latest loss—the burned woods around me, Dodger's disappearance and my guilt about it—hardly compared with what I'd experienced when Terry died, but it was enough of an echo to bring back some of that pain and grief and that sense of belonging nowhere anymore. Corbin's Landing had been a refuge, a place that allowed me to heal, but like everything else, it was impermanent, provisional. Something was saying to me that now it was time to move on.

26

I try not to engage in magical thinking, but sometimes events move you so decisively in a particular direction that it's hard not to think you were meant to go there.

The day after I decided I had to move away from Corbin's Landing, Carey called. "We were in Vancouver," she said, "and I didn't hear about the fire up there until we got back. Are you all right?"

I told her. "Yes, basically. My house didn't burn, but my neighbor's did. I think I need someplace to move to, for at least a while. My house has a good deal of water and smoke damage—and I just don't feel like staying up there right now."

"I understand the feeling," she said. "Are you going to stay in the area?"

"I don't know," I answered. "It's hard to find a place. Lot of displaced people, not enough housing, since the big fires last year."

"I don't know if you'd be interested," she said, "but as it happens, we have a friend who has a little house on the central coast. He's been keeping it as a vacation rental, but he told us the other day he was getting tired of managing it and considering finding a long-term tenant."

The central coast was a long way from where I was—but perhaps that wasn't such a bad thing. "You know I have two dogs and two cats. Will he accept pets?"

"I'll vouch for you," she said. "I'm sure you're very responsible."

Carey put me in touch with her friend, an easy-going mortgage broker in Ojai. He sent me photos of the house, and we worked out the details of rent and deposit. Ed and I, in our turn, talked arrangements for the house in Corbin's Landing, and we agreed he'd move in once his ankle was healed enough that he could drive. I spent the next couple of weeks packing what I wanted to take with me, mostly books and mementos and enough bedding, dishes, and kitchen stuff to get me started in the new place. From the house and shed I took loads of damp and smoke-damaged possessions—mostly boxes of papers, books, and tchotchkes I'd brought with me when I moved there from Berkeley, and never opened—and hauled them to the dump. I left whatever else was useful for Ed. Between that, work, and calls and visits from insurance adjusters, I had plenty to do to keep my thoughts at bay, at least during the day.

Harriet came back to check on her house, which was in an area the fire had somehow skipped. Even the trees around it were still green. I helped her pack up some things to take back to Reno, and we ate lunch at Vlad's.

"Bill and I decided we won't be moving back here," she said. "With his health problems, it's just not safe for us to live so far from town. We've decided to stay in Reno, near his son, buy or rent a nice condo somewhere. Put this place on the market, or maybe rent it until prices come back up."

"What about your gardening?" I asked.

She sighed. "Well, I'm getting awfully arthritic; it's hard to do all that these days. Maybe I'll grow some tomatoes and greens in containers on my deck. Dan—Bill's son—said he could make me a raised bed or two in their yard." She said this with determined cheerfulness. I admired again her resolve in the face of loss and change.

I rented a trailer, hitched it to the back of my Subaru, drove it up the winding highway to the house, and loaded into it all I was taking with me; there was room enough still for the boxes of legal files I had stored in Santa Rosa. The day before I left, the wind shifted, and cold, damp air, carrying the smell of the ocean, drifted over the hills. Clouds, white and gray, sailed slowly across a sky the delicate blue of a Watteau painting. The next morning, as I drank a last cup of coffee and watched out my living-room window, gray clouds covered the blue, and the sky seemed to sigh and, like a mother who hears her baby cry, let down a gentle flow of rain onto the ash-covered ground.

27

My new home was a square, charmless bungalow in a quiet little town called Holly Beach. The house had a compact kitchen and breakfast nook, a tiny living room, and two small bedrooms. On the plus side, it had a Meyer lemon tree in the front yard, and a mandarin orange, a fig, and some kind of plum tree in the back; and if I walked out to the sidewalk, a blue expanse of ocean beyond the end of the street.

I bought a bed frame, box spring, and mattress, and put them in the darker bedroom in the back of the house. I set up my office in the front bedroom, which had a window with a view of the lemon tree and the street beyond it, and another facing the driveway and the side of the house next door. I missed my wood stove on foggy mornings, but unlike Corbin's Landing, the weather here never seemed to get really cold.

Living in Holly Beach didn't require nearly as much planning as life in Corbin's Landing—in fact, it was hardly any work at all. It was five minutes' drive to the main street, which had thrift stores, coffee houses, restaurants, an ice cream shop, a pharmacy, a hardware store, an antique movie theater, and a small supermarket. A shopping mall, with a much bigger market and a Trader Joe's, was in the next town, ten minutes away. It was civilization on a small scale, but welcome just the same.

Slowly, I began to get to know my neighbors. The house on one side was a vacation home. During the week and on some weekends it was silent. Lights came on and went off on timers, and a pair of landscapers came now and then to rake the paths, trim the tidy hedges, and pull any weeds that came up in the wood chips of the low-maintenance front yard. When the owners showed up, they kept to themselves. Sometimes I'd know they were at the house only because their car, a white Lexus SUV, would be parked in the driveway. I glimpsed them only occasionally, a slender, gray-haired man and an equally slender woman with a perfect haircut and blond highlights. They always came alone, just the two of them, and spent most of the time indoors or gone in their car, though occasionally they took walks in the neighborhood. On the rare occasions when we met outdoors, they avoided engaging with me unless we actually happened to make eye contact; then they would nod and say hello with a perfunctory half-smile and move on.

My neighbors on the other side were more welcoming. Jackie, an ample woman who dressed in long skirts and big sweaters and still wore her gray hair long, was an artist who made watercolor paintings, cards, and jewelry. Her husband

Roger, gray-bearded and as comfortably built as she was, was a retired math teacher and train buff. When they weren't on the road at fairs and art shows or steam train excursions, they lived quietly in a cottage not unlike mine, filled with well-worn furniture, art of various sorts, houseplants, and books. They had a dog, a phlegmatic Rottweiler mix named Rhonda, who quickly made friends with Charlie and Lizzie. They also had a vegetable garden, which I could see over the fence between our yards: a pair of raised beds in which they seemed to be growing chard, kale, a tangle of cherry tomato plants, still with fruit even in late fall, and a rank collection of weeds. The rest of the yard was a wonderfully random scatter of bushes, vines, flowering plants, statuary and other odd ornaments, like pinwheels and a life-sized ceramic duck. Like me, they had a fig tree and a Meyer lemon, both of which hugged their back fence, and a huge angel's trumpet vine that cascaded giant pale yellow flowers down its length, into their yard and mine.

The holidays came, and I bought some strings of lights and an artificial tree—I'd left the others in my garage up north, for Ed to use or get rid of as he pleased. I'd brought some ornaments with me in a box that still smelled like smoke, but as I opened it and began hanging them on the tree, I started to feel strongly that sense of emotional free-fall that had haunted me after Terry's death. The bulbs, blown glass fruit, flowers, and Santas, carved wood animals, each held its tiny flash of memory of other Christmases—of Gavin as a kid, Terry as a young man, my parents visiting,

Christmas baking and dinners and presents. They filled me with homesickness, finally, for the time when I'd had a real home and a family, somewhere beyond the unbridgeable chasm created by time and death. I supposed someone, not me, could have put them away, closed the box and put it on a shelf. But I couldn't; it would have felt like abandoning them and their silent, beseeching messages. So I hung them on the tree, and then went to the mall and bought a bunch of new ones to mix with them, to remind myself that the present matters, and time can also make things new.

On the holiday I was alone. I put together for myself a fabulous breakfast of eggnog, croissants, Brie, fruitcake, and chocolates. In the afternoon, I drove to the nearest town with a multiplex open on the holiday and saw an animated comedy, in the midst of a restless audience of candy-fueled children and their parents.

That night I dreamed about Terry. He looked like he had not long before he killed himself, his dark hair starting to gray, a few lines softening his thin, handsome face. We were in a park somewhere, and he was walking with Pepper, a black lab from another time entirely, whom we'd acquired soon after buying our house. In the way of dreams, everything was in soft focus, and after a bit of mild surprise at running into one another, we walked together and talked—about what, I didn't remember on waking. But for some reason the dream left me feeling warmer and more comfortable, and it colored the next day with a sort of gentle serenity, as if something had been resolved, a circle closed.

The weeks after my move had been quiet—a respite that gave me time to get settled. The courts had cut me enough slack on my various appeals because of the fire and my move that I had some space to get my caseload under control again. The water and smoke damage to my old house in Corbin's Landing had turned out to be relatively minor, and Ed was handling the repairs while I dealt with the insurance company.

The holidays over, I made what felt like a long-deferred visit to San Quentin, to touch base with Arturo. San Quentin is a lot farther from Holly Beach than from Corbin's Landing, and a trip there meant I had to stay overnight. I paid Jackie and Roger, who could use the money, to dog and cat sit while I was away and offered to do the same for Rhonda, at no charge, if they had to leave her when they traveled.

I made the drive to San Francisco one drizzly afternoon. The prison outside Soledad where we'd visited Steve Eason was on the way, visible from the highway. I wondered idly what he was doing as I drove by, thinking of how our utterly separate lives had intersected that one afternoon. In the city, I stayed the night in a noisy motel, in a room that smelled like stale tobacco and seemed to be decorated in nothing but various shades of brown, then drove to San Quentin the next morning across the Golden Gate Bridge.

Arturo thanked me for helping his family find an immigration lawyer, but told me his father had been deported anyway, because of an old drunk-driving conviction. His mother was back at work, but afraid of losing her job sewing clothes in a sweatshop, and his little brother had been arrested and charged with assault. On the bright side, his sister had been able to stay in college and would be graduating this year. "So she can take care of my mother if she has to without having to leave school," he said. Arturo himself seemed to have grown up. I commented on the fact that it had been a long time since he'd been sent to administrative segregation for some bit of defiance or bad behavior. "I decided to chill," he explained. "Lady guard on my tier said to me a while ago, 'Arturo, why you so hardheaded? You know you always gonna lose. Guards here, we have to do our jobs whether you like it or not. Why not just program, get along with people? You're gonna be here a long time; no point in making your life harder than it needs to be.' And you know, I thought to myself, she has a point. I just keep getting mad, messing up, and it's not doing me any good. So now I try to see things differently, let people do what they gonna do, and not take it personal, you know?"

I figured it was as good a philosophy as any.

A couple of days after I got back to Holly Beach, Carey called. "I have a favor to ask you," she said. "We're close to getting a dismissal in Sunny's case."

I started to congratulate her, but she said, "Not quite yet. The DA, Mike Beatty, is still gun-shy about bad publicity. It would help seal the deal if we can tell him and the judge the Ferrantes are okay with it. Beatty says the family has been approached about a deal, but he was kind of cagey about what they said. It may be that they haven't given him a clear answer. I'd like to see them again and sound them out. Would you come with me?"

Harrison was actually a lot closer to Holly Beach than it was to Corbin's Landing; I could be there in less than half a day. "No problem," I said. "Just say when."

28

This time we met the Ferrantes at the big house on the hillside where Robert III now lived. We sat on chairs and sofas around a coffee table at one end of the living room, a lodge-like space with cathedral ceilings and a wall of windows framing a panorama of the valley and the highway running through it. On this winter day, the view had the pastel colors of an impressionist painting. At the end of the room where we were seated, a fire burned cheerfully in a big stone fireplace. Robert III—the one the family called Rob—and Marta, his wife, had brought us cups of tea and coffee and a plate of soft, spicy cookies drizzled with caramel-colored icing. "Marta's persimmon cookies," Rob said, with obvious pride.

"Marlene's recipe, actually," Marta said. "It's kind of a classic around here; they print it in the Harrison paper every persimmon season." I took one and bit into it. The soft cookie, redolent of cinnamon and ginger and not too sweet, made a perfect combination with the brown sugar flavor of the icing. I resolved to look it up.

It was a substantial group of family members who met us: Robert, Jr.—Bob—and his wife Marlene, Tony and Cindy, John and Barbara, as well as Rob and Marta. Rob was in his fifties, lean and dark like his father. After the initial small talk, he asked the first question. "I wasn't here when you met with everyone else last time. What is it you're looking for?"

I'd had a meeting like this with a victim's family once before, years ago, after a client of mine won a reversal of his death sentence. Our goal in that case had been to convince the family members not to object to resentencing our client to life in prison without possibility of parole, rather than have another trial on the issue of whether he should be sentenced to death again. What we were asking of the Ferrantes was a much bigger concession: to agree to let Sunny, who had been convicted once of murdering their brother, their uncle, walk free, with all the charges against her dropped.

Before going on, I thought I'd try to find out what the prosecutor had told them. "Things have changed a lot since we were here before," I began. "I understand the district attorney, Mr. Beatty, may have talked with you about what happened."

"Actually," Bob broke in, "it was the head honcho, Jim Chalmers. He kind of told us where things stand. We've all talked about it and what we might want to do. He says the case is going to be hard to retry. He still thinks Sunny's guilty, but he told us the same thing you said, that their star witness, the guy who said Todd told him Sunny hired him—signed a sworn declaration saying he lied about it all.

Chalmers said the guy is kind of backtracking now, but he says he's not worth much as a witness anymore, and their case against Sunny is a lot weaker without him. And now, he says, they have two people saying Sunny didn't have anything to do with it. Brittany says Braden got Todd to do the murder, and Braden says it was Brittany."

Chalmers' assessment was almost exactly in line with what I'd told Carol Schiavone. I breathed an inward sigh of relief.

"Brittany might just be saying that to help her mother," Rob said.

"Frankly, my money's on Braden," Tony said.

A couple of the others murmured their agreement.

"Braden's a conniver," John said. "I wouldn't have thought he'd have his father killed, though. But then he supposedly hired someone to kill his business partner, so go figure."

"Yeah, but he's accusing Brittany," Marlene said.

"Brittany? I don't see that," Barbara said. "She was just an ordinary teenager, as far as I could see."

"But she couldn't stand Greg," Cindy said. "I saw it whenever they were here together. She stayed away from him. Never talked to him if she didn't have to. Always referred to him as Greg, never Dad. And she'd just look daggers at him when he made some snide comment to Sunny."

"That's a long way from talking your boyfriend into murdering him," Marlene said.

"She wouldn't be the first," said Barbara. "A girl in my high school got together with her boyfriend and killed her stepfather. Turned out he'd been sexually molesting her. They sent her to juvenile hall."

"And there was that case here, six or seven years ago," Cindy added. "It was in Beanhollow, but still—"

"We'll probably never know," Bob said. "Let's get back to the business at hand. Near as I can tell, Chalmers wants to know how we'd all feel if they dropped the charges against Sunny."

Several people nodded.

"And my guess is, you'd like the same thing."

"That's right."

"Well, we've talked about it a lot in the family over the past few weeks," Robert said. "And at this point I believe we all pretty much agree. Correct me if I'm wrong," he said to the rest of the gathered relatives. "My mother—Tony's and mine—made it a mission of hers to get justice for Greg, as she said. Once the DA back then convinced her that Sunny was guilty, she was all in. She wanted Sunny convicted, and she wanted her dead, for killing her boy. We respected that—well, some of us did, some didn't agree, and it divided the family badly for a while. But she's passed on now, and the rest of us aren't as intent on avenging Greg as she was. And besides, with this new information, we're looking at the possibility that Sunny may actually be innocent."

Several murmurs of "Yes," and "Right," came from the group.

"Even Mama wouldn't have wanted her to be punished for a crime she didn't commit. Nobody's happy that it looks like either Braden or Brittany is responsible for the murder, and from what Chalmers said, it doesn't seem that either of them is going to be charged. But we're also thinking that we don't want to go through another family fight and another trial, with all the publicity. I guess this is kind of a roundabout way to reach the bottom line, but I believe we're all in agreement to let the DA drop the charges and all get on with our lives."

Again, several people around the table nodded or murmured their assent.

"Thank you," Carey and I said, with real feeling.

"So you can tell Chalmers or Beatty that on our behalf. And I'll confirm it if they want to know," Bob said.

We thanked everyone again. "We really believe Sunny is innocent," I said. "You've done a great thing for her."

I must have looked as if I was about to cry, because Cindy leaned toward me and said, "That's okay, honey. Would you like some more coffee? And have another cookie." She held up the plate, and I took one, and so did she. "I feel like we're all going to be better for this," she said.

And thus, the Ferrantes removed one of the last obstacles to allowing the case against Sunny to go away.

If this were a thriller, I thought, there would have been a point at which the hero found himself confronting someone willing to kill him to prevent him from revealing the truth. Sunny's case was almost the opposite. A lot of people, it seemed, suspected that an injustice had been done and hoped that the truth would somehow come to light. Sunny, of course, knew the truth, or part of it, but she had been afraid to raise the lid on the Pandora's box which held it; and Craig Newhouse had felt bound to inaction by her fear. The Ferrantes, for their part, had remained passive and kept their thoughts to themselves, to keep peace in their own family.

Belatedly, as we drove back to Harrison, it occurred to me that I ought to feel some moral ambivalence that we were allowing a woman who might have conspired in the murder of her stepfather to go unpunished. But, I thought, Sunny had sacrificed her own life for Brittany's. And Brittany had honored her mother's gift as best she could and done what she could to atone, and now she had a husband and children of her own. One person had already spent fifteen years in prison for the crime. Three families had already been broken by it. I couldn't see the point of letting the prosecution fix its mistake by doing the same thing, or worse, to yet another one.

The district attorney, still worried about publicity, set the hearing on his motion to dismiss the charges for the Friday before President's Day weekend. I drove back to Harrison to be there. Since I wasn't Sunny's attorney of record any more, I sat in the audience, between Natasha and Carol. Brittany wasn't there. When I asked Carol if she would be, she said that Sunny told her not to come, because she felt it would be better if she weren't seen in Harrison. "I think it's silly, but she's still worried. We're going to drive over to see her later today," she said.

Sunny, dressed in an off-white sweater and gray slacks

("I bought those for her yesterday," Carol whispered), was escorted by the bailiff to the counsel table, where she sat next to Carey. Soon afterward, the judge came out to the bench looking relaxed and even, in a subdued way, pleased. Not many hearings end as happily as this. When we sat again, Beatty, the prosecutor, stood and made the motion, simple in its language, that the charges against the defendant in *People v. Cheryl Ferrante*, Hartwell County case number A117061, be dismissed in the interest of justice. The judge granted the motion and declared the court adjourned.

Sunny and Carey turned and walked out the little gate between the front of the courtroom and the audience section, Sunny seeming a little stunned, as if she had just walked into bright sunlight from a darkened room. She saw Carol and walked into her arms, hugging her, and started to cry. Then she hugged each of the rest of us in turn, as we all smiled and cried and said silly things about how amazing and wonderful it was.

"You know," Carol said to Sunny, "we should all go to the Pepper Tree Café for breakfast."

Sunny turned to her, wide-eyed. "Really? Is it still around?"

"Yes," Carol said, "and as good as ever. I went there yesterday for dinner, to make sure."

Sunny dabbed her eyes and blew her nose with a Kleenex given to her by Carol. "Chorizo and eggs," she said. "That's what I want."

The Pepper Tree was in the old downtown, and we walked

there. The air was chilly, but Sunny didn't seem to notice. She kept gazing around her and commenting on how green everything was, and what had and hadn't changed since she'd been in jail. "Didn't that antique store used to be a television repair place? And that wine shop was a stationery store. I remember it; I used to buy birthday cards there."

She was delighted that the Pepper Tree appeared unchanged. Its décor was intensely western, with antique branding irons, bridles, and bits decorating the walls between posters of cattle brands and paintings and photos of ranch life. Over huge breakfasts of eggs and meat, home fried potatoes, and muffins, we asked Sunny if she had plans for what to do next.

"Kind of," she said. "First, Carol and I are going to drive over to Wofford Heights and spend the weekend with Brittany and Rick and the kids. Then we're all going down to LA and—you're gonna laugh at me, this is so hokey—we're going to Disneyland."

We did laugh; it sounded like a perfect California wish come true.

"We may drive out to Laguna Beach," Sunny went on, "while we're down there. I'd like to see the water again, even though it's February. And then—then Carol and I fly to New Mexico."

"Sunny's going to stay with Tom and me for a bit," Carol said. "But I have a line on an apartment and a job that would suit her really well. We'll take it a step at a time. Right now, I'm just glad to have her here."

As we walked back to our cars, I drew Carol aside. "Sunny's moving to New Mexico?" I asked.

Carol nodded. "I know it seems strange," she said, "but she asked me if she could come live near us."

"Did she say why? Not that I don't think it's a great idea—hey, I'd like to live in New Mexico—but I'd have thought she'd want to stay close to her family."

"Maybe eventually." Carol glanced at Sunny, walking and talking with Carey, then back at me, with a shake of her head. "I don't know everything she's feeling. I know she loves Brittany—consider what she did for her. I suspect she just needs some time to find forgiveness."

2 9

Word of the dismissal of Sunny's case traveled quickly on the grapevine, and Carey and I were minor celebrities at the death penalty conference that weekend. Exonerations—the ultimate victory—are rare, but they sustain us through long strings of losses, giving hope that justice sometimes does ride to the rescue when it's needed. Old acquaintances and people I'd never met came up to congratulate me and ask how we'd done it. I didn't know how to answer. I knew what had happened, but there was no simple why: a series of small steps, some strokes of luck, some clever strategizing, mostly by Carey. And I was as reluctant as Sunny herself to get into the questions raised about Brittany's role in the murder. So I said thank you and mumbled self-deprecating clichés about good luck and the contributions of a great team.

Not long afterward, I took another long weekend, bundled the dogs into the car, and drove up to Corbin's Landing, at Ed's invitation, to see how his work on the house had gone. The beauty of the last part of the drive, with steep green hills on one side and the ocean, crashing on rocky beaches, on the other, unknotted, as it always did, a lot of the cords of tension inside me. As I got close to Corbin's Landing, and into the fire zone, I made a joke to the dogs about returning to Manderley.

In this Mediterranean climate, winter, with its rains, is spring, the time of renewal, and new grass and weeds were sprouting, lush and green, among the burned trees and downed logs and the cleared areas around houses that had been saved and others that had not. The bulldozers had been at work along my road, and brush and logs had been gathered into piles, to be chipped and burned or scattered before the wet season ended. My lot was cleared, and so was Ed's, a flat patch of ground all that remained where his house had been. He had made sure the bulldozers steered clear of the orchards, though, and my little trees still stood, skeletal frames, knee deep in lush green grass, pointing thin blackened fingers into the air. My house, no longer surrounded by woods, sat exposed on the hillside, dominating the landscape.

The house, with new floors and new drywall, freshly painted, was cleaner and brighter inside than I remembered. I admired it and thanked Ed profusely. "What's happening with your place?" I asked.

"Nothing much," he said. "Working with the insurance company and a builder, but everyone is so backlogged, they don't know when they'll be able to get to me. Figure I'll be here for a while, if you don't mind." I didn't. For all its familiarity, the house seemed no longer mine, as if we had both, figuratively speaking, moved on in the months since our separation. I had felt much the same way, I remembered, the first time I came back to my parents' house in Anchorage after moving to California.

The dogs greeted each other as old friends and romped beside us as we walked around the lot. I was glad to see that the Meyer lemon tree, in its pot on the deck, had a crop of bright yellow fruit. Next to the kitchen door, I noticed a small dish of kibble. Ed saw my glance and said, "By the way, that orange cat of yours seems to be coming around again."

"Dodger? Oh, my God!" Impulsively, I gave Ed a hug. "I felt so bad about leaving him behind. I can't tell you how relieved I am."

"Well, he won't come near me, but I'm leaving him some food outside like you did. It doesn't hurt to have a good mouse hunter around."

"Yep," I said, remembering the vole corpses that had kept appearing outside my kitchen door. "He's your man for that." I wished him and Ed a happy life together.

In the orchard, I tried cutting some of the tree branches with a pair of borrowed pruners, hunting for live wood, finding their metal identification tags: Gravenstein, Golden Delicious, Belle de Boskoop, King David, Winter Pearmain. Some of the younger trees were dead at the grafts, but the older ones had living wood and buds on some branches. They'd been set back, but they'd probably survive and grow again. I felt a wave of nostalgia as we walked through the rank wet grass, smelling the green scent of it underfoot combined with the salt tang of the moist air.

I treated Ed to dinner at Vlad's and greeted a few old acquaintances there, who asked casually what I was up to and where I was living these days. Back at the house, Ed gave me his bed for the night and slept on the sofa in the living room. All the furniture he'd brought into the house was new, and a lot nicer than what he'd had in his old house. I wondered idly whether Laurie had helped him pick it out.

As I left the next morning, I took one more long look back at the house, not saying goodbye, because I knew I'd be back there again, if only to get it ready to sell, but wondering whether my life here was a closed chapter.

Back in Holly Beach, with no trees of my own to winter prune, I borrowed a ladder from Roger and pruned the neglected plum tree, which was growing a forest of shoots skyward from its top. Admiring my handiwork after an hour of heading and thinning cuts, I felt like a good tenant—not the best housekeeper, but at least a well-meaning steward.

Early in the spring, Gavin and Rita visited, on their way from seeing one group of friends in Los Angeles to another in Berkeley. They were an attractive couple: Gavin, spare, dark-haired, and reserved, resembled Terry more than ever. Rita, also dark and slender, shone with a kind of inner light. They had great news. "We're expecting," Gavin said, and I noticed again the hint of an Australian accent creeping into his California one. "We found out just before coming here." The baby was due in the fall; they didn't yet know if it would be a girl or a boy.

They asked about the fire, and I told them. "How are you doing?" Rita asked me, with genuine solicitousness. "Actually not at all badly," I said. "It could have been a lot worse."

We spent an afternoon playing with the dogs on the local dog beach and walking the hills above the ocean—not as high or wild as those on the north coast, but still forbiddingly beautiful—and ate dinner at a seafood restaurant. They stayed the night with me, sleeping in my bed, while I, emulating Ed's courtesy, took the living-room sofa, the two cats jockeying for space on my feet, and Charlie and Lizzie squeezed end to end in the narrow space between the sofa and the coffee table.

The next morning I treated Gavin and Rita to breakfast in town at Lucia's, a place recommended by Jackie, before they left to drive up through Big Sur to Monterey. "We probably won't be able to visit for a while," Rita said as we ate, "with the baby and all. Can you come see us? We have so many more places to show you; and my parents would love to get to know you better."

"You'll have to nag her," Gavin said to Rita, with a smile in my direction. "She's a workaholic, and it's really hard to get her to take a break."

Outside the house, their suitcases packed into the car, we exchanged hugs and well wishes. "Keep me up to date about the baby," I said.

"We will," they said, and Gavin added, "Come visit when he's born."

"He?" Rita said. "I keep thinking of her as a girl. But definitely come see us and the baby. We'll expect you."

I promised. I watched them drive off, and felt again that sharp ache of seeing your children leave, like birds taking flight, to take their places in a separate part of the world.

That evening, Jackie, Roger, and I drove together to the next town over, to hear a group ("they're just the best—you have to come hear them," Jackie had gushed) that played Scottish music.

The concert was in a retired church that had been turned into a coffee house and book store, with a makeshift stage where the altar had been. The band, three very ordinary-looking middle-aged men with graying hair and slight paunches, played old jigs, reels, strathspeys, and airs, and occasionally sang a song in Gaelic or stopped to tell drily funny stories in a soft Scottish burr. The audience sat on mismatched folding chairs and spent the intermission nibbling cookies washed down by cheap wine. The music was a lot like that I'd heard as a kid at my grandfather's house, on old records, or when he played the fiddle; my father also sometimes played it on CDs on weekend afternoons as he worked on some project around the house. It always had an edge of nostalgic melancholy, a minor note lurking under it; it was music of loss, lost love, lost wars, lost lands, the diaspora of people leaving a beloved country to live in exile.

It was raining when we left, and I guess I was quieter than usual on the drive home. "Penny for your thoughts," Jackie said from the front seat.

I could see the back of her head silhouetted against the flashes of headlights and the highway disappearing ahead of me in the rain-streaked darkness. "Nothing much," I said. "I guess I was thinking of home."

ACKNOWLEDGEMENTS

This book is something of an appreciation and defense of my adopted home state of California, from the north coast redwoods to the agricultural Eden of the Central Valley, iconic landscapes and hidden corners, sprawling mega-cities and ambitious small towns, and the country around them, an amazing diversity of people and cultures – and the largest prison system and death row in the United States. I have quite a few people to thank for helping me try to bring the book to fruition, particularly Sam Matthews and Miranda Jewess, my encouraging and patient editors, my always supportive agent Kimberley Cameron, and Michael Kurland, my life partner, who batted ideas around with me, took the time to read and critique drafts and the finished manuscript, and talked me through my personal crises about the book and my career as a writer. And I owe thanks to the capital defense attorneys I've known over the years, for teaching me how to practice in this complex and esoteric branch of the law (to which I doubt any novel could really do justice) and holding up the example of their idealism and dedication to the cause of criminal defense.

ABOUT THE AUTHOR

L.F. Robertson is a practicing defense attorney who for the last two decades has handled only death penalty appeals. Until recently she worked for the California Appellate Project, which oversees almost all the individual attorneys assigned to capital cases in California. She has written articles for the CACJ (California Attorneys for Criminal Justice) Forum, as well as op-ed pieces and feature articles for the *San Francisco Chronicle* and other papers. Linda is the co-author of *The Complete Idiot's Guide to Unsolved Mysteries*, and a contributor to the forensic handbooks *How to Try a Murder* and *Irrefutable Evidence*, and has had short stories published in the anthologies *My Sherlock Holmes, Sherlock Holmes: The Hidden Years* and *Sherlock Holmes: The American Years*. The first Janet Moodie book, *Two Lost Boys*, was her first novel.

TWO LOST BOYS
L.F. ROBERTSON

Janet Moodie has spent years as a death row appeals
attorney. Overworked and recently widowed, she's had
her fill of hopeless cases, and is determined that this will
be her last. Her client is Marion 'Andy' Hardy, convicted
along with his brother Emory of the rape and murder
of two women. But Emory received a life sentence
while Andy got the death penalty, labeled the ringleader
despite his low IQ and Emory's dominant personality.

Convinced that Andy's previous lawyers missed mitigating
evidence that would have kept him off death row, Janet
investigates Andy's past. She discovers a sordid and damaged
upbringing, a series of errors on the part of his previous
counsel, and most worrying of all, the possibility that
there is far more to the murders than was first thought.
Andy may be guilty, but does he deserve to die?

"This is a must-read"
KATE MORETTI, NEW YORK TIMES BESTSELLER

"Suspense at its finest"
GAYLE LYNDS, NEW YORK TIMES BESTSELLER